"Are you sure ~~Lee told~~ the **stand down? All of them seem mighty interested in the gap between your body and mine."**

"Then let's give them something to worry about." On the next turn, Penny snuggled in. "How's that?"

Sky dragged in air. "Spectacular. Jake and Matt just gave me the evil eye. If I go missing, check the alley. I'll be lying in a bloody heap."

"No, you won't. These guys are not violent. They might give you a talking-to, but they don't beat people up. They're extra protective right now because I recently broke off my engagement after I discovered my fiancé was cheating on me."

"On *you*? Is he nuts?"

"You just made my evening."

"Then listen closely. You're beautiful, smart, and caring. He's a fool. Anybody who got a *yes* from you is one lucky bastard. I can't believe he messed it up."

She sighed. "See? I told them dancing with you would be good for my battered ego. The song's almost over, but can we do this again soon?"

"Yes, ma'am, we certainly—"

"But not right away. You turn me on, and I need to catch my breath." The music stopped and she wiggled out of his arms. "Catch you later, cowboy."

GIFT-GIVING COWBOY

THE BUCKSKIN BROTHERHOOD

Vicki Lewis Thompson

Ocean Dance Press

GIFT-GIVING COWBOY
© 2021 Vicki Lewis Thompson

ISBN: 978-1-63803-957-0

Ocean Dance Press LLC
PO Box 69901
Oro Valley, AZ 85737

Visit the author's website at
VickiLewisThompson.com

Want more cowboys? Check out these other titles by
Vicki Lewis Thompson

The Buckskin Brotherhood
Sweet-Talking Cowboy
Big-Hearted Cowboy
Baby-Daddy Cowboy
True-Blue Cowboy
Strong-Willed Cowboy
Secret-Santa Cowboy
Stand-Up Cowboy
Single-Dad Cowboy
Marriage-Minded Cowboy
Gift-Giving Cowboy

The McGavin Brothers
A Cowboy's Strength
A Cowboy's Honor
A Cowboy's Return
A Cowboy's Heart
A Cowboy's Courage
A Cowboy's Christmas
A Cowboy's Kiss
A Cowboy's Luck
A Cowboy's Charm
A Cowboy's Challenge
A Cowboy's Baby
A Cowboy's Holiday
A Cowboy's Choice
A Cowboy's Worth
A Cowboy's Destiny
A Cowboy's Secret
A Cowboy's Homecoming

1

So this was Apple Grove. Skyler McLintock pressed gently on the brakes of his F-250 as he rolled to a stop at the corner of the festive town square. An overcast sky had triggered the lamppost lights and a Christmas tree sparkled in the gazebo. A snowplow had been through and the blacktop gleamed with what was likely a layer of ice.

His mom leaned forward to peer through the windshield. "Sure is freaky to be back here. Let's take a turn around the square before you drop me at the hotel. I want to see what's changed."

"Yes, ma'am." He checked for traffic and pulled slowly through the intersection.

Sky's brother Beau unsnapped his seat belt and leaned between the driver and passenger seats to get a better view. "Have they always decorated like this for Christmas?"

"Probably. It was already an established tradition when I lived here. Seems like they've taken it up a notch, though. I remember the lighted tree in the gazebo, but not the greenery and bows. Or the wreaths on the lampposts."

"Looks nice." Sky glanced to his right as they passed a large brick building with a row of windows decorated with lights and greenery. "What's the Choosy Moose?"

"The town watering hole."

"Is it anything like the Fluffy Buffalo?"

"Very much so. Unless it's changed, they have good food, live country music and a decent dance floor. We should check it out while we're here."

"Assuming that's more than just one night." Sky wasn't counting on anything. His phone conversation this week with Buckskin Ranch owner Henri Fox hadn't promised him a warm welcome. Clearly she was suspicious of his story. "If it doesn't go well, I doubt we'll feel like partying."

"Don't be a Gloomy Gus." His mother gave his shoulder a squeeze. "It'll go well. Charley fell in love with Henri, so logically she's a good sort. And if it doesn't go well, some hard apple cider and a fast two-step will fix us right up."

Beau laughed. "Since when do you like hard cider? I thought you were strictly a whisky-drinkin' gal."

"I am, normally, but seeing this town is making me nostalgic for the taste of apple cider. That's what I used to drink when I lived here."

"Alrighty, then." Sky glanced over at her. "It won't take Beau and me long to assess whether we're a hit or a miss with Henri. It's a little after three, so either way, we'll be back in town by five. If we're a hit, we'll all head to the Buckskin for a celebration. If not, the three of us will mosey down to the Choosy Moose and get plastered."

His mom gave him a look of approval. "That's my boy."

He smiled. Life with Desiree Annabel McLintock was a never-ending adventure. That's how he'd chosen to view this trip she was so keen on. He didn't need it, but she did, so he'd go along for the ride.

"Wow, the yarn store on the corner is now a coffee shop. Looks cute. The Apple Grove Gazette is still in business. That's cool." His mom's nose was an inch from the window. She was clearly enthralled.

Yeah, this trip was worth it, if only to give her a walk down memory lane.

"The Apple Barrel is still here! It looks *exactly* the same. We have to go in there before we leave and get caramel apples. And we'll stop by Logan's Leather, too. I used to dream of buying one of their saddles."

"And now you could." Sky was always up for browsing a top-notch tack store.

Beau chuckled as they passed the next shop. "*Racy Lace*. I'll bet that wasn't on the square thirty years ago."

"No, sir, it was not. I'm glad to see it, though. That's progress. But they *still* don't have a bookstore. That pains me."

Sky glanced at her. "Gonna open one?"

"You know, I just might, depending on how things go."

After a turn around the holiday-themed square, Sky followed his mom's directions to the historic Apple Grove Hotel a block away.

"Oh, good, they've kept it the way it was." His mother sighed with obvious pleasure. "It's even more beautiful than I remember."

"It's pretty, all right." A pristine white clapboard exterior glowed in the light from antique lamp posts set into the sidewalk. Sky waited while an SUV backed out of a spot near the door of the three-story hotel. A second-floor porch created a sheltering overhang for the front entrance, which was flanked by two slim Christmas trees decorated in gold.

"I never could justify spending the money to stay here, but sometimes I'd sit in the lobby and read a book so I could bask in the atmosphere."

"A Louis L'Amour book, I assume," Beau said.

"The perfect read for a hotel like this. I used to pretend he'd spent the night here in his travels with his family. It could have happened."

The SUV drove away and Sky pulled into the vacant space. "I didn't know staying here would be such a big deal for you."

"I didn't say anything in case we arrived to find some modernized nightmare instead of the stately elegance I remember. Thank goodness they've maintained it the way it was meant to look. That's a good omen."

"Didja hear that, Sky?" Beau tapped him on the shoulder. "We got us a good omen. Nothing to worry about, now."

"That's a relief."

"Make fun if you want, but once a venture is off to a good start, you've set the stage for more positive outcomes."

"I'm willing to go with that." Beau opened the back door. "I'll get Mom, bro. You get the luggage."

"Will do." He climbed down just as a tall cowboy about the age of his youngest brother Rance came out of the hotel wheeling a luggage trolley.

His hat and shearling coat looked new and his tooled boots were spit-shined. "Need some help, folks?"

Sky almost told him they could handle it. Those boots didn't need to get messed up fetching their luggage. But the guy already had the trolley out the door and he could probably use a nice tip. "Thanks. Appreciate it."

"Yes, sir."

"Suitcases are in the back. I'll get the tailgate for you." Then he winced as the cowboy planted those fancy boots in the muck and wheeled the luggage rack through the glop, spattering his new jeans in the process. A guest needed service and he'd by golly provide it.

Rance had been known to do the same thing when he was trying to make a good impression. Sky reached for his wallet and pulled out more than he'd originally intended, just because the kid reminded him so much of his little brother.

The cowboy pocketed the money with a shy smile and a soft *thank you*. Once he'd lifted the loaded trolley up over the curb, Sky's mom got into the act, making over the kid, asking his name and handing him more money. Then she turned back to her two sons. "Rusty, I'd like you to meet my sons, Skyler and Beau."

Rusty left the trolley by the entrance, pulled off his glove and trudged back through the slush, bare hand extended. He shook Beau's hand and then Sky's. "You've got a great mom."

"We know that," Beau said. "Treat her like a queen, okay?" He handed over another bill.

"Absolutely, sir."

"Rusty and I have everything under control, boys," she called out. "He'll help me get checked in. I'll see you two later."

Sky shared a look with Beau and they both grinned. Sky was the first to speak. "Sure thing, Mom. Any last instructions?"

"Just don't forget to give Henri the book. And my letter."

"I won't."

"Then I'll see you in a couple of hours." She smiled at her new friend Rusty. "Has anyone ever told you that you look like a young Brad Paisley?"

As Rusty blushed, tongue-tied and under her spell, Sky signaled his brother. Minutes later they were back in the truck heading out of town.

Beau glanced at him. "That kid made enough off us to get another pair of those fancy boots."

"Yeah, I know." Sky chuckled. "Remind you of Rance?"

"Sure did. Almost as good-looking as our little brother, too." He unbuckled his seatbelt, moved the seat back to accommodate his long legs and buckled up again. "Think Mom was wishing she was thirty years younger?"

"I doubt it. She's always saying she loves being this age, at the height of her career, with all of us able to take care of ourselves. More or less."

"Yeah. Bret's still finding his way, and Rance—hell, he's only twenty-five. I remember what that's like. Anyway, it feels weird to me that she's stopped dating. It's like the end of an era."

"Not surprising, though, after the last one wore that spandex thing to hold in his gut. and the one before—"

"What idiot talks about his colonoscopy on a first date?" Beau sighed. "I still think she should try somebody younger, but—"

"Nope. Not her style." Sky braced his hands against the wheel and leaned back, stretching the kinks out. "I kind of admire her decision. She's not willing to settle for a clueless geezer just to have a man around. Like she says, she's had more than her share of fun."

"Well, she has a point. And I've liked 'em all, the ones I remember, anyway. I have no memory of Clint and Cheyenne's dad. His pictures don't ring a bell. But beginning with Marsh's father, I have good memories of each one."

"I tell myself I remember yours, but I'm probably kidding myself. I was only a year old."

"This deal with Charley Fox has me thinking about my dad."

"You curious?"

"Sort of." He smiled. "But after Mom's experience with girdle guy and colonoscopy guy, I don't wanna risk destroying my fantasy. My dad will always be the handsome cowboy in the pictures Mom took."

Sky had no pictures. Might be for the best. "At least I don't have to worry about coming face-to-face with a sixty-something Charley Fox."

"Just his very suspicious widow."

"I can see why she is. The Buckskin's a thriving business. I looked it up online. For all Henri knows, I could be trying to scam my way into a piece of her ranch."

"The book should do the trick."

"Where is it? Please tell me you didn't put it in your duffle, because I gave that kid everything that was in the—"

"Relax, bro. It's tucked in the pocket behind my seat, along with Mom's letter."

"Are you sure?"

"Want me to haul it up here so you can lay eyes on it?"

"Yes, please. Without it I'm just some guy who's using a vague resemblance to her late husband to cheat her out of her property."

2

"I'm not sure I'm qualified to be your right-hand woman." Penny Marston sat at Henri's kitchen table sipping a mug of cinnamon tea while she and Henri waited for Skyler McLintock's arrival.

"Sure you are." Henri left her mug on the table and got up to stir the chili they'd made as a productive distraction. "You're the least likely to punch him if he turns out to be a fraud."

"I don't know about that. Just because I haven't spent as much time here as everybody else, I'm pretty invested."

"Are you saying you would punch him?" Henri tapped the spoon on the side of the pot, covered it and came back to the table.

She sighed. "Probably not. Leo would, but I'm not as impulsive as my brother. I'm a slow burn kind of person. I didn't punch my cheating ex-fiancé, much as he deserved it. But I might when I go back to L.A."

"He's lucky he's twelve hundred miles away. The Brotherhood would gladly take care of that for you."

She smiled. "I love that about those guys. I used to have one big brother ready to defend my honor. Now I have a bunch." Spending Christmas at the Buckskin had improved her morale about five hundred percent.

"They're a protective bunch, too. That's why I couldn't let any of them be here this afternoon."

"What about Ben? Don't you want your husband to be here in case—"

"Same story." She cradled her mug in both hands. "If the guy's hoping to weasel his way in using Charley's good name, Ben would likely sock him. Maybe more than once."

"Then Ben's not in the house somewhere, ready to rush to your aid?"

"He's down at the barn, where I've asked him to stay until he hears from me."

"What about the rest of the gang?"

"Staying close to their phones but keeping their distance."

Penny gazed at her with new respect. She cut a regal figure, nearly six feet tall in her boots, her body fit, her silver hair cut stylishly short. "I knew you were the boss, but damn. That's impressive."

Henri just smiled.

"So it's just you and me against Skyler McClintock."

"That's the idea. I'll do the talking and you do the listening. Compare his appearance with the pictures I showed you. If he's a pro at this, he might have dyed his hair and put in colored contacts to make him look more legit. See if you can find the holes in his story."

"I appreciate your confidence in me, but if I were any good at spotting liars, I wouldn't have dated Barry, let alone ended up engaged to the bastard."

"It's harder when someone's intent on bamboozling you. That was Barry, for sure. We all saw it when you came for Leo and Fiona's wedding."

"Why didn't anybody effing *tell* me?"

"Would you have listened?"

She hesitated, toying with her mug. "Yeah, probably not. I had to discover it on my own."

"I freely admit I'm vulnerable to this story of Skyler's. I want it to be true. To have Charley's long-lost son appear... makes me breathless every time I let myself think about it."

Penny glanced up and caught the yearning in her expression. She was a tough lady who could take what life dished out. Her self-possession was common knowledge in Apple Grove. When Henri Fox allowed her feelings to show, that was huge.

"This guy will be focused on charming me." Henri sucked in air and steadied herself. "That'll give you a chance to quietly study his tone, his gestures, anything to tip us off that he's working a con. Do your sweet, innocent bit and he'll never suspect you have him under a microscope."

She laughed.

"You know what I'm talking about."

"I do. Everyone underestimates a cute blonde, especially if she has long hair." Penny finished off her tea and stood. "Okay, then. Bring on

Skyler McLintock. It's an unusual last name. I wonder if he's using it so we'll associate him with that old John Wayne movie." She put her mug in the dishwasher.

"Exactly. I've never met a McLintock except on the big screen. He even spells it the same way."

"What's the game plan? Going to invite him to sit? Offer him a beverage?"

"I'll let him sit but I'm not serving refreshments. This isn't a social call."

"What is it, then?"

"That's what we're about to find out. I hear the rumble of an F-250." She pushed back her chair and stood.

"You can tell what model truck it is by the sound of the engine?"

"Mostly. Sometimes I'm fooled." She poured out the rest of her tea and tucked the mug in the dishwasher.

"I take it we're not going to the window to peek out."

"Definitely not. In fact, why don't you head upstairs? You can come down when you hear me answer the door, like you're curious about who's there." She threw a dishtowel over her shoulder. "I plan to look as if I was in the middle of drying the dishes. Totally unconcerned about this upstart McLintock dude coming to call."

"Gotcha." Penny scampered up the stairs. Truth be told, she was honored that Henri had chosen to make her a deputy in this enterprise. And bonus, it demanded all her attention, leaving no room at all for Barry. The slimy creep didn't deserve another micro-second in her head.

She ducked into her room at the top of the stairs just as Skyler McLintock gave the front door knocker a soft tap. Her heart sped up the way it used to when she'd acted in school plays and it was her turn to take the stage.

Did her hair look okay? Sweet and innocent enough? As she tucked it behind her ears, a deep baritone spoke Henri's name. Nice voice. She wouldn't let that influence her. Con men would cultivate a smooth delivery to charm the victim.

Then another man greeted Henri, his tone similar but with a different cadence. Two guys?

Grabbing her phone, she hurried down the stairs. They likely meant Henri no harm, but if Skyler had brought some muscle along, the Brotherhood needed to know about it. She'd text Leo the first chance she got.

The two men paused in the act of taking off their sheepskin jackets and glanced up at her abrupt entrance. Holy moly, they looked even better than they sounded. The sandy-haired one flashed her a smile that crinkled the corners of his blue, blue eyes. "Howdy, ma'am."

Her brain stuttered. If he was a fake, he was the best fake ever. The guy from Henri's picture album was standing in the foyer. Her tongue refused to work. "H-hi. I'm... uh..."

"Let me introduce my dear friend Penelope Marston." Henri's words were clipped, as if she couldn't get enough air. "Penny, meet Skyler and Beau McLintock." She swept a hand first toward the sandy-haired Charley look-alike, and then in the direction of a dark-haired cowboy with a face right out of the movies.

As both responded with a polite *pleased to meet you, ma'am*, Penny kept glancing from one to the other. "You're *brothers*?" Their body type was similar—as in yummy to the max, but their features were nothing alike.

"Yes, ma'am." Skyler met her gaze.

Damn. Those were Charley's eyes. No wonder Henri was white as a sheet. "I didn't mean to be rude. It's just that you—"

"Don't resemble each other. It's because we have the same mom, but different... fathers." He swallowed and turned to Henri. "I'm sure you have questions about that subject."

"You have no idea." Henri stared at him, her hand flattened against her chest. "Come in and sit down." It was more of an order than an invitation.

They quickly draped their jackets and hats on the coat tree. Beau handed Skyler a book as Henri marched into the living room.

A book? What a strange thing to bring. A folder with a birth certificate would make more sense. Except Skyler didn't need more proof.

She followed Henri into the living room and sat in the wingback chair next to the one where Henri perched, her hands clenched, her body rigid and her attention locked on Skyler.

He cleared his throat and held up the book. "My mom asked me to bring you this because—"

"It's *The Sackett Brand*, isn't it?"

"Yes, and she—"

"Charley didn't have that one." Henri tightened her fingers until her knuckles were white. "I bought it for him because it's such a good book and I thought he hadn't read it. Turns out he'd given his original copy to a... friend."

"My mom."

Henri's voice quivered. "When were you born?"

"Five months after he married you." Skyler's voice softened. "She never told him. He didn't know about me."

"*Of course he didn't!*" Henri swiped at her eyes with trembling hands. "Charley Fox would *never* have abandoned his son!" Rising unsteadily to her feet, she took a quick breath.

Both men stood, too. Skyler started toward her.

She held up a hand. "You'll have to excuse me. I need to...." Clearly fighting tears, she sent a pleading glance in Penny's direction. "Will you..."

"Yes." She left her seat. "I'll handle things here. Go see Ben."

<u>3</u>

Gut clenched, Sky watched Henri run from him like he was the devil incarnate. She dashed toward the entry, grabbed a leather coat off the rack and disappeared into the gathering dusk. Her distress cut deep. Did she hate the idea of him that much?

Beau put a hand on his shoulder. "She probably just needs some time. It's a lot to—"

"Or she's horrified by my existence."

"No, she's not."

The gentle voice of Henri's friend broke through the noise in his head. He turned toward her.

Her gray eyes glowed with warmth and kindness. "She's not horrified. Less than fifteen minutes ago she told me how much she wanted this to be true. She said the idea took her breath away."

"But..." He paused, scrubbed a hand over his face. "I'm sorry. I've forgotten your name."

"Penelope. But everybody calls me Penny except for my... well, never mind the exceptions. It's Penny."

"Well, Penny, if she was so eager for me to be the real deal, why did she take off like she couldn't stand the sight of me?"

"She was about to lose her cool and she didn't want to do that in front of you and Beau. Or me, for that matter. She's Henri Fox, the port in a storm, the life raft everyone clings to when they're going under."

"Oh." The steel bands gripping his chest loosened slightly.

Beau gave him a look. "Sounds like someone I know."

Penny smiled. "Your mom, maybe?"

"No, ma'am." Beau shook his head. "Our mother's fantastic and she's always there when we need her, but I was referring to this guy." He jerked a thumb in Sky's direction.

Heat rose from Sky's collar. "Hey, Beau, I'm not—"

"The hell you're not. You're an effing Rock of Gibraltar." Beau glanced in Penny's direction. "Beg pardon, ma'am."

She grinned and crossed her arms. "I'm not as sweet and innocent as I look."

That got Sky's attention. He'd pegged her as Miss Goody Two-Shoes — not much makeup, straight blonde hair in a simple style, a loose black turtleneck, wide-legged pants and loafers. His mother dressed more seductively than Penny.

Clearly this pretty, conservatively dressed woman wasn't trying to attract male attention. That intrigued him. "Who's Ben?"

"Her husband."

"She remarried?" Funny how that pricked him. Like it was an act of disloyalty to his father. A father he'd never known. Dumb reaction.

"They had a simple ceremony in July. She told me she'd never expected to marry again, but— anyway, let me show you something." She walked over to a massive antique desk with a sizable number of small drawers and cubbies.

His mom would go nuts over that desk, assuming she was invited to visit this place. He wouldn't hazard a guess on that one.

Penny picked up a nine-by-twelve photo album lying on the desk, the kind of album folks put together before digital cameras changed the game. She brought it over. "Have you seen pictures of your dad?"

"Oddly enough, I haven't. Mom wasn't into the picture thing then. She started that with Beau's dad."

"Is that who she's with, now?"

"Uh, no." He exchanged a glance with Beau. Might be better to avoid that level of detail at this point. "She's single." Always and forever.

"Henri put this together from shots the guests took when she married Charley. She showed it to me today because in these pictures, Charley's about the age you are now. She wanted me to know what he looked like back then."

"How come?"

"I was supposed to help her figure out if you were a fraud."

"Why'd she leave it out?"

"In case you weren't making this up."

Henri didn't hate him, then. That mattered. To his surprise, it mattered a whole hell of a lot.

Penny held out the album.

He was dying to look at it, but he hesitated. "Should we wait until she gets back?"

"Do you want to?"

"Maybe we could glance at a couple of pages. Just so I can see if I look like him."

She started to say something, but stopped. Instead she handed over the album. "Let's sit on the couch. It's mostly self-explanatory, but Henri gave me some background."

"Sure." He held the album gingerly, keeping it flat like a serving tray while she walked around the rustic coffee table and settled on the end couch cushion.

Beau gestured for him to claim the middle spot. Then he sat to his right.

Sky balanced the album on his thighs. "I feel like I'm holding a ticking time bomb. Maybe we should wait."

Penny shifted, her shoulder brushing his. "Want my advice?"

He liked that she'd asked before giving it. He also liked being close to her. She smelled nice, like spice and pine. Oh, wait, the pine scent came from the big Christmas tree in the corner. But the spice was definitely her. "What's your advice?"

"Diffuse the bomb. Look at a few pages now. Save the rest for when she gets back."

"Good compromise." He opened the album. And the air left his lungs.

"Damn, bro." His brother's voice was hushed. "That could be you."

Emotion swelled in his chest and tightened his throat. For one awful moment, he teared up. *Get it together, dude.* He blinked and cleared his throat. "I didn't expect... yeah, he's... we're..."

"Clearly related." The smile in Penny's voice helped. "Your mom didn't mention that you looked like your dad?"

"She said I did, but she couldn't say for sure how much. It's been thirty-two years. And a lot of... water under the bridge." The first page of the album held a single five-by-seven picture, a younger version of Henri smiling up at a man who looked just like him. He stared at it so hard it began to blur. "I thought I might have the same nose or the same chin."

"You have the same everything, bro."

"It's startling how much you resemble him." Penny leaned closer to the album, bringing her spicy scent closer, too. "It's amazing Henri didn't run out the door the minute she laid eyes on you."

"She did look a little peaked," Beau said. "Like she could've used a shot of whiskey."

"I could sure use one." Sky dragged in a breath. His father looked so happy, so *alive*. But he wasn't. Damn. Damn it to hell. He should have driven over here.

"What kind of booze do you like?" Penny pushed to her feet. "I'll check the liquor cabinet."

"No, never mind." He had the insane urge to touch the picture, but he might leave a smudge. The photo didn't have any kind of plastic sleeve. It was stuck on the page with the same kind of black corners his mother had used when she'd made the daddy albums for each of the kids.

"Take her up on the offer." Beau nudged him gently with his elbow. "I'll have one with you."

Sky glanced at Penny. "My mom mentioned that hard apple cider is the thing around here."

"Oh, yeah, and there's plenty of that. Henri keeps a second fridge back in the laundry room stocked with it."

"Will you join us?"

"Yes." She smiled. "Be right back."

Beau lowered his voice. "That's a good-looking woman right there."

"I have eyes."

"Just checking that you noticed."

"But she's not trying to get noticed."

"Those are the ones to watch out for. You think she isn't all that hot, and then *bam*, she gives you a smile like Penny just did and it's all over."

"You interested?"

"No, sir. My heart belongs to Jessica."

"It does? You two are serious?"

"Gettin' there. Even if we weren't, I'm not starting up with someone who's a four-hour drive from Wagon Train. And that's in good weather. Plenty of prospects closer to home." He glanced at Sky. "How 'bout you? Wanna be a travelin' man?"

Sky dredged up a smile. "I know what you're doing and I appreciate it, but—"

"You needed a distraction. You were looking pitiful, bro, like somebody died."

"Somebody did. I already knew that, but seeing his picture... he wasn't real to me before. Now he is."

"Yeah. It sucks. I wish there was something—"

"Here you go." Penny walked in carrying three open bottles by the necks. Each one had a knit red sleeve cupping the lower part of the bottle. A felt Santa face decorated the sleeves.

Beau stood and relieved her of two of them. "Thank you, ma'am. Festive presentation."

"I put those on so we won't drip on the album." As she resumed her seat, her thigh made contact with Sky's. "Sorry." She edged away.

"No worries." Firm thigh. The lady was in shape. He closed the album and set it on the coffee table. "I'm not taking any chances on drips or spilling. I found out what I needed to know." He took the bottle Beau handed him. "Thanks. Seems like we need to toast Charley Fox."

"To Charley." Penny tapped the neck of her bottle against his.

Beau reached over and touched the lip of his bottle to Sky's. "To your dad."

"To my dad, Charley Fox." He took a gulp of the cider and swallowed past a lump of guilt. "Wish I'd come over here earlier."

"Why didn't you?" Penny's question hung in the air.

He took another swig. "Told myself it would serve no good purpose. Mom left it up to me and I just thought it would be disruptive. Potentially upsetting."

"Then why come now? He's gone, but you've thrown Henri for a loop."

"It's my mom's idea. She just published her fiftieth book and she—"

"*What?*" Penny swiveled to face him, bumping him with her knee in the process. She didn't bother to apologize this time. "Your mom has written *fifty* books?"

"Yes, ma'am." He was so used to living with a full-time writer that he forgot the number would seem excessive to most folks.

"What kind of books?"

"Westerns."

"No kidding. That's my area."

"Your area? What does that—"

"What name does she use?"

"It's—"

"Hang on." Beau left his seat and crossed to a bookcase that occupied one wall. "Let's do a show-and-tell." Pulling out a paperback, he took it to Penny. "This is one of my favorites, but Henri has a slew of others. Or maybe Charley bought 'em. Either way, Mom's been here all along."

"Your mother is M.R. Morrison?"

"Yes, ma'am." Sky glanced up at Beau and smiled. "One of your favorites, huh? I wonder why?"

"Excellent story. Courageous cowboy hero."

"Who just happens to be named Beau."

"Really?" Penny flipped over the book and read the back blurb. "Sure enough. There you are. Your first name, anyway."

"Sky gets the place of honor, though. She used his name in the first book she sold."

"Sky?" Penny trained those mesmerizing gray eyes on him. "That's your nickname?"

"It is."

"I think I read that book. Maybe that's why your name sounded familiar. I like it."

"So do I." And he was beginning to like Penny.

"Your last name, though, that seems... improbable."

"You'll have to take that up with our mom. When she turned twenty-one, she ditched the name Doris Ann Miller and reinvented herself as Desiree Annabel McLintock."

The light dawned in Penny's gray eyes. "Just like Marion Robert Morrison reinvented himself as John Wayne."

"Just like that."

"That's so cool. And clever. M.R. Morrison. A subtle tip of the hat to the Duke." Then she looked confused. "But why would you and Beau show up here because your mother hit a publishing milestone?"

"We didn't come alone."

"Tell me you didn't leave her out in your truck."

"She's at the Apple Grove Hotel. She didn't know how Henri would feel about this, so we're the scouting party."

"I still don't get why—"

"The person who told her to submit her work to a publisher, the one who handed her a

Louis L'Amour book and said she could write just as well... that person was Charley Fox."

4

"Does your mom know Charley's passed on?" Penny held her breath. How sad if Sky's mother thought the guy was still around.

He nodded. "Yes, ma'am, she knows."

"Oh, good." Her breath whooshed out in relief. "I mean, not good that he's gone, but if she'd come here hoping to thank him in person..."

"She always intended to make a production of it when she published her fiftieth book. Then she came across his obituary online five years ago. Hit her pretty hard."

"Yeah, it did." Beau drained his cider. "We were all worried about her."

"All?" So the family was bigger than these two guys and their mom.

"Well, there's—"

"We live on a big ranch." Sky's interruption came across as deliberate.

She let it go. This wasn't the time to cross-examine them. "I'm not surprised you live on a big ranch. That's appropriate for a successful writer of Westerns. Makes for great promo, too."

"To a point," Beau said. "All her fans think she's a man."

"I guess that makes sense. Most of the successful authors in the genre are male."

"She figured that out real early," Sky said. "You won't find pictures of M.R. Morrison anywhere. Not inside the book and not online."

"So her identity is a secret?"

Sky nodded. "And I'm sure we can count on you to keep it that way."

"Of course I will. So will Henri. And the Brotherhood."

"Brotherhood?" Beau sat forward, his dark gaze alert. "Have we stumbled on some underground society?"

"No, no. Nothing like that. It's just the wranglers who work at the Buckskin. Nothing ominous."

"Might not be ominous," Beau said, "but I've never heard of ranch employees calling themselves a brotherhood."

"Charley and Henri had a habit of hiring young men who needed... stability. A loving home. They've bonded because they have similar histories."

Sky frowned. "But didn't Charley and Henri have kids of their own, too?"

"No."

"Then why did the obituary say he was survived by his wife and sons?"

"Henri and Charley treated them like sons, but it's not a legal thing. When Charley died, they created the Brotherhood as a tribute to him. He was the closest thing to a father they'd ever had."

"I see." His gaze dropped. "He must have been a great guy."

"That's what I hear from my brother Leo. He's a member of the Brotherhood. He was devoted to Charley."

"Your brother?" Sky glanced up again. "Is that why you're here, too? You didn't have a place to go, either."

"No, I'm visiting from California. I've never lived—" She stopped talking as the front door opened, letting in a gust of frigid air.

"We're here," Ben called out. "Got the horses all situated for the night. Brisk out there." Rustling noises indicated they were dispensing with their coats.

Beau put down his empty cider bottle, stood and moved away from the couch.

Sky set his bottle next to Beau's, got to his feet and turned to offer Penny a hand.

The gesture startled her. She still hadn't acclimated to cowboy manners. Very few male members of the UCLA faculty would have done what was clearly automatic behavior for this guy. She let him help her up and gave him a smile. "It'll be fine."

"Hope so."

She'd started out as Henri's ally, but now she was Skyler's, too. She rounded the coffee table, unsure of her next move. Then Henri walked into the living room looking like she'd been run over by a truck. All doubt vanished. Penny went to her and held out both hands.

Henri grabbed them with a grip like iron. "How's it going?"

"Great. I served them bottles of cider. I hope that's okay."

"Perfect. I—"

"Good Lord." Ben froze, his gaze on Sky. "You told me he was the spittin' image, but I didn't..." He huffed out a breath, straightened his shoulders and made for the two brothers. "Skyler and Beau, welcome to the Buckskin. I'm Ben Malone."

A tiny smile lifted the corners of Henri's mouth. "That's my Ben. Excellent recovery time." She gave Penny a quick nod and let go of her hands. "I can do this."

"I know you can." Turning, Penny watched as Henri joined Ben and shook hands with each of the brothers. No hugs, though. Henri reserved her hugs for those she cherished. These two men weren't in that category. Time would tell if they'd ever be.

Henri glanced back at Penny and beckoned her closer. "I didn't properly introduce you before."

"Of course you did."

"Not really. Knowing you, you didn't talk about yourself, either."

"I told them I was Leo's sister."

"Bet you didn't mention that you teach at UCLA."

"No, she did not." Sky regarded her with lifted eyebrows. "What subject?"

"American Lit. With a specialty in the Western genre."

"So that's why you've read M.R. Morrison."

She nodded. "And I think that's your cue."

"I think you're right." He walked to the wingback chair Henri had occupied, picked up the Louis L'Amour book she'd left there and offered it to her. "My mother asked me to give you this. She wanted you to know that... Charley changed her life."

"Clearly." Henri's head was high, but her voice quivered just a little. She made no move to take the book. "He gave her a son."

Had Henri longed to have babies with Charley? If they'd tried with no success, this revelation had to sting.

"That's true. But he gave her something else, confidence in herself and her talent. Please read what he wrote to her inside this book. There's a letter, too, from my mother to you."

A tense silence descended as Henri accepted the book and slowly opened it. Handing the envelope to Ben, she glanced at the words written on the inside cover. "That's definitely his writing."

"Yes, ma'am." Sky's expression softened. "More like his printing. I guess he liked to use all caps."

Penny's chest hurt. Did he realize how much he'd treasured this small sample of his dad's handwriting? He'd likely studied it, maybe even memorized it. Now the book and its inscription belonged to Henri.

Closing the book, Henri swallowed and wrapped her arms around it, holding it tight against her chest. "He... he was like that. Encouraging others to be their best selves."

"He was," Ben said. "Best friend in the world. He told me I was a fool if I didn't buy the Choosy Moose when it went up for sale. Best business decision I ever made, but I was ready to chicken out. Charley wouldn't let me."

Beau perked up. "You own that place?"

"For twenty-four years, now." He looked at Henri and held up the envelope. "Want to tackle this or leave it for another time?"

She took a shaky breath. "I'm not sure I'm up for it."

"Um, Henri?" Penny prayed she wasn't sticking her nose in where it didn't belong. "I think you'll want to know what's in that letter."

Henri gave her a sharp glance. "You've read it?"

"No, but after talking to Sky and Beau, I have some idea of what it says."

"Let me take a guess. She'll make a case for why she didn't tell Charley she was pregnant with his child." Anger vibrated through her words as she gazed at Sky. "She cheated Charley out of that experience. And she cheated you."

To his credit, he didn't flinch. "Not really. I've always known who my father was. I could have come over any time. Before I could drive, she would have brought me if I'd asked. I didn't. This trip was her idea, not mine."

"She sent you to Apple Grove?"

"No. She came, too."

Henri gasped and looked around, as if expected her to jump out of a closet. "Where is she?"

"Settling in at the Apple Grove Hotel."

"Oh, my God, Skyler! First I thought it was just you, and then it turned out to be you and Beau, and now you tell me your *mother's* in town? What next? An impromptu Christmas concert by Faith Hill and Tim McGraw?"

Beau chuckled. "Wait here. I'll go tell them it's time to set up."

5

Beau could be counted on to make comments like that, whether they were appropriate or not. This time Sky was grateful. The temperature in the room lowered considerably.

Even Henri gave Beau a brief smile.

Maybe he could build on that. "My mom was hoping you'd read the letter and feel more kindly toward her. Then we could let you know she was at the hotel."

"I see." Clearly Henri wasn't thinking kindly of his mother just yet.

"Sometimes she forgets that people in real life don't act the way she would have written the scene in a book."

"So I take it she became an author?"

"Yes, ma'am. She writes Westerns."

"Under what name?" Henri flicked an uneasy glance at the bookcase. Then she zeroed in on the paperback Penny had left lying on the coffee table. "*M.R. Morrison*?" Her eyes widened.

He couldn't tell if she was shocked or appalled. Maybe a little of both. In any case, she didn't look pleased. He gestured toward the letter

Ben continued to hold. "I'm pretty sure she put the pertinent info in there if you'd be willing to—"

"I'll read it." She plucked the buff-colored rectangular envelope from Ben's fingers. Pulling out the matching sheet of Rowdy Ranch stationery, she unfolded it. "Damn, I need my—"

"I'll get 'em." Ben crossed to the desk and picked up her glasses.

"Why Rowdy Ranch?" Henri made eye contact with Sky. "Are you and Beau the rambunctious sort?"

"No, ma'am."

"Sometimes." Beau grinned.

Clearing his throat, Sky gave him a look that said *not now*. It would do no good. Beau was Beau. "She named the ranch after Rowdy Yates, the Clint Eastwood character in—"

"*Rawhide.* I'm familiar with the show." She didn't act like she was happy to hear that piece of information, either.

The potential for turning this visit into a positive occasion was fading fast. He and Beau might have to get sloshed with their mom tonight, after all.

Henri thanked Ben for bringing over her glasses, slid them on and began to read his mom's letter. She'd revised it several times and had asked his opinion on each version. She'd agonized over those words more than any scene she'd written.

He had to be prepared for Henri to tear it up. Needing a bit of comfort, he looked at Penny.

Turned out she was looking right back. She gave him an encouraging smile that eased the heaviness in his chest, a smile that prompted him to give her one in return. She'd been terrific in the clutch and despite what he'd told Beau, he'd like to get to know her better.

Not much point in that, though. She made her home in California. A four-hour drive from Wagon Train to Apple Grove would be an iffy arrangement. Round-trip jaunts to L.A. were out of the question.

On top of that, her brother lived on this ranch. Her brother and his posse. Sky was familiar with that dynamic.

He and his brothers interrogated every male who dared cast an eye in their little sister Angelique's direction. No doubt Penny was similarly well-guarded by Leo and this Brotherhood bunch.

"Well." Henri glanced up. "So you're Skyler Charles McLintock."

"Yes, ma'am. I always knew my dad's name was Charles."

"Most folks called him Charley." Henri heaved a sigh and folded the letter. "I can say one thing for Desiree Annabel McLintock, aka M.R. Morrison. She's a good writer."

"She'd be happy to hear you think so." Sky figured there was a *but* coming.

"But I still have a problem with her decision to keep her pregnancy a secret from Charley. He would have been over the moon about you, Skyler."

"Most folks call me Sky." Yep, the jury was in. Henri didn't want to play. He'd be at the Choosy Moose with his mom and his brother sucking down hard cider tonight.

"I should have guessed it was Sky. Just like in the book where you're the hero."

"You read it?"

"I've read all M.R. Morrison's books. Beau's in that one." Henri pointed to the paperback on the coffee table.

"Yes, ma'am." Beau smiled. Clearly he thought the battle could still be won. "And that's not the whole of it. She named me after Louis L'Amour's son. Isn't that something?"

"That's something, all right." Henri's expression didn't change.

"I have a lot to live up to, although not as much as Clint. He's—"

"You have a brother named Clint?"

Oh, boy. Sky shot Beau a warning look but he was on a roll, determined that Henri would admire his amazing, creative mother.

"Sure do. We're only eleven months apart. He's named for Clint Walker and Clint Eastwood, so that one does double duty. And here's where my mom got crazy clever. She named Clint's twin Cheyenne, Clint Walker's character in—"

"*Cheyenne.* I know that one, too." Henri studied him. "Sounds like your mother has quite a brood."

"Yes, ma'am." Beau gave Sky a quick glance, as if he'd finally grabbed a clue that the game was over and he needed to shut his trap. "And I just remembered that we promised her we'd be back before five, so we'd best be going, right, Sky?"

"I was just about to say that."

Henri blinked. "Hang on. We haven't discussed how long you'll be in town."

Beau gestured for him to answer.

Easy one. "I expect we'll shove off in the morning." The hour would depend on how long they stayed at the Choosy Moose drowning their sorrows.

"I have some people who will want to meet you."

Too bad for her, he wasn't in a socializing mood. "The Brotherhood?"

"You know about the Brotherhood?"

"I filled them in a little," Penny said. "They were confused because the notice about Charley mentioned he had sons."

"Yes, well... he did. And they'll have a fit if I don't arrange for them to meet you. Millie will also be upset if she misses seeing you. And Lucy. They knew and loved Charley."

Ben touched her shoulder. "Don't forget the Babes."

"Right. The Babes." She rubbed her forehead. "Maybe the answer is for all of us to gather at the Moose tonight." She looked over at Ben. "Isn't this the night you're testing out your buffet idea?"

"As a matter of fact."

"That might be perfect for this situation." She glanced at Sky. "Would that work for you? An evening at the Moose to meet some folks?" A hint of vulnerability flickered in her eyes. She needed this from him.

That gave him leverage. He used it. "Only if my mother is invited. And made to feel welcome."

Henri's jaw tightened.

"She risked a lot coming here. She didn't have to, but she felt it was important to acknowledge Charley's part in her success. She has fond memories of Apple Grove. I'm not leaving her alone in the hotel while the rest of us party at the Choosy Moose."

Taking a deep breath, Henri nodded. "Well said. I admire your loyalty and respect. And your protective instincts. You do her proud. Please bring her."

"Yes, ma'am. What time should we be there?"

"Let's say an hour from now. I should be able to round up the gang by then. When they hear what it's about, they'll drop everything."

Sky checked his phone. "An hour it is." He looked over at Penny. "You'll be there, won't you?"

"Wouldn't miss it."

"Good." He held her gaze for a moment and enjoyed the sweet rush of warmth in his chest. Too bad nothing could come of it. But maybe they could have a dance or two tonight. "See you then." He headed for the entryway. "Let's make tracks, Beau."

"I'm right behind you."

"We'll reserve a couple of adjoining booths and tables," Henri called after them. "Just tell them you're with the Buckskin gang."

"Great. Thanks." He kept going.

"Oh, and Sky?"

He turned back as Beau fetched their jackets and hats from the coat tree. "Ma'am?"

"Don't worry about the Brotherhood. They'll be thrilled to meet you. None of them know..." She swallowed. "Charley and I really wanted kids. We tried everything. We were all set to adopt when Matt—well, that's a long story. And you need to go."

"Yes, ma'am." He took the jacket Beau handed him and crammed his Stetson on his head. "See you soon." Buttoning his jacket as he went out the door, he pulled the door closed with a soft click. "Damn."

"Yeah." Beau hurried down the steps. "Gonna tell Mom that bit of info?"

"She needs to know." He followed Beau over to the truck, digging his keys out of his pocket. "She probably assumed he'd have kids with Henri. Then the obit confirmed that he'd had sons, so no worries on that score."

"Now I'm feeling extra bad that I mentioned Clint and Cheyenne. Good thing I didn't list the others."

"Yeah, that would have made it worse." He sighed. "Like Mom says, she's excelled at two things — writing books and having babies."

<u>6</u>

Penny caught a ride to the Moose with Leo and Fiona. They'd offered, and when she'd checked with Henri, her hostess had looked relieved. The drive into town likely would give her an opportunity for a private conversation with Ben.

Leo had been running errands in Great Falls and got held up by a semi that had jackknifed, temporarily blocking the highway. He texted Penny that he and Fiona would be a little late picking her up. Fine with her. She had time to put on makeup and change into the outfit she'd bought at the town's Western wear shop.

The minute she settled into the back seat of Leo's truck, he and Fiona wanted the whole story. She shared everything except Henri's last revelation. She'd promised Henri she'd keep that to herself. If the information made its way to the rest of the Buckskin gang, it wouldn't be her doing.

"This is like something out of a movie." Fiona twisted around so she could look at Penny while they talked. "Did Henri say whether she'd ever heard of this ex-girlfriend?"

"No, but she didn't act like it. I think Desiree McLintock was news to her. And she was totally shocked to find out the author she'd been reading for years was Charley's ex."

"I don't picture Charley discussing other girlfriends with the love of his life." Leo slowed down as he took a curve in the ranch road that was famous for being slippery. "He had class. Once he fell for Henri, there was no other woman in the world as far as he was concerned."

"Henri's not naïve, though," Fiona said. "She had to assume he'd had other relationships, even if he didn't talk about them."

"I'm sure." Penny unbuttoned her jacket as the truck's heater warmed up the cab. "But who would expect something like this? It really threw her."

"Yeah, I'll bet." Leo glanced in the rearview mirror. "How's she doing, sis? I don't want to get wrapped up in the drama and forget about Henri."

"She's coping, but it's been difficult. She's not feeling kindly toward Desiree for depriving Charley of the chance to know his son."

"That's a tough one." Leo sighed. "Charley would have loved to be part of his life. Hell, the Brotherhood would have loved it, especially when we lost Charley. His son could have been so much comfort. To Henri, for sure, but to all of us, really."

"You'll think that even more when you see him. That phrase *a chip off the old block* is perfect for Sky. He looks exactly like the pictures of Charley in their wedding album."

"Which isn't how I remember him, so that might keep me from totally freaking out. Charley was fifteen years older when I hired on, so I might not have the same reaction as Henri."

"Ben looked like he was seeing a ghost."

"Of course he did. He was Charley's best friend. I think he was the best man at their wedding. I'm glad Henri has Ben to help her through this."

"And you guys," Fiona said. "And the Babes. Did Henri ask them to come tonight, too?"

"She did, but she asked them to show up a little later. They're eager to meet Sky, but his mother is a different story. Henri decided it wasn't fair to bring in the Babes right off the bat."

"That's kind, under the circumstances," Leo said. "She could have just turned the Babes loose on Desiree. Facing Henri is one thing. Facing Henri when she's surrounded by her posse is a whole other thing. Desiree wouldn't be prepared for that."

"I wonder if she's prepared for the Buckskin gang, to be honest. I was a little overwhelmed when I came here for your wedding in October, and yet I knew I'd have a warm welcome. Desiree has no such guarantee. For that matter, neither does Sky."

"Which is the point of this gathering." Leo pulled out on the paved two-lane that led into town. "We'll all be nice, but we'll be watching, too. He might look a bit like Charley, but that doesn't matter if he's a jerk."

"He's not a jerk."

"Time will tell, sis."

"Yeah, okay. I blew the call on Barry. But I'll go out on a limb and say he's a good person."

"I hope you're right, for everyone's sake. I wonder if he has Charley's eyes. That's what I remember when I think of him. So blue, and you could tell the wheels were always turning."

"Skyler has great eyes." Whoops. Had she said that out loud? And let out a sigh, on top of it?

Leo sat up straighter and peered in the rearview mirror again. "Does he, now?"

"Don't go all big brother on me. I didn't mean that the way it sounded."

"I hope not. We've taken a vote and you're on restriction for at least six months."

"*We*? You mean you and Fiona?"

"The Brotherhood."

"Ah. That makes more sense. I didn't think that sounded like you, Fi."

"Thanks." She gave her a smile.

"And for your information, Leo, you guys aren't the boss of me."

"Don't we know it. But seriously, six months is a good idea. A year would be even better."

"Gonna lock me in my room?"

"If only we could. I've told them you're extremely intelligent and sensible, though. You're not the type to go crazy and do the rebound thing. Please don't make a liar out of me with some cowboy who has great eyes."

"As you wish, brother dear."

"You're not taking this seriously, are you?"

"Why should I? Last I heard he's leaving town in the morning."

"Famous last words. I'm gonna alert the Brotherhood to keep an eye on this dude, make sure he doesn't step out of line."

Fiona groaned. "Leo, really?"

"What?"

"I thought you were smarter than this." She glanced back at Penny and shrugged. "Evidently not."

"I could have told you."

Leo looked over at Fiona. "I have no idea what you two are talking about."

"Which is sad, my darling. News flash — putting all this emphasis on a situation that would likely have resolved itself turns it into a tempting challenge."

Penny grinned. She'd won the sister-in-law lottery when she got Fiona.

Leo huffed out a breath. "That's ridiculous." He glanced in the rearview mirror again. "Come on, Penny. You know as well as I do that after a bad breakup, it's best to avoid relationships for a while."

"You're so right, Leo." She ducked her head so he couldn't see her face.

If a certain cowboy asked her to dance tonight, and she was reasonably sure he would, she planned to accept. She appreciated the support and protective instincts of Leo and the rest of the Brotherhood, but if they thought they could dictate how she conducted her love life, they had another think coming.

***

Penny had never seen the Choosy Moose done up for Christmas, but she'd heard about it from her brother. Ben and his staff's liberal use of evergreen boughs, holly and festive lights created a warm holiday atmosphere.

A Christmas tree stood in a corner behind the bandstand, and the large plush moose head mounted over the bar was covered in sticky bows courtesy of the Brotherhood's recent toy-wrapping session.

Fiona looked at it and chuckled. "You guys did an excellent job with the bows."

"Thanks. We got a little slap-happy. The community donated a boatload of toys, which is great, but wrapping them took for*ever*." He helped Fiona and Penny with their jackets. "I'll haul these to the coat room. Be right back."

"I love Operation Santa," Penny said. "It's a good cause, but I love it mostly because it brought you two together."

"I love it, too." Fiona smiled. "I would have happily done the Santa and elf thing again this year, but Ben loves it so much."

"I could tell. He was as excited as a kid last night when he got dressed in the suit and drove off in his freshly washed red Santa truck. He looked adorable."

"But not as adorable as I looked, I'll bet." Leo returned, adjusting the fit of his Stetson. It was customary for the guys to leave their hats on at the Moose.

"I can't say. I wasn't here." Penny gave him a teasing glance. "Since when did you start fishing for compliments? The brother I knew hated people mentioning his looks."

"I still do, but being in costume is different. I was proud of my Santa routine."

"You were adorable, too, sweetie." Fiona patted him on the cheek. "You rocked that red suit."

"Thanks. You're prejudiced, but I'll take it." He surveyed the room. "I just spotted the Buckskin gang over in the corner. Is that Skyler, the one sitting at the far end of the booth? He's turned away from me."

"That's him." She'd picked him out immediately. Catching sight of him gave her heart rate a boost.

Then he looked their way and Leo sucked in a breath. "Damn. Put streaks of gray in that guy's hair, a few more lines on his face, and he's Charley Fox."

"Told you."

"Yeah, I know, but..."

"Ready to head over?" She was, especially after the welcoming smile Sky had just given her. A fifty-something woman with an upswept arrangement of auburn curls sat next to him. Had to be Desiree.

Sky started to get out of the booth, his gaze on her, when Jake, the unofficial co-captain of the Brotherhood, intercepted him, keeping him in his seat.

He'd been on his way over. She'd swear to it. She pinned Leo with a look. "Did you by chance text the Brotherhood while you were taking care of our jackets?"

"Who, me?"

"You did! Jake just kept Sky from coming over to meet us."

"Could've been a coincidence."

"Yeah, right." She was tall, but still six inches shorter than her brother. Getting in his face was tricky, but she did her best. "Listen up. I'm an adult. An adult with a fair amount of blackmail material on you. If I want to spend time with Skyler McLintock tonight, I will. Got it?"

"But—"

"I mean it, Leo. Pull out your phone and call off the Brotherhood. I love them dearly, but they don't get to stop me from having a lovely evening dancing with a handsome cowboy. I could use an ego boost. Quite likely he'll be gone tomorrow and I don't want to miss my chance."

Fiona nudged him. "Do it, Leo. Penny's right about this."

He held his wife's gaze. "Okay." Taking his phone from his pocket, he tapped the screen a few times. "Done."

"Done?" Penny lifted her eyebrows. "You sure? That was awfully fast."

"Just needed a code word."

"What code word?"

"Don't bother asking," Fiona said. "When it comes to the Brotherhood, he's a vault."

"Oh, I could break the code if I wanted to." She glanced at Leo. "Keep the Brotherhood in check and I won't use my code-breaking superpowers. Understood?"

A glimmer of amusement lit his eyes. "Yes, ma'am."

7

Delicate situation. Sky had his hands full monitoring the stilted conversation between his mother and Henri while he watched for Penny. By stationing himself at the end of the curved booth, he'd have an easier time of getting out so he could walk over and invite her to sit with him.

Just his luck she'd arrived late. Being on the end also meant he was fair game. A constant stream of Buckskin folks from the neighboring booth and nearby tables had stopped by to look him over while they made small talk and figured out if they liked him or not. He couldn't say whether he'd made a good impression, but he'd enjoyed the heck out of this bunch so far.

Too bad he couldn't relax and just hang with them, but the underlying tension between his mom and Henri kept him on alert. The booze was flowing — everyone had either a glass of wine or a bottle of cider — but liquor hadn't worked its magic on Henri and his mom.

Happy-go-lucky Beau likely was oblivious to the dynamic. He sat between Ben and a guy named CJ, one of the Buckskin wranglers who also played guitar. CJ's wife Isabel had tucked in next to her husband and those four had a lively discussion about music going on.

His mom and Henri had settled on a somewhat neutral topic—what had changed in Apple Grove over the last thirty years and what hadn't. They'd almost exhausted that subject and they were no friendlier than they'd been at the start of it. His mom was making an effort, but Henri remained frosty.

Penny would be a big help. She had a positive effect on Henri and his mother would be tickled at Penny's academic choice. As for him, he couldn't wait to see her again. But when she finally walked in, Jake appeared from the other booth and settled in next to him, blocking his way out.

Jake had introduced himself earlier and they'd found common ground talking about the raptor rescue program. This time Jake launched into a story involving Charley's love of dinosaurs and root beer floats. Weird as hell, almost as if he'd been told to head over and keep Sky in his seat.

And away from Penny? Maybe. If so, they'd have to work damn hard. At a bare minimum, he planned to dance with her tonight. The band was setting up and should begin playing soon.

In the middle of his root-beer float monologue, Jake's phone pinged. Excusing himself, he glanced at it and stood. "Nice talking to you. As a point of interest, do *you* like root beer floats?"

"Not crazy about them." The minute Jake gave him enough room, he slid out of the booth. "Dinosaurs are cool, though."

Jake stared at him. "You even sound like Charley, dude."

"I wouldn't know."

"Take my word for it. He was soft-spoken, but we had no trouble understanding him. He took care with his words. You do that." Jake shook his head. "Crazy."

"He's right," Henri said. "I've noticed that, too. If I close my eyes, I can almost convince myself Charley's here talking."

Jake shivered. "That would give me the gollywobbles. I'm keeping my eyes wide open." He turned as Penny approached the booth with a couple Sky hadn't met. "Well, if it isn't Dr. Marston."

Dr. Marston? That was news to Sky. But he didn't have time to dwell on the new bit of information in the flurry of introductions that followed.

"I'm so pleased to meet you all." His mom scooted out of the booth so she could shake hands with Penny, Leo and Fiona. "Now I can identify every member of the Buckskin gang."

"Except I'm not a member," Penny said.

"Oh, yes, you are." Leo wrapped an arm around her shoulders. "You're my little sister. You're automatically in."

His mom smiled. "That's sweet. And did I hear Jake call you Dr. Marston?"

"Yes, ma'am."

"That's quite an accomplishment."

"Thank you. So is writing fifty books. Congratulations."

"Thanks. It's the result of hard work sprinkled with fairy dust. I've also had generous help and advice from friends in publishing. I'll bet you've had the same at the university."

"Um, yes. I've been... very fortunate."

"Sky told me you've read—oh, my goodness!" She swung toward the bandstand. "That's the intro to *A Better Man.* Sky, did you request it for me?"

"I might've." It had been her favorite for years. If hearing it tonight gave her a lift, that was more than worth the tip he'd given the band.

"Thank you, son." She glanced at Penny. "Do you dance country?"

"I'm working on it."

"Then get out there with Sky. I'll snag—" She looked up as Beau appeared by her side. "Just the man I was looking for."

He laughed. "I figured that the minute I heard this. Let's go."

"I'm gonna learn to play this one," CJ said as he passed by with Isabel. "I forgot how much I like Clint Black. Thanks for jostling my memory, Sky."

"Welcome." Evidently the Buckskin gang shared CJ's opinion of the song because everybody was heading to the dance floor.

"Are you going to ask my sister to dance or aren't you?"

He met Leo's gaze. Quietly taking Penny out on the floor while everyone else was occupied had been his original plan. Revealing his interest in her right under her big brother's nose might not be the wisest course of action. "Will it get me into trouble?"

"No." Penny said it with firm authority. "I've handled that. Come on."

He chuckled. "Alrighty, then." He tucked his arm around her waist and followed the rest of the gang. "I'm glad you handled whatever needed to be handled." He twirled her onto the dance floor.

"Leo asked the Brotherhood to keep an eye on you, make sure you didn't step out of line."

"Can't say I'm surprised." Holding her was like wrapping his arms around sunshine.

"Do they know something incriminating about you?"

"No, ma'am. But I'm a stranger and you're Leo's little sister. I know how that works."

"How do you know? Do you have a sister?"

"Matter of fact, I do. My brothers and I watch Angelique like a hawk."

"Isn't Angelique the name of Louis L'Amour's daughter?"

"It is but I'm surprised you—oh, wait. That's your area." This song was way too short. He knew it well, and they were already at the midpoint. "I like your cowgirl duds."

"Not too much bling?"

"I like sparkles." And the snug fit of her jeans, but he wasn't going to say that.

"I went a little crazy at Jeans Junction."

"Looks good on you." Mouth-watering.

"Thanks. So how are things going with Henri and your mom?"

"Not great. My mom's fantasy of becoming best buddies with Henri seems doomed."

"Which means you'll definitely be taking off in the morning?"

"I'm afraid so." He hesitated. "Listen, I don't want to get crossways with your brother or the rest of the gang, but I'm hoping we can spend some time together tonight."

"We can. I told Leo to back off. I have dirt on that boy, things the Brotherhood would tease him mercilessly about."

He laughed. "You and Angelique would get along."

"How old is she?"

"Twenty-three going on thirty-three."

"I'd love to meet her. I could give her some tips."

"Which tells me I need to keep you two far, far apart. Not that it will be difficult. Sounds like you're well and truly planted in L.A." He drew her closer, just a little bit. The entire Brotherhood was on the dance floor monitoring his every move. "Are you sure Leo told this Buckskin group to stand down?"

"He said he did. Why?"

"All of them seem mighty interested in the gap between your body and mine."

"Then let's give them something to worry about." On the next turn, she snuggled in. "How's that?"

He dragged in air. They fit perfectly. "Spectacular. Jake and Matt just gave me the evil eye. If I go missing, check the alley out back. I'll be lying in a bloody heap."

"No, you won't. These guys are not violent. They might give you a talking-to, but they don't beat people up. They have a creed — *What Would Charley Do?* I gather he wasn't the violent type, either."

"I'm slightly comforted by that."

"They're extra protective right now because I recently broke off my engagement after I discovered my fiancé was cheating on me."

"On *you*? Is he nuts?"

"You just made my evening."

"Then listen closely. You're beautiful, smart, and caring. He's a fool. Anybody who got a *yes* from you is one lucky bastard. I can't believe he messed it up."

She sighed. "See? I told them dancing with you would be good for my battered ego. The song's almost over, but can we do this again sometime soon?"

"Yes, ma'am, we certainly—"

"But not right away. You turn me on, and I need to catch my breath." The music stopped and she wiggled out of his arms. "Catch you later, cowboy."

Her departure was so abrupt that he stood there for a few seconds, stunned by her admission and the impossibility of doing anything about it.

Beau and his mom came toward him with matching frowns. Beau got in the first comment. "What did you do?"

"Nothing. She just—"

"She ran away," his mother said. "Did you upset her?"

"Evidently I turned her on."

"No, you didn't." Beau shook his head. "Women don't run *from* a guy who turns them on. They run *to* him."

"She said she needed to catch her breath."

"Ah." His mother smiled. "You're too potent for her."

"You think so?"

"I don't." Beau tipped his head toward their mom. "She does. I think you screwed up."

"Not necessarily, Beau. Maybe she recently broke up with someone."

"Good guess," Sky said. "Her fiancé cheated on her."

Beau winced. "Bummer."

"Then she's probably a bit fragile." His mother gazed at him. "You like her, don't you?"

"I do, but it's pointless."

"Nothing of a romantic nature is pointless, but some things are ill-advised. She might not be in the right place to get involved with you."

"Oh, she's definitely not. She lives in L.A."

"I wasn't talking about geography, son."

"I am. That factors into it."

"People can work around geographic hurdles. You're two intelligent people. You'd find a way. Her recent breakup is a bigger problem."

"I hate that she got slammed like that."

"I know you do." She laid a hand on his chest. "You have a good heart. But you could get yourself in trouble if you try to fix hers."

8

Penny needed some girl talk. Normally she'd turn to Henri, but that fine lady had enough on her plate. Penny collared Fiona before she and Leo reclaimed their seats. "I'm making a trip to the ladies' room. Want to go with me?"

"I don't really—"

"It's urgent."

"Oh. Then, sure. Let me grab my purse." She glanced at Leo. "Nature calls."

"Uh-uh. I know this routine." He looked at Penny. "I saw how cozy you and Sky were getting out there. You're asking for trouble."

"Like I said, he's a good person."

"I don't think you're in the right frame of mind to—"

"This is why I'm talking to your lovely wife instead of you. See you later." She led the way to the restroom with Fiona close behind.

Luckily, it was empty. The buffet had just opened and folks were lining up.

Fiona reached in her purse and pulled out a brush. "You didn't bring your purse?"

"I needed to grab you quick so I didn't go back for it."

"Then, here. Borrow my eyebrow pencil so it looks like we have a purpose for this visit if someone comes in."

"I've never owned one of these."

"Invest in one. Blonde eyebrows make us look like innocent waifs."

"And I'm neither." She experimented with the pencil. "I have the hots for Sky."

Fiona pulled the brush through her thick hair. "I figured. Whatcha going to do about it?"

"Logically I should do nothing. He'll go home in the morning and I'll never see him again. I'm not crazy about one-night stands."

"Me, either." Fiona met her gaze in the mirror. "That's plenty of eyebrow pencil. Too much, in fact. Grab a tissue and rub some off."

"I never got into this makeup stuff."

"I didn't used to be into it, either. Then I started hanging out with Eva."

"Nick's girlfriend? Blue hair? Stylist at Tres Beau?"

"That's her. She's taught me a lot. But never mind that. Do you want more time with Sky?"

"I do, even if there's no future in it. I hate to think of him leaving tomorrow."

"I'll bet you're not the only one."

"Henri?"

"She keeps looking at him. She'd probably love to have him stick around so they could get to know each other, but not if it means dealing with his mother the whole time."

"If only there was a way to get them to go home and leave him here for a few days. But…

Christmas. It sounds like their family is close. They'd want him back for the holiday."

"Of course they would. But they've had him for thirty-plus years. Isn't it Henri's turn?"

She met Fiona's gaze in the mirror. "Yes. Yes, it is. I have a selfish reason for wanting him to stay, but you're so right. Henri deserves to spend Christmas with Charley's son. Should we just suggest that to her?"

"Someone should, but not you. Your motives would be suspect."

"My motives *are* suspect. But it's still a great idea. Do you want to talk to her?"

"I could, but after that conversation in the truck, Leo would think I have ulterior motives, too. I'll get Eva to do it, however she thinks best, sometime this evening."

"The more I think about this, the better the idea gets. Henri won't need much convincing. She'd get to spend more time with Sky and make a point with Desiree. It's Henri's turn."

"My thoughts, exactly. The Brotherhood seems to like him so far. They'll be in favor of more time to examine him closely. They can put him through his paces, test his wrangler skills."

Penny grinned. "I'll make sure I'm on hand for that. Uh-oh. Just thought of something. Guess he'd be staying in Henri's house."

"That's logical."

"Right down the hall." Her heart rate picked up. "Not that I'd do anything about it. And neither would he. We both have manners."

"And like you said, there's no future."

"I'm sure he's figured that out, too."

"On the other hand, there's the present."

Penny smiled. "And it's Christmas, after all."

"Come on." Fiona tucked her brush in her purse. "Time to put this plan into action."

* * *

Penny and Fiona split up after they left the restroom. Fi grabbed Eva and Nick as they walked off the dance floor and Penny went back to the empty booth to retrieve her purse.

Everyone was in the buffet line, but her small shoulder bag still lay on the seat. After twenty-six years in L.A., she got a kick out of leaving her belongings lying around in a public place. Because this was Apple Grove, she could do that.

But since she might end up eating in another spot, she slung it over her shoulder as she crossed the room and joined the buffet line. Then she surveyed the room, looking for Sky.

Ah, there he was, leaning against the bar in a confab with Beau, Matt and Jake. Getting a talking-to? If so, it must be the most hilarious dressing-down ever, judging from all the laughing going on.

Although she was too excited to eat, she put a few things on her plate. What now?

"Penny, come sit with me." Desiree came toward her. "My boys are otherwise occupied so we have room at the table. You and I haven't had a chance to talk."

"No, we haven't. And I have a ton of questions regarding your books." Carrying her plate, napkin and silverware, she followed Desiree to the booth. Henri and Ben were back in their former spot. CJ and Isabel had been joined by Rafe and Kate.

Beau and Sky hadn't left plates there. Maybe they'd excused themselves and taken their dinner over to the bar. Or Matt and Jake had come to get them. By now Fiona would have set the wheels in motion for Eva to broach the subject to Henri. Better if Desiree's sons weren't there.

Penny waited for Desiree to slide in next to Henri. *Next to* was a relative term. About eighteen inches separated the two women. Desiree made a polite comment about how delicious the food looked. Henri thanked her and gave the credit to Ben. Then she took a long swallow of her apple cider.

Penny hated seeing Henri upset. Yes, Desiree had bravely taken a risk, one she could have skipped. But Henri had a right to feel cheated, both for Charley's sake and her own. Friendship between these two was a long way off and might never happen.

"You need another bottle of cider, Penny." Desiree motioned to a waiter. He hurried over, all smiles. "How can I help you, Miss McLintock?"

"Two more of those amazing ciders, please, Joey."

"Yes, ma'am."

"There you go again, sounding like Steve McQueen. I swear you could do an impersonation of him if you worked on it a little bit."

Joey beamed. "I just might try that, ma'am."

After he left, Desiree sighed. "I fell in love with a man years ago because he sounded exactly like Steve McQueen's character in *The Magnificent Seven*."

"He was great in that."

"You're telling me. Hero material."

"It sounds like you've been strongly influenced by the old Western movies and TV shows."

"Couldn't have made it through my childhood without them." She broke eye contact and gazed out at the milling crowd. "No dad around and my mom... wasn't into me all that much. Brave, handsome cowboys were my role models. They gave me a base to build my dreams on."

"And now you do the same for others."

"I've been told that, but honestly, I do it for me, too. This writing gig is the most fun you can have with your clothes on." She turned back, her expression friendly. "What fueled your dreams, Penny?"

"As a kid, I got deeply into *Lord of the Rings*."

Her perfect eyebrows rose. "So why didn't you study that? Why focus on the Western genre, instead?"

"*LOTR* has been analyzed so much. I wanted to get into a popular fiction niche that wasn't already bulging with dissertations. Besides, I like it. Plenty of heroes."

"I know. I love being surrounded by them."

"Fifty heroes. Is that your favorite part of the writing, creating those honorable characters?"

"Absolutely."

"Do you still draw your inspiration from those old Westerns?"

"I do, but also from my boys. And my daughter. And then there's—"

"Desiree."

She turned toward Henri. "Yes?"

"Sorry to interrupt. The friends I told you about—"

"The Babes on Buckskins? The barrel racers?"

"They just arrived. They're coming over to meet you."

"You said that with a note of warning in your voice. Should I stand up? Arm myself?"

"No need to arm yourself, but you might want to stand. It's hard to make decent eye contact when you're staring at a belt buckle."

"Okay, if you think—my goodness, I see what you mean. I haven't encountered this many tall women in one place except on a college basketball court."

Penny stood, too, and moved out of the booth to greet the Babes. Matt's wife Lucy came over from a nearby table. The youngest and shortest member of the group, she'd become an excellent barrel racer.

CJ and Rafe popped up to greet their beloved aunties. By the time the Babes made it to the far corner of the Choosy Moose, the booth had emptied out, poised to give them a proper welcome.

Henri took care of the introductions.

Ed, the eighty-six-years-young leader of the group, held out her hand to Desiree. "And all this time I thought M.R. Morrison was a man."

Desiree shook Ed's hand. "That's what you're supposed to think. I've taken great care to keep it that way."

"Don't worry. None of us will squeal on you. But personally, I think your fans would enjoy the heck out of the truth. Especially your women readers. Like me."

"I'll think about it. And thanks for reading."

"You're welcome. Oh, and one other thing. We discussed this situation on the drive over. We're troubled because Henri's upset."

"I know she is, and I wish—"

"Would you like to take a stab at making amends?"

"Amends? What's done is done. I don't see how I—"

"Leave Skyler here over Christmas. It doesn't wipe the slate clean, but it's a start."

Penny blinked. Had the Babes come up with it on their own? That was some coincidence.

Then she connected the dots. Eva co-owned Tres Beau with Josette. Josette was one of the Babes. Eva had texted Josette while the Babes were on the road and given them the job of presenting this idea. Awesome decision.

Desiree took a deep breath. "Christmas is a special time at Rowdy Ranch."

"It's special at the Buckskin, too." Henri threw her shoulders back and lifted her chin. She was down with this plan.

"I've never spent a Christmas without Sky."

"I've never spent a Christmas with him. And Charley never got the chance."

"You make a valid point." Desiree's cheeks flushed and her eyes took on a steely glint. "But Sky's a grown man. Neither of us gets to decide. It's his choice."

"Agreed."

Rafe swung into action. "I'll fetch him for you."

Sky arrived, with Beau, Matt and Jake right on his heels. "What's up, Mom?"

"I have a question for you. Henri would like you to stay here for Christmas. Do you want to do that?"

He gazed at his mother. Then his attention flicked briefly to Penny.

If she didn't have a poker face, it wasn't for lack of trying.

Finally, he looked at Henri. "Thank you for the invitation. I would like that very much."

Penny ducked her head to hide a grin of triumph. The jury was in. She had the smartest, best sister-in-law ever. And the combo of the Buckskin gang and the Babes wasn't too shabby, either.

9

Sky was immediately surrounded by Henri and the Babes. Everyone talked at once, reeling off a list of holiday activities — fire pit nights, barrel racing demonstrations, a Christmas Eve party at Ed's, a video of something called Operation Santa.

"I'm up for all of it. Can't wait." He gave them a big smile. "But if you'll excuse me for a bit, the band's playing one of my mom's favorites and I owe her a dance." Tipping his hat, he went in search of her.

She hadn't gone far. She and Penny stood near the booth, deep in conversation. Had Penny stepped in to provide his mother with a distraction? That would be like her.

When he approached, his mom paused in mid-sentence and turned. "Hey, son."

"Sorry to interrupt."

"No worries. What's up?"

"Thought you might like to dance to this one."

"Love to." She looked at Penny. "Thank you for rescuing me, sweetheart. You're a kind woman."

He'd second that. And add a few more things. Beautiful. Smart. Tempting as hell.

Penny's face lit up with pleasure at his mother's praise. "Are you kidding? I've been dying to get your take on that movie."

"Then we'll pick up where we left off when I get back."

"That's a deal. Enjoy your dance."

"I always do. He's an excellent dancer. His sense of rhythm is—"

"Time to go." He flashed Penny a grin and touched the brim of his hat. Then he laid his hand on the small of his mother's back in a show of guiding her through the cluster of people to the dance floor.

She didn't need the guidance. He'd never known a more self-sufficient woman. But she'd taught him it was a polite gesture and it was automatic, now. "Bet you were talking about *McLintock.*"

"Uh-huh. The Shakespearian aspect. She's sharp. I really like her."

"I really like her, too."

"Too bad about the timing."

"Yes, ma'am." He swung her into a quick two-step. They'd been dancing together ever since he could remember. When he was little, she'd hold his hands while she taught him the steps.

"I'll miss you like the devil, Sky."

"I'll miss you, too."

"It's probably the right call."

"I believe it is. But when you asked if I wanted to stay, I almost told Henri I'd come back after Christmas."

"Why didn't you?"

"The Brotherhood was... *is*... devoted to Charley, or to his memory, at any rate. Now that he's gone, they're closer to Henri than ever. If I'd turned her down on this Christmas thing, they wouldn't like it."

"I suppose not."

"I doubt I'd be as welcome if I came back in January. The Brotherhood is starting to like me enough to share stories about Charley. I want to hear them."

"Sure, you do." His mother sighed. "You know, if I'd encouraged you to come over here ten years ago, you—"

"No second guessing, Mom. That's not where I'm going with this."

"Maybe not, but I can't help thinking—"

"You gave me the choice. You didn't encourage or discourage me. I appreciate that you gave me the freedom to decide."

"I sure didn't expect him to die on us."

"Neither did they. They were devoted to him."

"So was I." Her soft comment sounded... wistful.

"Do you think maybe, if he hadn't met Henri—"

"Oh, I would have told him about you. I would have married him in a heartbeat."

"Wow."

"Please keep that to yourself, okay?"

"Of course."

"I kept looking for another Charley. Never found him. So I... made do." She gazed up at him.

"Henri couldn't have babies, and I'm sorry about that, but I'd say we're even. She got Charley."

His throat tightened. All this time she'd kept this under wraps. She'd lost the love of her life. "You almost had it all."

"Almost." Her expression softened. "But I'm not sad, Sky. Don't ever think that. I love you kids so much, and my writing brings me such joy. I'm very lucky."

"Me, too. You've given me — all of us — a great life. I'm glad we made this trip and I'm excited to get more info on my dad, but then I'll be ready to come home."

"You'll need someone to fetch you."

"I figured Beau would."

"I might ride along. Depending. Do you think Henri and I will ever be friends? Because I like her, too."

"I don't know if you'll end up friends or not, but she got what she wanted with this Christmas visit. That might take the edge off her resentment."

"If I'd known she and Charley couldn't have children, I would have played this differently."

"But you couldn't know."

"I should have suspected something was fishy when the obit said *survived by his wife Henri and his sons* without naming them. I assumed whoever wrote it didn't know any better."

"If you're trying to pin the blame on yourself, you need to stop. You came here with a glad heart, hoping that Henri would take the news about me and your tribute to Charley as a positive."

"I was naïve."

"And optimistic. Which I love about you. Look at it this way. For the next few days, you'll have me here, subtly painting a favorable picture of you for Henri. I'll be your goodwill ambassador."

"Don't overdo it."

"Notice I said *subtly.*"

"I did, but your concept of subtle might be different from mine."

"You're thinking of Beau. I'm the one with the light touch."

She chuckled. "You and Beau are so different. But then, so were your fathers."

"Makes life interesting."

"True. Our family is many things, but boring isn't one of them." She glanced up at him. "Staying with Henri over the Christmas break will put you in proximity to her other house guest." She looked him in the eye. "I hope I don't have to tell you—"

"You don't, Mom. You taught me better than that."

"She's very pretty."

"And I'm very self-disciplined."

She smiled. "The woman who breaks through that famous self-discipline will be the one for you."

"Hasn't happened yet." He gave her one last twirl as the music ended. "Maybe it never will."

"Oh, it will. You'll meet your match. Wait and see." Standing on tiptoe, she kissed his cheek. "Thanks for the dance. Guess we'd better return to the fray."

"Guess so. Although here comes Beau. He's wearing his *I need to warn you* face."

She chuckled. "So he does. What's going on, Beau?"

"Major discussion in progress. Wanted to give you a heads-up, bro."

"What kind of discussion?"

"Regarding your sleeping arrangements."

"Huh?"

"Seems the Brotherhood finally tweaked to the fact that if you stay in Henri's house, you'll be right down the hall from Penny."

"So what? I can be trusted. Did you tell them I could be—"

"Oh, I told them, alright. They insist that's not the issue, but any idiot can see it is. They're just framing it to sound like a bid for brotherly camaraderie."

"Can you be more specific?"

"Seems there's a bunkhouse on the property which is where they used to live. Now it's more like a clubhouse where they gather for Brotherhood meetings, cook dinner sometimes, light up the fire pit out back."

"I've heard about fire pit nights. And the tradition of monthly Brotherhood gatherings at the bunkhouse."

"Yeah, well, they're making sleeping in that bunkhouse sound like a night at the Ritz. It's within walking distance of the barn and they assume you'll want to help out with barn chores."

"I'm happy to do my share, but are you saying they want me to sleep in the bunkhouse? By myself?"

"Oh, no, not by yourself. This is where it gets interesting. They'll rotate guys in and out, one at a time. Gives each of them a chance to get to know you better while you get a taste of what the Brotherhood is all about."

"But you think it's really guard duty so I can't sneak up to the house and get cozy with Penny."

"Bingo."

"Oh, for God's sake."

His mom started laughing. "Personally, I think it's a fabulous idea."

"Uh-huh, you would." Sky turned back to Beau. "Is everybody going along with this dumb stunt?"

"Most seem okay with it. Penny looks fit to be tied, though."

"Really?" That brightened his spirits.

"Yeah, she dragged her brother into a corner and she's telling him how the cow eats the cabbage. His wife is giving him the stink-eye, too. Come to think of it, none of the Brotherhood wives and girlfriends are acting happy."

"You did say you wanted to hear more stories about Charley." His mom's eyes sparkled with amusement.

"You're enjoying this, aren't you?"

"I am. It's like a chess game. I wish I could stick around and see how it comes out."

Beau perked up. "Could we?"

"Nobody says you have to leave right away." And he could use some backup.

"I say so, Sky. We weren't asked to stay. I'd bet the royalties on my current book that Henri can't wait for me to get out of town."

"She just doesn't know you well enough. If you—"

"Mom's right," Beau said. "We need to shove off tomorrow morning. But listen, bro, you have to text us pictures of you living in the bunkhouse."

"You're assuming that's where I'll end up."

"I don't see any way you can weasel out of this plan without looking like a pansy-ass. It's an impressive maneuver on the part of the Brotherhood."

"And unnecessary. Considering Penny's circumstances, we have no business getting involved."

Beau nodded. "Very noble of you, big brother. But judging from what I've observed, Penny doesn't agree. You might want to keep your powder dry."

"Meaning?"

"You know, be prepared." He waggled his eyebrows. "For whatever."

10

Penny and Fiona pulled Leo away from the group and boxed him into a corner for a talking-to. Penny crossed her arms to keep rom throttling him until he turned blue. "Leo, how could you? Do you and the Brotherhood honestly think I'd do the wild thing with Sky when we're Henri's invited guests?"

"It's not you we're worried about." Leo kept his voice low.

"That's insulting to both of us. He's not that kind of man, but even if he is, do you think I'm a helpless female who would simply let him ravish me?"

"No, that's not why—"

"Oh, yes, that's exactly what they think." Fiona met Penny's gaze. "Their actions make that very clear."

"Agreed."

Leo glanced at his wife. "Don't look at me like that, Fi. I was outvoted."

"If the ladies of the Brotherhood took a vote right now, it would be unanimous. You guys suck."

"Is that a thing? Do the ladies have a group?"

"It's not official, but this stunt could motivate us to organize. You're treating Penny like a child and Sky like a predator."

"The plan isn't just about them. The Brotherhood wants a chance to get to know him, one-on-one. We might have come up with the idea even if Penny didn't happen to be here."

Penny snorted. "I'm so sure." She struck a pose and thrust out one hand. "Oh, look! Charley's long-lost son is here. We can't let him sleep on a soft bed in Henri's guest room and allow her to fuss over him. We must stick him in the drafty old bunkhouse to see if he's capable of fending for himself!"

"It's not drafty," her brother muttered. "And the wood stove works great. That place has character."

"Which is more than I can say for you, Leo."

"Ouch."

"Seriously. Couldn't you have talked them out of this? I'm your sister. That should give you leverage."

"I tried. I knew you'd be upset. But they got hold of this concept and fell in love with it."

"When? How did you guys manage to concoct a plan so quickly?"

"We got a tip the Babes might be up to something."

"What kind of tip?"

"Nick saw Eva text Josette."

Penny's gaze briefly locked with Fiona's. She looked away, but Leo had caught the exchange.

"You two knew Eva texted Josette, didn't you?"

"No." Penny could look him in the eye because it was the truth.

Fiona shrugged. "News to me, too."

"I say you're both hiding something. You had a hand in this, didn't you?"

Penny made her face blank.

"Oh, yeah, sis. I know that stony-faced look. You're guilty as hell. It was the bathroom visit, wasn't it? You two cooked up the scheme to keep Sky here over Christmas. Then you got Eva to contact Josette."

"We had nothing to do with Eva contacting Josette."

"But one of you talked to Eva." He zeroed in on Fi. "Logically that was you. She's your buddy."

Fi's cheeks turned pink. "I—"

"But aren't you glad we took action?" Penny rushed to help her sister-in-law. "If we hadn't, Sky would have left in the morning. Now the Brotherhood will have more time to—"

"Exactly. And we'll have a better chance to talk with him man-to-man if he's living in the bunkhouse." He faced Penny, a gleam in his eyes. "Care to tell me why you and Fi engineered this Christmas visit?"

"We were thinking of Henri."

"Henri, huh?" He nudged back his hat. "That's it? A good deed for Henri?"

"Okay! I didn't want Sky to leave in the morning. Happy, now?"

"No, I'm not. You're liable to—"

"It doesn't mean I'll jump his bones at the first opportunity."

"Ah, but the second opportunity, that's totally up for—"

"No, it's not, Leo. I want to get to know him."

"Why? You know damn well this relationship, friendship, whatever it is, has no future."

"I'm aware of that."

"Then what the hell are you doing?"

"I don't know."

"That's what I thought. You—"

"I don't know what I'm doing, but I know that Skyler isn't just some random guy."

"I don't care if he's the Prince of Wales!"

Fiona chuckled. "I think he's taken."

"I know. My point is—"

"I get your point. I'm not going to fall in love and flush all my plans down the toilet. But I don't want to miss out on... Sky."

Leo groaned. "You're heading for a cliff."

"I don't see it that way. And if you'll please excuse me, I gotta go."

"Go where?"

"To intercept him. He's not in lockdown yet, and I want another dance."

"Penny—" He reached for her.

She dodged his attempt to grab her arm. "Hands off, Leo. So help me, if you or your brothers mess with this dance, you'll be sorry."

"Yeah, okay. I'll keep them away."

"Good." She turned and hurried over to Sky before he could be swallowed up by the Buckskin gang.

His beautiful blue eyes widened. "Hey, Penny. What—"

"Dance with me."

"Now? But—"

"They can all wait." She slipped her hand in his and tugged him back toward the dance floor.

"Yes, ma'am." His fingers tightened. "Good move."

"You have to be fast around here. And alert."

"I'm getting that."

"Just so you know, I have no plans to seduce you while you're staying at the Buckskin."

"That's disappointing news."

"That said, I want us to become better friends."

"So that's it? You're shooting for a platonic relationship?"

"I don't know what I'm shooting for." She led him onto the floor. "I just want more time with you."

He drew her into his arms. "Is this a confession? Are you the one who got me invited to stay for Christmas?"

"Not exactly." Heat spread from every point of contact and her breath caught. "But I had something to do with it. I told Fiona I didn't want you to leave and we knew Henri didn't want you to leave either, so..."

He held her gaze. "And why didn't you want me to leave?"

"I don't know if I should tell you."

"Why not?"

"You might laugh. You might not believe me. You might think I'm crazy."

His grip tightened, bringing her closer as they moved through the smooth steps of a waltz. "Try me."

"I think we were destined to meet. I don't know whether our time together will be platonic or not." Her heart thundered as she held his gaze. "I only know I couldn't bear the idea of you driving away tomorrow."

11

Sky's pulse leaped at the intensity in Penny's gaze. Fragile? Broken-hearted? Not tonight. He held one fired-up woman in his arms. Lucky him.

"You're staring. Do you think I'm delusional?"

He took a shaky breath. "I think you're amazing."

"Doesn't answer my question." Her mouth curved in a soft smile. "Do you think I'm going off the deep end?"

He ached to taste those tempting lips. "If you are, I'll take the plunge with you. And I don't think platonic is the way this'll turn out."

"Just so we're clear, I'm only talking about these few days. Stealing a moment out of time. If you're not okay with that..."

"I'm okay with it." For now, anyway. No question she was out of reach. But things could change. People could change.

"We'll have to get creative."

"Because of the plan to keep me under guard at all times?"

"Beau told you?"

"Yes, ma'am. I'm expecting the Brotherhood to hit the dance floor with their ladies any second."

"They won't. Leo promised to keep them away."

"No kidding?"

"It was the least he could do." She grinned. "Although the Brotherhood may discover their ladies don't feel like dancing."

"Interesting." He checked the sight lines. The crowded dance floor gave them excellent cover. "Then we're gonna disappear."

"Disappear?"

"Not for good. Just until the tune is over. Fortunately, it's a long one. I'm not ready to openly defy the Brotherhood. Not yet, anyway. Just follow my lead."

"Happy to."

"We'll dance around the side of the bandstand, acting like we just want more room to maneuver. The footing won't be the same. Watch your step."

"Lead on."

Encouraged by the anticipation in her voice, he tucked her in closer while he navigated past the edge of the dance floor. The wooden planks beneath their feet were rougher and slightly uneven. He didn't want her to stumble.

Her breathing quickened. "This is great fun so far."

"I promise it'll get better." He maintained the pretense of dancing until they reached the shadows of the narrow hallway. Too bad he didn't know the building layout.

A door at the end had no label. "This way." He took her hand and hurried toward the closed door. They had about two minutes before the number ended.

The knob turned. But when he opened the door, frigid air swept in. The alley. He started to close it again. "Bad idea."

"No, it's not." She grabbed the edge of the door. "My guess is you want to kiss me."

"Good guess."

"I suspect it'll be a hot kiss."

He chuckled. "Planning on it."

"We won't have time to get cold." She slipped through the opening and pulled him after her. The door closed behind them with a soft click. "Now, about that kiss..."

Shoving back his hat, he tugged her close. "We have about a minute and a half."

"Then make it count."

"Yes, ma'am." His grip tightened around her waist as he cradled her silken cheek in one hand and lowered his head. Her breathy sigh warmed his face. Moist, plump lips welcomed him.

His heart thundered as he settled in. This was going to be good. Extremely... good. He groaned as she nestled closer, setting off tiny explosions in his chest, his gut, his groin.

When she gripped the back of his head and parted her lips, a surge of heat wiped out any lingering restraint. He took possession of her mouth with a firm thrust of his tongue.

The kiss heated up fast after that. She whimpered and shifted the angle. He delved deeper, splaying his fingers over her firm bottom and bringing her in tight. Ahhh. Right *there*. The denim barrier muted the sensation, but not much.

Making love to her would be an adventure, the kind that would turn him inside out and leave him craving more. As if she'd read his mind, she shifted her hips in a blatantly suggestive move.

Gasping, he drew back, his breath fogging the air. "If that's not seduction—"

"You inspire me." She pulled him down to her eager mouth, her hunger fueling his.

Any second he'd have to stop. He wasn't ready to stop. He'd never be—*Time's up.* The alarm went off in his brain, a self-discipline trick he'd mastered long ago. Breathing hard, he lifted his lips a fraction from hers. "We have to go."

"I wish—"

"Me, too." Taking a step back, he kept his arm around her shoulders and pivoted toward the door. The ice-cold knob turned partway and stopped. He tugged. The door didn't budge. Not frozen shut. That couldn't happen in two minutes. "Uh-oh."

"Locked?"

He tried again, just to be sure. "Yes, ma'am. I'm afraid so. Probably does that automatically. I should have thought of that."

"I didn't give you a chance to think. I practically dragged you out here and short-circuited your brain with sexy talk."

He laughed. "I'm glad you did. We just need to figure out how to get back inside."

"We could bang on the door and hope somebody comes to open it."

"They might not. The band's loud. I can hear them even now. We could walk around the building and go in the front door."

She gave a little snort of amusement. "Because that won't be weird."

"You're right. We'd have to come up with a hell of a good story."

"Can we snuggle a bit while we debate this? It's freezing."

"We sure can." He pulled her close. "I don't dare kiss you, though. It makes me forget everything else."

"Yeah?" Sliding her arms around his neck, she gazed up at him.

"Yes, ma'am." He wrapped her in his arms and fought the urge to do exactly what he'd said was a bad idea.

"Then how did you know it was time to go back in?"

"I taught myself that when I was a kid. I set an alarm in my brain and it goes off on schedule."

"Impressive."

"Annoying. I hated when it went off just now. Almost ignored it. You're incredible, lady."

"Backatcha, cowboy."

"Warmer?"

"Much warmer. You?"

"Heating up fast."

"But we haven't solved our problem."

He sighed. "I could text Beau."

"You don't sound thrilled with that option."

"I'll never hear the end of it."

"Then are we walking around to the front?"

"We couldn't finesse that in a million years. But if Beau lets us in, we can claim that we danced the next one. He'll cover for us." He pulled out his phone and quickly sent the text.

"Will he see it?"

"Hope so. He's not looking for a text from anyone, let alone me." He rubbed her back with his free hand, hoping the friction would help keep her warm. "I think this is the part where I'm supposed to loan you my jacket."

"I'll pretend you did."

"I could take off my shirt and loan you that."

"I should let you." She pressed closer. "I can tell you have lovely chest muscles. I'll bet you'd look hot without a shirt."

"I'll bet I'd look cold."

"I meant *hot* as in sexy."

"Trust me, there's nothing sexy about a shirtless, shivering cowboy."

"But if you were in a nice warm room, would you look hot if you took off your shirt?"

"I was taught not to brag on myself." His phone remained quiet. *Come on, Beau.*

"Which is a *yes*. A man knows if he looks good naked." She regarded him with a teasing light in those beautiful gray eyes.

"So does a woman." Not kissing her was becoming a full-time occupation.

"Are you asking?"

"Don't have to. Not after you ditched your other outfit for this one."

"I was hoping to catch your attention."

"You did. I thought maybe you didn't like showing off your figure."

"That was my college-professor look."

"Then what's this?"

"My ready-for-anything look."

"I'll keep that in mind." *Damn.* If only they were having this conversation under better circumstances. It could lead to all kinds of wonderful activities. "I—ah, there's Beau. He's on his way." His brother had added about ten laughing-my-ass-off emojis. Nice guy.

12

When Beau opened the back door, he was grinning. He touched the brim of his hat. "Howdy, ma'am." He held the door open and stood back. "Glad I could rescue you before hypothermia set in."

"I'm fine, Beau." Penny held back a sigh of relief as she walked into the warm hallway. No point in giving Sky's brother more ammunition. "Thanks for letting us back in."

"Yeah, thanks, Beau." Sky sounded contrite. "I owe you one."

"Oh, you certainly do, big brother. I've already told two big fat lies on your behalf. I said I'd glimpsed you two mashed in with the other dancers during the tune they're playing now. Then I pretended I desperately needed to use the facilities so I could ride to your rescue."

"I'm grateful, bro. Penny, if we get out there before the number ends, we might pull this off."

"You just might, thanks to my quick thinking," Beau said. "As opposed to your extremely slow thinking, brother-of-mine, so slow as to be classified as not a brain cell working."

Penny ducked her head. Sky didn't need to see her laughing.

"I agree it was a lame stunt, but Penny and I need to—"

"Before you go, I want to show you something." Beau put a hand on Sky's shoulder and turned him toward a sign beside the door. A rather prominent sign. *Warning! Door locks automatically.* "See that?"

"I do, now."

Beau glanced at Penny. "You'll have to excuse him. He's not used to these newfangled inventions."

"I didn't see the sign, either." She gulped back another laugh.

Beau shook his head. "If this is how you two operate, you don't have a prayer of outwitting the Brotherhood."

Sky exhaled. "I don't really plan to—"

"I'm offering my services, dude. I can lay out a game plan for your visit when I drive you back to the hotel to get your stuff. We'll go over it on the way back to the Moose."

"I'm spending tonight at the Buckskin? I thought I'd be at the hotel with you guys."

"No sir. You'll be in the bunkhouse with the first of your keepers... I mean, congenial members of the Brotherhood."

"Which one?"

"I didn't get that info. But you need a strategy and I'm prepared to help you come up with it. Although I won't be physically on the scene, we can stay in touch by phone and text. I'll see you through this."

Sky just looked at him. "I don't need a strategy."

"That's where you're wrong. They intend to keep you from doing what you just did with Penny. If you want to continue that activity with this lovely lady, you need counter moves."

She jumped in. "We didn't do anything. It was just a kiss."

"*Just* a kiss?" Beau threw up his hands. "You're not only missing brain cells, bro, you're losing your touch. If she can describe what happened as *just a kiss* you might as well hang it up."

"That's not what I meant." Penny fought to keep from laughing, but Beau was hysterical. "It was a fabulous kiss. A very hot kiss." She looked over at Sky. "A panty-dampening kiss."

He gave her a quick smile. "Good to know."

"If you hadn't called a halt, no telling what—"

"Time out." Beau gave the referee signal. "I don't require this level of information. You can discuss your specific state of arousal on the dance floor. All I'm saying is, you need help and I'm willing to provide it."

Sky looked at him with a mixture of amusement and frustration. "I'll think about it. We'd better get out there and corroborate your story."

Beau waved them off. "Corroborate away. Oh, wait. I need to check you for kissing evidence." His gaze swept over them. "As I suspected, we have lipstick transference." He pulled out a bandana and handed it to Sky.

"Good call. Thanks." He wiped his mouth.

Beau nodded. "You're good to go." Then he glanced at Penny. "You donated all yours to him. Do you have a tube in your jeans pocket?"

"I don't."

"You might want to consider carrying it at all times. That's my first tip. Lipstick always available for a touch-up."

"I'll do my best, coach."

"Have you traded digits with my brother?"

"Uh, no. Sky, send me a text." She reeled off the number.

"Got it. Texting you. Done."

"Can't believe I had to remind you guys of such a basic move. Listen, bro, you never know when opportunity will knock. You need to carry—"

"You don't have to spell it out."

"Except you missed that sign beside the door. Clearly you're not firing on all cylinders, bro."

"Come on, Penny." Sky caught her hand. "Let's go dance."

"You're welcome," Beau called after them.

Penny was still laughing as Sky hustled her around the bandstand and maneuvered them neatly into the swirl of two-stepping couples on the floor. "Your brother's a riot.'

"And we just made his day, or rather, his evening. He lives for moments like this."

"I'll take a wild guess that they don't come often."

"Not if I can help it."

"Guess I'm a bad influence. Sorry, not sorry."

"I'm not the least bit sorry. I'd do it all again, humiliation included."

"I'm honored. Clearly it's not your usual M.O."

"I've always tried to set a good example for my brothers and sister."

"Because your mom told you to?"

"I'm sure she didn't. That's not like her. I think it's all me, trying to be the man of the house."

Carrying the weight of the world on those broad shoulders. Made her heart hurt.

"Meanwhile they're hoping I'll screw up so I don't look so blasted perfect all the time."

"I'll go out on a limb and say Beau secretly worships the ground you walk on."

His startled gaze met hers. "Mom says the same thing. Seems crazy to me, but—"

"It isn't crazy at all. I feel the same about Leo. Lord knows we fight, and right now I'm irritated because he's collaborating with the Brotherhood on this deal, but I would go to the mat for the guy."

"I don't want to tick him off, Penny. Or the rest of them. When it comes right down to it, I'm a guest on the ranch."

"And you want to be a perfect guest."

He sighed. "Exactly."

"I'm Henri's guest, too. I don't want to abuse that privilege any more than you do. I wasn't planning to sneak down to your room if you'd ended up staying at her house. I doubt you had that idea, either."

"Oh, I had it. But I wasn't going to act on it."

"That said, if we'd been in the same house, we would at least have been able to see each other often."

"True."

"Sharing meals, sitting in front of the fire..."

"Long walks in the snow."

She laughed. "You and I do think alike. But that option's gone."

"Sure is. I didn't expect the Brotherhood to be so paranoid. I'm protective of Angelique, but—"

"What if she'd just broken an engagement with a cheating fiancé?"

He took a deep breath. "You're right. I'd want to vet every guy who came within twenty yards of her."

"Would she like that?"

"Probably not. But I'd want to. I get where they're coming from. They don't want you to get hurt again."

"Except I'm not hurt, other than my pride. My heart is in good shape. I've figured out I wasn't in love. I was grateful. He was my mentor."

"Have you shared this revelation with Leo?"

"He agrees, but he still thinks I need time off to recalibrate. Learn to trust my instincts again."

"Hm."

"He's probably right. I made a huge mistake in judgment by accepting Barry's proposal. A part of me knew he'd cheat on me. I ignored it."

"You didn't kiss like a woman who wants time off."

"I'm thinking I'll start my time off in the New Year."

He chuckled. "Lucky me."

"Maybe not. Unless Beau has some useful tricks up his sleeve."

"I'll let you know if he does." He pulled her close as the song ended. "Keep your phone handy."

13

When Beau dropped Sky at the bunkhouse, a truck was already parked in front of it.

"Looks like your babysitter's in place." Beau left the motor running. "Nice truck. Any bets on who's taking the first shift?"

"Could be Matt. He's the head honcho."

"Offer him some of that cider. Chances are he's been up since dawn. One bottle of cider and he'll conk out, leaving you to work the program."

"Yeah."

"Look, it's a romantic idea. Think Romeo and Juliet."

Sky glanced at Beau. "They both die in the end."

"Because they were young and kinda stupid, if you want my opinion. My plan's doable."

"It would be for you." Sky held his brother's gaze. "I don't have your gift for this kind of thing."

"Eye on the prize, bro. Eye on the prize." He lifted his hand. "See you in seven days."

Sky gripped it and squeezed. "Tell everybody Merry Christmas."

"Will do. Like Mom said, we'll have Christmas, Part Two, after I haul your ass home again on the twenty-ninth."

"I appreciate it." He climbed out of the truck with his duffle and a six-pack of cider.

"Go get 'em, tiger."

He chuckled. "You make it sound like I'm about to take the field."

"Aren't you?"

"I'm not sure. Later, bro." He shut the door.

Beau flicked the lights and pulled away.

Sucking in a breath, Sky headed for the front door of the bunkhouse. Lights glowed from the windows and smoke drifted from the chimney of the low-slung building. Opening the screen, he knocked on the weathered door.

Penny's brother opened it. That changed the odds. Guaranteed Leo would sleep with one eye open.

Stepping back to let him enter, Leo glanced at the six-pack. "I take it you approve of the local brew." For some reason he was still wearing his Stetson.

"It's good stuff." A fire blazed in the pot-bellied stove directly across from the door. "Cozy setup."

"We think so. I'll take that six-pack off your hands. Pick your bunk." Leo gestured to the sleeping area to the right. Four built-in single beds lined each wall with an aisle in between. Leo's duffle sat on the one closest to the door. Strategic.

Making the diplomatic move, Sky put his on the bunk across the narrow aisle, acting like he had no thoughts of sneaking out once Leo fell asleep. Or borrowing a gelding named Lucky Ducky so he could whisk Penny from Henri's house to a warm barn.

Beau had obtained info on which horse to choose by chatting with members of the Brotherhood. He'd secured a layout of the ranch from the Buckskin website and texted it to Sky's phone. Could Beau pull off a bold stunt like that? Oh, yeah. But he wasn't Beau.

He left his jacket on the bunk, too, but retained his hat. If it was good enough for Leo, it was good enough for him.

His roommate came out of the kitchen with two open bottles of cider and handed over one. "Might as well get started. No telling when the others will get here."

"The others?"

"Penny and Fiona gave me grief over this plan, so I called a meeting of the Brotherhood to talk things over." He lifted his bottle. "Here's to a peaceful resolution."

Sky tensed. "Am I about to get beat up?"

"What gave you that idea?"

"The opposite of a peaceful resolution is a fight."

"Whoa, dude." Leo nudged back his hat, a friendly gesture. "We're not brawlers. We don't gang up on people. Your dad taught us better than that."

"Glad to hear it." Okay, so the hat was a signaling device. Good thing he'd left his on.

"We seem to have a difference of opinion on how to handle this. How to handle your continued presence here, more to the point. That requires a meeting."

"I see." Despite Leo's reassurances, his gut tightened.

A truck's engine rumbled outside and Leo perked up. "That'll be Jake." He sounded happy about it. "He's bringing his little brother Zeke, Matt and CJ. Rafe was gonna pick up Nick and Garrett. You met everybody, right?"

"I did."

"You might want to chug-a-lug that cider. You'll need it. Could be a long night."

"If you're trying to intimidate me, it's working."

Leo gazed at him. "Intimidation's not my goal. But a little healthy respect isn't a bad thing. We all think a lot of my little sister."

The glint in Leo's eyes struck a chord. "Understood. And if it's all the same to you, I'll take it easy on the booze."

"Suit yourself."

Truck doors slammed outside and Matt came in carrying a six-pack in each hand and a third under his arm. "Drink up, cowboy. Negotiating goes smoother with lubrication."

"Listen to the man." Jake appeared behind him with another three six-packs and headed for the kitchen. "We'll either crack this nut or have a hell of a good time trying."

Sky winced. "Wish you hadn't put it quite that way, Jake."

"Nervous, McLintock?" Jake grinned.

"You could say that."

"Smart man." He continued into the kitchen.

CJ and Zeke arrived with more cider, bringing the count to a dozen six-packs. CJ paused. "Hey there, Sky. You look a tad discombobulated."

"It's a lot of booze."

"No worries. Nick's bringing the pizza. That'll soak up the alcohol."

"Pizza? After all the food at the buffet?"

"I do my best thinking with a slice of pizza in one hand and a cold brew in the other." Jake walked out of the kitchen with a bottle of cider. He set it on the small table near the pot-bellied stove, took off his jacket and carried it to the bunk behind Sky's. "Seeing as how you took my spot, I'll just claim this one." He tossed his jacket down and returned to pick up his cider.

"You're staying over?"

"Might need to." He lifted his hat and settled it more firmly on his head. "This here's a sticky wicket."

"Bet you couldn't wait to say that." Matt emerged from the kitchen.

"It's a great expression!"

"Jake had some British folks visit Raptors Rise and now everything's a sticky wicket."

"You gotta admit it's way classier than ballbuster."

"But it comes from *cricket*." CJ made a face. "Cowboys don't play cricket, bro."

"Not yet, but those ol' boys made it sound fun. And dangerous. I like me a little danger now and then." He looked over at Sky and flashed him another grin.

"Pizza's here!" Rafe came through the door carrying two flat boxes followed by Nick and Garrett, who each had two apiece. "Get it while it's hot!"

CJ laughed. "Yeah, sure it is."

"While it's *lukewarm*, then. It's winter. Deal with it." Rafe carried the boxes into the kitchen.

Garrett came in last and closed the door while balancing his boxes one-handed. "Why don't we buy the frozen kind and cook 'em here?"

Nick glanced over his shoulder. "Gotta stick with tradition, bro. I can't picture Charley going the frozen pizza route."

"Ah. Got it." Garrett looked at Sky. "Only my second winter. Still learning."

"Okay, everybody." Matt raised his voice. "I'm calling this meeting to order. Gather around the table."

Sky let the group assemble before he walked into the kitchen. Chances were good everyone would have a designated chair. He'd already claimed Jake's bunk. He didn't want to take someone's seat at the table.

Rafe sat at the far end, the logical place for whoever was running the meeting. Matt, who acted like the one in charge, sat on the left side between Jake, on the end, and Garrett. The others occupied the rest of the chairs on either side, leaving the other end for Sky. The hot seat? He took it as everyone grabbed some pizza. He pulled a piece out of the nearest box. Likely wouldn't eat it.

Matt glanced across the table at Leo, who sat on Sky's right. "Since you asked for the meeting, you've got the floor."

Leo finished chewing and swallowed. "To borrow Fiona's words, we suck."

Sky did a double-take. Hadn't seen *that* coming.

"Eva told me the same thing." Nick made a face. "She's not happy with us."

"Neither is Kate." Rafe sighed. "I got an earful. She has a point, too. Maybe we shouldn't have—"

"Hang on, there." Jake put down his half-eaten slice. "We took a vote. We agreed this was the best—"

"Penny's fully capable of deciding for herself whether to get involved with Sky." Leo leaned forward. "We're treating her like a delicate flower and she doesn't appreciate it."

Matt frowned. "But that's not the only reason we wanted to do this."

Leo met his gaze. "Come on, Matt. Setting up a Brotherhood gathering, either tonight or some other night Sky's here, would have done the trick. A poker game, booze and pizza — that's all we need to get acquainted."

"We're two for three on that," Rafe said. "Let's break out the cards. I wanna see if Sky plays poker like Charley did."

"Not so fast." Matt surveyed the table. "Are we abandoning the plan, then? And if so, now what?"

"Exactly." CJ shoved back his hat and picked up his cider. "We made a big deal about Sky livin' the bunkhouse life. How're we gonna walk that one back?"

"No problem," Sky said. "I like it here. I'm happy to stay." Being at the bunkhouse instead of Henri's could be a plus.

Nick gave him a pleased smile. "Isn't it awesome? Eva and I live in her Victorian because she loves it, but this bunkhouse is just... beautifully simple."

"Yeah." Rafe nodded. "Bunkhouse simplicity. Gotta love it. Kate, though, she likes the cottage, soft rugs and pretty curtains and such." He shrugged. "And I love Kate, so there you go."

Jake looked at them as if they'd lost their minds. "I'll take the cabin Millie and I built over this place any day. Stepping on a soft rug on a cold morning suits me just fine."

"I'm with you, bro." Garrett lifted his bottle in Jake's direction. "Nothing wrong with rugs."

"Millie and I have a fluffy one in front of the fireplace. We—"

"We're veering off the subject," Matt said.

"I don't know what the subject is, anymore." CJ waved a slice of pizza in Sky's direction. "Are we giving him the green light or what?"

"I wouldn't say that." Jake tugged on his hat and pinned Sky with a hard look. "The yellow light is more like it. Penny's a special lady."

Sky met that look with one of his own. "I know."

"You can't possibly know," Leo said. "Not after a few hours and one stolen kiss."

His breath caught.

"Aha!" Jake pointed a finger at him. "So you did take her back behind the bandstand. We didn't know for sure, but—"

"We made bets on it," CJ said. "I lost money on you, dude."

"Me, too," Garrett said.

"But the rest of us guessed right." Jake continued to hold his gaze. "So proceed with caution, sir. We'll be watching."

"Understood." They weren't all-seeing, though. Evidently they didn't know about the locked door incident.

"Great, then we're done." Rafe pushed back his chair. "I'll fetch the cards. Nicholas, take the leaf out of the table, please."

"Will do. Everybody up."

"We might not have much to worry about regarding this romance." CJ stood and started collecting pizza boxes. "Sky doesn't have wheels."

"He doesn't need 'em." Matt looked over at Sky, a knowing gleam in his eyes. "He's figured that one out."

14

Penny slept with her phone on the bedside table, but it remained silent through the night. She woke to the smell of coffee and something sweet in the oven, maybe muffins or cinnamon rolls.

Picking up the phone, she checked to make sure she hadn't missed a text. Nothing. Might as well jump in the shower. She put on her bathrobe and tucked her phone in the pocket, just in case.

Although Henri and Charley had updated the hall bathroom fixtures, it was still a tiny space. Barry had complained about it when they'd stayed with Henri back in October. He'd complained about nearly everything, in fact.

What a joy to be at the Buckskin without him. She laid her phone on the counter and untied her robe. She'd stripped off her flannel nightgown when her phone rang. Not a text. A call from the cowboy she'd been dreaming about all night.

Heart thumping, she answered. "Hey."

"Good morning."

His voice gave her goosebumps. Or maybe it was the chill in the air, but she gave credit to Sky's deep baritone. "Good morning to you."

"Am I interrupting anything?"

"I was about to hop in the shower."

"Is that so?"

"Uh-huh." Oh, this was delicious. "What's on your mind?"

"You, seconds away from climbing in the shower."

"You did ask."

"Glad I did."

"Just so you know, I'm not into sending pictures over the internet."

"Totally unnecessary. I have an excellent imagination."

She'd never tried talking sexy on the phone. Kind of fun. "Will this be a long conversation? It's chilly in here. I need either warm water, my bathrobe, or—"

"Wish I was closer. I'd help you out."

His husky tone made her shiver. "Wouldn't that be lovely?"

"Yes, ma'am, it surely would. I'm a fan of shared showers."

"Saves water."

"Sometimes. Depends on how long you stay in there."

She swallowed. "Do you like taking long showers?"

"Under certain circumstances." He took a breath. "Still chilly?"

"Not so much." She pressed a hand to her chest. "Why did you call?"

"I... let me think... oh, yeah. Would you like to take a horseback ride this morning?"

"Yes."

"How soon can you be ready?"

"Ten minutes."

"You've had breakfast?"

"Not yet."

"Then let's say thirty minutes, so you can grab something to eat."

"I'll be on the porch."

"Can't wait." He disconnected.

Quivering from anticipation, she glanced at her phone, put it down and turned on the water. Thirty minutes.

Coffee and one of those sweet things baking in the oven would qualify as breakfast. She didn't have the time or inclination for more. Not when Sky was saddling the horses, preparing to sweep her away to... somewhere private.

* * *

The trip to Jeans Junction a few days ago had yielded more than the outfit Penny had worn to go dancing at the Moose. She'd picked up serviceable jeans for riding, a lined denim jacket and a Stetson.

When she only wanted coffee and a cinnamon roll, Henri fussed about her skimpy breakfast. Penny savored every word. Her parents had been too busy turning Leo into a child star to fuss over her. If Sky hadn't been on his way, she would have gladly eaten all the healthy food Henri offered.

Instead, she powered through the roll and coffee so she could be on the porch when he rode up. Frost and the remnants of the last snowfall lay on the ground under a clear blue sky. What a glorious day, one made even better when Sky rounded the bend at a brisk trot, riding one buckskin and leading another.

Clouds of moisture coming from the horses' nostrils added a dramatic touch, as if they were fire-breathing steeds. Shivering with excitement, she moved to the top of the steps to get a better view.

He sure looked good with his sheepskin-lined collar turned up and his Stetson pulled low. One gloved hand gripped the lead rope and the other held the reins with steady confidence. His movements smooth, he neck-reined his horse into the turn at Henri's driveway. The second horse tucked in perfectly.

She glanced over her shoulder when the front door opened.

Henri walked out on the porch, pulling on a jacket that she held together rather than taking the time to button it. "I won't keep you. I just had to see him riding up on King."

Penny's breath caught. "You let him ride Charley's horse?"

"Matt called to ask about this outing and I told him to let Sky have King and have him bring over Prince for you." She cleared her throat. "Told him to dust off Charley's saddle, too."

Penny slipped an arm around her shoulders. "What do you think?"

"He looks fabulous on King." She swallowed. "Dammit. Charley would have loved to know his son. He would have had so much fun teaching him... everything."

"I'm sure he would have." She danced a thin line, determined not to take sides. Henri had good reason to be angry, but Desiree deserved the benefit of the doubt.

Sky trotted the horses to the foot of the steps and reined in the magnificent buckskin. "He's a dream to ride, Henri. Thank you for trusting me with him."

The horse looked good, but the rider claimed all Penny's attention. Cheeks ruddy from the cold, his blue gaze seeking hers, Sky McLintock embodied a fantasy she'd kept locked away for years.

She'd told herself that men like this only existed in fiction, the product of an author's fertile mind. Yet here he was, flesh and blood, a broad-shouldered cowboy who wanted... her. Giddy with anticipation, she walked down the steps as he unclipped Prince's lead rope and coiled it.

Then he started to dismount. "Let me help you—"

"Thanks, but I can manage. I've been riding since I was six." Mostly dressage, but she'd coaxed her parents into adding Western saddle lessons, too.

"She can ride," Henri said. "We went out several times when she came for Leo's wedding."

"Okay, then. I wasn't sure. Got gloves?"

"In my pocket." Along with the tube of lipstick Beau had advised her to carry.

"Will you two wait a minute while I get my phone? I want a picture."

Sky's *yes, ma'am* blended with Penny's.

As Henri whipped through the front door in search of her phone, Penny walked up to Prince. "Hey, big guy." She stroked his nose. Because he'd been led over, he wore both a bridle and a halter. "Should I leave the halter on him?" She glanced up.

"Might as well."

"Okey-doke." She swung into the saddle and unwound the reins from the horn.

"Are your stirrups okay? I had to guesstimate."

"Good job. They're perfect. How'd your night go?"

"Very interesting. The Brotherhood—"

"Located my phone." Henri came out and positioned herself at the top of the porch steps. "Indulge me by holding hands."

Sky pulled off his glove and extended his bare hand. Penny slipped hers into his. Whoa. The jolt of that skin-to-skin connection was intense. She'd built up a store of lust if simply holding his hand could produce a buzz.

"That's great." Henri lowered her phone. "When you've finished your ride, shoot me a text and I'll drive down to the barn and pick you up. We can come back here for lunch."

Sky gave her a smile. "Sounds terrific."

"I'll show you some pictures of Charley and me in that same pose. You'll think it's you guys. I was a blonde back then."

"Can't wait to see 'em." Sky gave Penny's hand a squeeze and let go. "Thanks again for loaning us King and Prince."

"Seemed like Charley would want me to."

"Is this his saddle?"

"It's King's saddle, custom made for him and fitted to Charley's butt." She glanced at him. "How does it feel?"

"Like it was made for me."

Henri nodded. "Thought so. I'll take a guess you didn't have to adjust the stirrups."

"No, ma'am." He hesitated. "Are you saying nobody's used it since—"

"Ben rides King and he... well, he claimed the saddle didn't feel right, so he had Jared at Logan's Leather make him a new one."

Sky glanced down and laid his hand on the tooled leather. "It's... an honor." He looked up at Henri. "A special honor. Thank you."

"You're welcome." Henry's voice wasn't quite steady. "Let me know when you need to be picked up."

"We will. Should be around noon."

"Perfect."

He touched the brim of his hat. "See you then." He turned to Penny. "Gloves on?"

She held up one gloved hand.

"Then let's do this."

"Alrighty." She had questions, but she waited until they were side-by-side at the bottom of the drive. "Do you know where you're going?"

"Yes, ma'am. We'll take a left here. Should be able to ride abreast if there's no traffic."

"I just wondered because you've never been here before. Since I have, I wondered if you needed me to guide you."

"Don't believe so. I have a map on my phone."

"That was enterprising of you."

He chuckled. "Beau gets the credit for it."

"Beau? He found you a map? Why would he—"

"Part of the plan he created for me. For us."

"Is this it? Taking a morning ride?"

He flashed her a grin. "Hardly. Beau wanted me to sneak out of the bunkhouse last night once my guard fell asleep, borrow a horse, ride to Henri's, pick you up and—"

"Pick me up? When it's below freezing?"

"He said if we kept moving until we made it to the barn, the rewards would be worth a little discomfort."

"*Discomfort*? We'd get frostbite!" But the implications of Beau's statement sent a rush of heat to her lady parts, so he might have been right about that. "And you were okay with this goofy scheme?"

"I didn't have a better idea."

"But I notice you didn't work that plan, unless you threw pebbles at my window and I slept through it."

"Nope. I didn't have just one guard last night. The entire Brotherhood showed up. I think the poker game ended around four."

"Good grief. You must be exhausted."

"Funny thing about that. I've never felt more awake."

"You're probably overtired."

"Or overstimulated."

"Oh?" Her pulse was off to the races.

"Long-story short, Leo convinced the Brotherhood to back off."

"No kidding?" Her voice squeaked. Just a little. She cleared her throat. "So you're moving into Henri's other guest room?"

"Actually, I'm not. I realized it makes more sense to stay at the bunkhouse." He reined in his horse and turned toward her. "Now that I have it all to myself."

She met his intense gaze. And forgot how to breathe.

15

Sky couldn't tell if Penny's wide eyes and sudden gasp stemmed from lust or panic. Those two emotions could look about the same. What if she didn't want to move this fast?

He'd pulled King to a halt a few yards from the bunkhouse turnoff. Better not make assumptions about their route. "I invited you for a horseback ride."

She nodded. Still speechless, though.

"If we keep going down this road, we'll come to a nice trail that leads to a meadow with a great view of the mountains. I checked that out on the website this morning." If all she wanted was a few kisses, that was Plan B.

She took another quick breath. "Been there." Her voice quivered.

"Want to do that?"

She spoke in a breathless rush. "Instead of going straight to the bunkhouse?"

That startled a laugh out of him. "Well, I—"

"Because that's what I thought you—"
"I do, but—"

"Then let's go." She nudged Prince into a trot and veered onto the bunkhouse road.

Transfixed by her unexpected move, he sat there grinning like an idiot.

She glanced back at him. "You coming?"

"Hell, yeah." King only required a touch of Sky's heels to break into a trot and catch up with Prince. "You took me by surprise."

"Don't know why. After last night, I thought you knew I—"

"I was hoping. But we've only known each other—"

"Long enough." She smiled.

"Evidently."

"Is this why you wanted to leave the halter on Prince?"

"Yes, ma'am. We'll tie 'em to a tree when we get there. I hung another halter and lead rope on a branch for King."

"Nobody's at the bunkhouse?"

"They've promised not to show up unannounced."

"I'm amazed. What a turnaround."

"You and Fiona did it. You changed Leo's mind and then he got everyone else thinking differently. A few were tending in that direction already. The Brotherhood plan wasn't popular with the ladies."

"I could tell, but still... those guys seemed determined to keep us apart."

"Because they care about you. I can't blame them for that. If they get any indication I'm not treating you right, or causing you distress, I'll be in big trouble. Like Jake said, I don't have a green light. I have a yellow one."

"It's better than a red one."

"Yes, ma'am." He didn't attempt conversation after that. Filled to the brim with desire and gratitude, he had no words good enough for the occasion.

The bunkhouse came into view through the trees, sending his already elevated heart rate up another several notches. "The tree's over to the right of the building."

He untied the lead rope and handed it to her.

"Last time I saw this parking area, it was wall-to-wall pickups." She guided Prince to the tree, looped the reins around the horn and dismounted.

"Have you been inside?"

"No, we just walked out to the fire pit. That's where the party was."

No doubt the *we* in that sentence included her cheating ex. His jaw tightened. "Fun party?" He secured the reins and swung down.

"I had a great time. Barry didn't enjoy himself all that much."

That was gratifying.

Grabbing the halter he'd left hooked on a branch, he slipped it on over King's bridle, clipped the rope on and tethered the gelding to the bare-leafed tree. An animal this well-trained likely didn't need to be tied, but he wasn't taking any chances with his dad's horse.

He checked to make sure Prince was secure, too. "Good job on the knot." He rounded the buckskin's rump and nearly ran into Penny.

"Thanks. I'm a pretty good hand."

"I can tell." He smiled. "I see you've got a stampede string on your hat." She'd taken off her Stetson and it hung down her back.

"I wanted one to make sure I didn't lose it. I didn't know it was called a stampede string." She slid her palms up the front of his jacket.

"So it doesn't fall off during a stampede." Thumbing back his hat, he wrapped her in his arms and pulled her close. "Or a particularly energetic kiss."

"Is that what we're about to have?"

"Yes, ma'am."

She took hold of his shearling collar as she gazed up at him, her gray eyes luminous. "Brilliant decision to stay down here."

"I was highly motivated to find a solution." Dipping his head, he captured those smiling lips. They parted for him as he'd known they would.

Paradise. He delved into the honeyed depths of her mouth with a groan of pleasure and shoved his hands in the hip pockets of her jeans so he could bring her into alignment with his aching package. Oh, yeah. Right... *there.*

He lost track of everything but the taste of her mouth, the slide of her tongue against his, the heat of her body pressed close, the spicy scent of her skin... *Penny.*

She pulled away from the kiss, breathing hard. "We should go in."

"We should." Shifting his hold, he scooped her up.

"You don't have to carry—"

"I want to. Makes up for the twin bed situation.'

"I don't care if it's a kitchen table. I just—"

"There's a thought."

"I wasn't really suggesting—"

"If you could just grab the handle on the screen..."

"Got it."

"And open the door, please."

She started laughing as she reached down and turned the knob. "Carrying me is kind of a production, Sky. I think—"

His kiss ended further discussion. The bunkhouse wasn't the most romantic place in the world, although for now it was the most private.

The bunk he'd claimed was made up with clean sheets and an army blanket—a utilitarian arrangement until he lowered Penny to the mattress. Then it became the most beautiful bed in the world.

He broke the kiss long enough to unhook her hat and help her out of her coat. One motion and both items were hanging from hooks on the wall beside the bed.

She smiled. "Handy."

"Bunkhouse simplicity." His jacket and hat quickly joined hers on the wall and he was back to the joy of kissing Penny.

Covering her body with his, he left just enough room to unbutton her blouse and the front catch of her bra. She moaned and clutched his shoulders as he stroked her satin skin, his fingertips sending urgent signals to his groin.

His jeans needed to go. Hers, too. But first... oh, yeah... this. He cupped the yielding weight of her breast. Rubbing his thumb over her taut nipple almost made him come. He lifted his mouth a fraction from hers. "I love touching you."

She gulped. "Kiss me... there."

"Gladly." Moving down, he touched his lips to the hollow of her throat and ran his tongue along the delicate ridge of her collarbone. He nuzzled the valley between her breasts, the fullness brushing his cheeks. Then he licked his way up and over that plump mound, eyes open, drinking in the sight of her passion-flushed skin and the deep burgundy of her aroused nipple.

Closing his lips over it, he tugged gently. She whimpered and arched her back, her fingers digging into his shoulders. *Ah, Penny.* He slid his arm under her, holding her steady as he made love to her breasts.

She began to pant. "Sky..."

"I know." He kissed his way back to her lips. "Time to get rid of more clothes."

"All of them." She started to sit up.

"Wait." He pushed her gently back down. "You're the best gift I'll get this Christmas." He feasted on the beauty of her rosy, perfect breasts, damp from his kisses. "Let me unwrap the rest of you."

Her gray eyes darkened. "I'm all yours."

Her words hit him with unexpected force, tightening his chest. Dear God, did he want...? No, not possible. Not the plan.

Her expression softened and she cupped his cheek. "For now," she murmured. "Didn't mean to scare you."

He sucked in a breath, got his head on straight. "I'm not scared." Blindsided. "But I can't remember the last time I—"

She frowned. "Had sex?"

"*No.*" He gave her a mock frown back. "That isn't what I was about to say, thank you very much."

"Sorry."

Leaning down, he nibbled on her mouth. "I can't remember the last time I wanted someone this much."

"Me, either. So start unwrapping."

"Yes, ma'am." Reluctantly leaving the pleasures of her tempting lips, he sat on the side of the bed so he could ease her arms out of the sleeves of her shirt and the bra straps off her creamy shoulders.

Tugging them out from under her, he reached over and made more use of the hooks on the wall. Then he moved to the end of the bunk to tug off her boots. "Are you ticklish?"

"No."

"We'll see about that." He started slowly peeling off her sock.

"Taking off my sock like that feels erotic, though."

"I'll bet you're ticklish." He unrolled the last bit of her sock and tucked it into one of her boots. Her toenails were painted alternate colors, red, then green. Lifting her foot, he leaned over and licked those enticing toes.

She laughed and jerked away. "*That* tickles."

"Told you." The ache of longing in his chest was back. The ache behind his fly had become more persistent, too. Taking off her other sock, he propped her heels on his thigh. "Nice feet." He stroked the arch of each one with his thumbs. "How does that feel?"

"Like I need you to unwrap the rest of me."

"I do believe I will." Getting up, he set her feet back down on the army blanket. "Good thing I spent some time unveiling your pretty toes, though. If I'd rushed through that part, I might have missed those festive colors."

"I'm able to show them off in L.A., but it's too cold for that here."

"You can show them off for me."

"Are you into toes?"

"Not in general. Just yours." Perching on the side of the bed, he leaned down and indulged in another kiss, another caress, his palm sweeping over the sensuous landscape of her breasts.

She cupped the back of his head and pulled him deeper into the kiss. Then she sucked on his tongue in an extremely suggestive manner.

He could only take a few seconds of that before agony set in below his belt. He drew back, breathing hard. "Got the message." He reached for the button on her jeans.

"I hope so." She gulped in air. "Your gift is about to explode."

"I want to be there when that happens." Pulling down the zipper, he divested her of the jeans and some very damp panties. The scent of arousal from those panties nearly shredded his control. He squeezed his eyes shut and clamped down on the demands of his body.

When he could look at her without losing his cool, he turned back. And went still. He had a goddess in his bed.

"You're incredible." He barely got the words out through a throat tight with awe. His gaze traveled upward and met hers. "Thank you."

"You're welcome." She gestured in his direction. "And you're way overdressed for this party."

"So I am." He forced himself to glance away from the mesmerizing view of Penny lying there. Waiting for him. He pulled off his boots and socks.

"Aw, no holiday toes." She peered over the edge of the bunk. "What a shame."

"Sorry about that." He stood, undid his cuffs, unsnapped his shirt partway and pulled it over his head. "I'll make it up to you somehow." He glanced at the army blanket. "That blanket is a little rough. Maybe we should—"

"I'll move it out of the way."

Watching her sit up, scoot back and toss the blanket to the foot of the bed was a great motivator. Putting the foil condom package between his teeth, he shucked his jeans and briefs in one motion.

Her quick intake of breath drew his attention. He paused in the middle of ripping open the packet. "Something wrong?"

"Something's very right." Her focus was on his cock. "You don't need holiday toes. You're party-ready just as you are."

"Almost." He ripped open the package and rolled on the condom. Took him a bit longer because he was shaking. He glanced at her. "I'm not nervous. I don't know why I'm—"

"It's okay. I'm shaking, too." She held out her hand. "Make love to me, Sky."

And there it was again, the tightness in his chest. He wanted this, wanted her, way too much. Yeah, he could be asking for heartbreak. But she was worth the risk.

<u>16</u>

No two ways about it, Penny lusted after Sky's gorgeous body. When he climbed into bed, she wanted to touch every inch she could reach.

That turned out to be only about half of him, since the narrow bunk left little room for maneuvering. He had nowhere to put himself except the obvious, his hips between her thighs and his chest inches from hers.

She started her explorations there, savoring the texture of dark blond hair that lightly decorated his impressive pecs. Then she ran her hands down his broad back and gazed up at him, dizzy with anticipation. "Cozy."

"Mm-hm." Heat flared in his blue eyes and his throat moved in a slow swallow. "I want to take it easy this first time, but..." His chest heaved. "I might not."

Heart pounding, she slid her palms lower and curled her fingers over his tight buns. "You might get wild?" She squeezed gently.

He shuddered. "It's likely."

Her body clenched. He hadn't deployed his amazing equipment yet and she was ready to fly apart. "Bring it, cowboy. Or I'll start this celebration without you."

"Can't have that." He lowered his hips.

She held her breath. Despite what he'd said about wild behavior, he slid in slowly, his gaze locked with hers as he sank deep. And deeper yet.

She let out her breath in a long, quivering sigh of delight. This would be good. And the first wave of happiness would hit soon.

"Okay?"

She couldn't hold back a grin. "You know it is, you poser. That's a top-of-the-line lady pleaser you have there."

He chuckled.

The slight movement of his pelvis brought on by his laughter was all she needed. With a startled exclamation, she climaxed, digging her fingertips into his glutes and gasping for breath.

His breath hissed out as he gritted his teeth. Then he gulped in air and stared into space. "I will not come, I will not come, I will not come."

"Poor guy." She cleared the huskiness from her throat. "You can if you want."

"But I don't want." Looking down at her, he managed a quick smile. "I'm determined to hold on long enough to make that happen again. Maybe even once more after that."

She stroked his back, now damp with sweat. "Over-achiever, are you?"

A flash of laughter sparkled in his eyes. "It's been said."

"Well, now it's been said again."

His gaze warmed. "It's not because I want to impress you with my skill. I just—"

"To be honest, you don't need much skill. I could have an orgasm just looking at you. Then when you plug in your lady pleaser, I'm toast."

His mouth turned up at the corners. "Sounds like we're cooking breakfast."

"Most important meal of the day."

"I just want to make love to you, Penny."

"That's what you're doing."

"But I can do it better." Easing back, he pushed in again. "Thanks for talking me down."

"You're not the least bit down. I can tell." Could she ever. Preparations were in progress for another round of fireworks.

"You have a way with words." He created an easy rhythm that didn't quite jibe with the heat in his eyes.

"I'm an English major." She wrapped her legs around his, increasing the friction. Ahhh.

His breath hitched. "With moves like a gymnast."

"I might've taken a few classes."

"Thought so." Leaning down, he feathered a kiss over her lips. "Winding your legs around mine makes me—"

"Wild?" She lifted her hips to meet his next thrust.

He groaned. "Yes, ma'am."

"Be wild. Go for it."

Raising his head, his gaze burned into hers. "Buckle up."

Excitement stole her breath. She nodded. And gasped as the first few rapid strokes hurled her over the edge into another orgasm. Crying out, she held on as he continued to plunge into her. The climax roared, blotting out everything but the incredible sensation of oneness as he rode the waves undulating within her core.

Then his thrusts came faster, even more insistent. Incredibly, her joyous center of operations offered up another thrilling episode. He shouted in triumph and pushed home, his muscular body rocked with the tremors of release, his breathing tortured, his forehead beaded with sweat.

She lay limp and panting beneath him, her gaze unfocused. No one else had ever... she'd never... nothing had ever been so....

Now what, genius girl?

* * *

Penny propped herself up on her elbows so she could watch Sky come back from the bunkhouse bathroom located at the far end of the row of beds. Poetry in motion. An abundance of riches.

She was in over her head, but there wasn't much she could do about it now except let the current take her and enjoy the thrills along the way. "We probably need to shower at some point."

"In a bit. Let's not rush into it. No telling how often we'll get to be alone while I'm here."

"How long will it take us to ride over to the barn and groom the horses?"

"Not long. We've got at least another hour before we have to be dressed and out of here." He stood beside the bed. "Think you have room for me in there?"

"Sure." She rolled to her side and scooted over against the wall. "Plenty of room." She patted the narrow spot that was left.

Lying on his side facing her, he wedged himself into the space. "That's not what I call plenty of room."

She slipped an arm around his waist. "I'm not complaining."

"Me, either. Best bed ever. You can't escape."

"Oh, I could if I wanted to."

"Betcha couldn't."

"Bet I could." She reached down and pinched his butt.

"Ouch."

"That was nothing." She nudged him with her knee. "If I really wanted you to move and you wouldn't let me, I'd go for the family jewels."

"Please don't." He caressed the curve of her hip. "I have plans for those."

"Kids?"

"I'd like to. Depends on how my partner feels about it. Do you want any?"

"With the right guy. The kind who wants to split childcare fifty-fifty."

"Sounds fair. Your brother has strong opinions about kids. I got some of his story last night."

"Yeah, his childhood sucked." She brushed her fingers over his chest hair. "I didn't understand when I was young. He got all the attention as the budding child star and I was jealous of that."

"Do you get along with your folks, now?"

"Mostly. I won't let them put Leo down anymore. And ironically, I don't like it when they're bragging on me, like I'm the most brilliant professor at UCLA."

He smiled. "I'm willing to believe you are."

"I absolutely am not."

"You recognize the cultural value in my mom's books. That takes brilliance."

His loyalty to his mother touched her. "So I have flashes of brilliance." She glanced up at him. "She fascinates me. After reading her books, I would have sworn she was a man."

"In some ways she acts like one."

"How?"

"Her kids come first. Her career second. The men in her life, except for her sons, rank a distant third."

"Do you mean ex-husbands?"

"No husbands. She swears she'll never marry."

"But clearly she wanted to have kids."

"You don't have to be married to have kids. She discovered that early on."

"I guess so."

"Evidently being pregnant with me was a joy. She felt great, wrote like crazy and sold a book for a decent amount. Having me was a breeze, too. She wanted to repeat that process."

"A kid for every book? How many siblings do you have?"

"I don't have forty-nine, if that's what you're asking."

She laughed. "She'd end up in the Guinness Book of World Records."

"That babies and books routine lasted about ten years. I have eight brothers and one sister. Mom shut down the operation when she got a girl."

"Beau mentioned twins."

"Yes, and one of my brothers is adopted."

"And the fathers of this brood? What—"

"That's a complicated subject."

"And you don't have to explain anything. I'm just being nosy."

"I'll be happy to explain everything." Tilting her face up, he gazed into her eyes. "But I would love to table the subject of my crazy family for the time being."

She grinned. "I wonder why?"

"I don't know if you've noticed, but we've had some interesting developments during this discussion."

"I've noticed." The hard ridge of his cock pressed against her belly.

"Want to do anything about it?"

Reaching between them, she curled her fingers around his pride and joy. "I could be persuaded."

"Then let me fetch something from my stash of supplies." Leaning away from her, he reached under the bunk and opened it. "Here we go." He closed the drawer and turned back to her, a condom packet in his hand.

"Handy."

"Bunkhouse simplicity."

"I didn't think to ask. How is it that you have these? I don't picture you as the sort of man who always travels with—"

"I don't, but Beau does."

"How many did he give you?"

"If this week works out as I hope, not enough."

"That could get tricky. Neither one of us has transportation, unless we're prepared to ride a horse to town."

He smiled. "Trust me, if we start running low, I'll come up with something more efficient than that."

He would, too. She'd already learned that he was goal oriented. What a wonderful trait in a lover.

17

Sky would always cherish the first time he made love to Penny. A slight shudder of his hips when he'd laughed and bingo, she'd come apart in his arms. The wild ride that followed had been spectacular, too.

But this moment, easing over her eager body for the second time, returning to the moist warmth, the snug fit, the familiar squeeze as she welcomed him — this was the gold standard.

She wrapped her arms around him, her hug both sensual and friendly. "I like this."

"Good. So do I." He held her gaze as he began to move. "I like you." He'd finally discovered a woman who fit like a glove — someone to laugh with and make love to for... a very long time. And she wasn't for him.

"Same here." Her hips rose to meet his thrusts. "What a lovely Christmas surprise you are."

"You, too." When a slight ripple caressed his *lady pleaser* as she called it, he pumped faster. "I must have been a good boy to deserve this."

Her breathing quickened. "I can't vouch for the whole year, but this morning you've been a very

good…" She moaned. "Sky, you have such a way of—
"

"Go with it." He shifted the angle, increased the pace, watched her eyes grow stormy with passion.

Color bloomed on her cheeks. "Come with me this time."

"But if I hold back, you might—"

"Don't wait. I don't need to have more than… just be with me."

Her breathless plea grabbed him by the heart. Well, okay, lower down, too. "Tell me when."

"Almost. There. *Now.*"

Instead of resisting the seductive tug of her climax, he relaxed into it with a groan of surrender. His body did the rest, happily responding as nature intended. He snuggled with her, more content than he'd been… ever.

* * *

A sexy shower break wasn't in the cards. They'd run out of time. He straightened up the bunk and picked up his clothes from the floor while she showered. Then he took his turn while she dressed.

When he came back from the bathroom, a towel around his hips, she was sitting on his bunk, texting on her phone.

She glanced up and grinned. "I hope you know that walking around with a towel draped over your privates turns you into a female fantasy."

"Thanks for the tip. I'll try to do it whenever you're here. And I hope that's a lot." He picked through the clothes that he'd left on the bunk across the aisle and located his briefs.

"I guess I'll be here tonight for the Brotherhood Christmas celebration around the fire pit. Leo just texted to remind me of it."

"FYI, I won't be attending wrapped in a towel."

"Awww. What a shame. Think we'll be able to disappear into the shadows for some mouth-to-mouth?"

"Maybe." Her comment shifted his attention from the briefs in his hand to the fullness of her lips. She hadn't put on lipstick yet. "Should be a big crowd. We might be able to get lost in it." Visions of kissing her now and later tonight threatened to reverse the shrinkage he'd achieved with a cold shower.

It didn't help that her gaze had dropped to the towel around his hips. "Penny, you're staring."

"Can't help it. The towel's moving."

"You're the one making that happen."

"I know." She looked up, her grey eyes full of mischief. "I'm moving it with my mind. I never could bend a spoon, but I'm moving that towel."

He laughed. "Guess I'll be getting dressed in the bathroom. It's the only way I'll be able to zip my jeans." Grabbing his clothes and picking up his boots, he walked away.

"Didn't mean to inconvenience you," she called after him. "I seem to have a little obsession going on."

"No worries. You're good for my ego." By the time he'd put on his socks and briefs, he mostly had the problem under control. He finished dressing before he left the bathroom, though, just in case she had more saucy comments to make.

When he returned, she was still engrossed in her phone. "More from Leo?"

"No, that was Fiona, texting during a break at the stationery store. Wanted to know how everything was going."

"And you said..."

She held up her phone so he could see her reply to Fiona — a thumbs-up emoji and a smiley sporting a big grin.

He chuckled. "I guess that about covers it." He plucked his Stetson and jacket from the hooks on the wall. "Ready to go?"

"Not really." She stood and unhooked her jacket and hat, too. "I can't help fantasizing what it would be like to spend a whole day together."

He sighed. "Yeah. Don't know if that's in the cards. Tonight's the fire pit deal. Tomorrow I'll need to do some shopping and there's the Christmas Eve bash at Ed's."

"And a birthday party tomorrow afternoon for CJ and Isabel's little girl. She turns one tomorrow."

"CJ mentioned that last night. Henri's pulling out all the stops for Cleo Marie. Besides Christmas gifts, I need to pick up a birthday present. Tomorrow's packed. And then it's Christmas Day already."

"You're not leaving on the twenty-sixth, I hope?"

"Beau's picking me up on the twenty-ninth."

"Whew. I didn't think to ask when you were leaving. Maybe the pace will be slower after Christmas and we'll be able to — why are you smiling at me like that?"

He blinked. "Didn't know I was smiling."

"Well, you were, with a dreamy look on your face."

"Just happy, I guess. Clearly you had a good time this morning if you're looking forward to more of the same."

"So are you, judging from your expression just now."

"You have no idea. If I weren't such a damned responsible human being, I'd be texting Henri to ask for a rain check. Then I'd climb right back in that bunk with you."

"And skip lunch?"

"There's food in the refrigerator. We wouldn't have to clear out until late this afternoon."

"But we couldn't leave the horses tied to a tree all that time."

"No. But you could rest up while I handled that situation. The barn's not that far away."

"Henri really wants to show you those photo albums."

"And I really want to see them. Except I forget all about that when I think about what we could be—"

"We need to vamoose." She put on her hat with the stampede string dangling under her chin.

"Yes, ma'am." He helped her into her coat. He loved that she'd opted for the string so she wouldn't lose that hat, likely the first Stetson she'd ever owned. She was adorably earnest, a quality he cherished and didn't often find. "By the way, I doubt we'll be alone at the barn. At least that's how it works at Rowdy Ranch. Someone's always around."

She turned to face him. "Then how about one more for the road?"

"My thoughts exactly." Sliding his hands inside her open coat, he drew her close and dipped under the brim of her hat. He knocked it off, anyway.

She smiled. "See how well that stampede string works?"

"I do." He touched down gently, then lifted his mouth a fraction from hers. "What soft lips you have."

She cupped the back of his head. "The better to kiss you with." She closed the distance, her passion restrained, her lips moving against his with infinite tenderness.

Warmth spread through him as he sank into the honeyed sweetness of a kiss different from any she'd given him before.

She ended it slowly and eased out of his arms. "Thank you for an incredible morning."

Opening his eyes, he gazed into the depths of hers. His breath caught. The way she was looking at him almost made him think... but that was crazy. He was seeing what he wanted to see.

He cleared his throat. "You're welcome."

_18_

Kissing Sky like that might have been a mistake. Penny had time to reconsider her actions as they rode over to the barn. Was it a misstep? They laughed and joked like before as they unsaddled and groomed the horses before turning them out to join their buddies in the snowy pasture.

But what if she'd changed the dynamic with that kiss? Every so often she caught him looking at her, a thoughtful expression on his handsome face. She couldn't prove that he was thinking about her kiss, but he hadn't acted that way prior to it.

Gratitude had driven the impulse. With Fiona's help, she'd instigated this Christmas visit. Only hours into it, Sky had provided an adventure beyond her wildest dreams. That deserved a sincere thank you. She hadn't intended to mess with him, though.

Soon after they turned out the horses, CJ showed up with his tow-headed daughter in his arms. She was decked out in a bright red snowsuit with a hood and tiny cowgirl boots. "Hey, there! How was your ride?" He said it with a straight face.

But he glanced at Penny with a teasing glimmer in his eyes. "Have fun, your highness?"

"I did. Big fun."

CJ snorted. "Alrighty. How about you, cowboy? Good times?"

"Unbelievable."

"Glad to hear it, dude. Now come meet the birthday girl. Cleo Marie, this is your Uncle Sky."

She looked him up and down, her blue gaze assessing, her rosebud mouth pursed.

"I get uncle status?" Sky acted surprised.

"Biologically speaking, you have more of a claim than any of us."

"Biology doesn't figure into this."

"Well, it does, but it's generous of you to say that."

"Will she come to me?"

"Let's hope so. She's my Geiger counter. If she won't let someone hold her, I figure they're radioactive."

"No pressure then." He approached slowly. "Hey, Cleo Marie. I need to look good, here. What'll it take? A giant teddy bear? What about a pony?"

"She already has a truckload of bears and Henri's promised her a pony eventually. It could even show up tomorrow. Try again."

Sky shoved back his hat. "How about piggyback rides for life? How about that?"

She lit up, babbling a steady stream of unrelated syllables as she bounced in CJ's grip and stretched her arms toward Sky.

"You've done it now, buddy. She knows exactly what you said and it's her favorite thing. You're gonna regret that promise."

"Not for a minute." He turned to Penny. "Hold my hat?"

"You bet."

Grinning, he took the little girl by her arms and lowered her over his head. She clung to him like Velcro, wrapping her pudgy hands around his neck as he hooked his arms under her legs. "Off we go!" He trotted toward the barn, then swerved toward the corral. Making a U-turn, he headed back to the barn and repeated the pattern as she squealed with delight.

CJ shoved his gloved hands in his coat pockets. "He's done this a time or two."

"He's the oldest of ten."

"He made some reference to that last night. Not sure I totally get the setup at their place, but whatever works for people is fine with me." He glanced at her. "It's going well with you two?"

"Yes. Fortunately, we're both realistic. We know it's temporary." Assuming she hadn't given him the wrong impression with that kiss.

"I had a temporary situation like that." He gestured to the laughing child on Sky's back. "Cleo Marie's the result."

"She wasn't planned?"

"No, ma'am. Total shock to both of us."

"I had no idea. You and Isabel clearly adore each other."

"Never was supposed to be, though. Separate lives and all that. Then Cleo Marie happened, thank God. She brought us to our senses."

"So if Isabel hadn't ended up pregnant, you wouldn't be together?"

"That's right. I can't imagine it, now. How could I have walked away from that woman? How could she have walked away from me? But we'd left each other for good."

"Incredible." She peered at him. "Did you come by so you could tell me about—"

"Heck, no. Total coincidence. I have daddy time today and Cleo loves going to the barn. Didn't know you'd be here."

"You almost missed us. Henri should arrive any minute to pick us up. We're going up to the house for lunch so Sky can look at her photo albums."

"Good. It's funny how the rest of us had either bad fathers or no father, but Sky had the best father ever and he didn't even know him. He should at least find out how great Charley was."

"I agree."

He took a breath. "Listen, Penny, I'm sure your situation is nothing like ours. It's just when I hear *it's temporary*, I wonder if someone's fooling themselves." He glanced at her. "No offense."

"None taken. You make a good point. I'm incredibly drawn to that man, and it's very... inconvenient."

CJ smiled. "I imagine it is. I—" He turned as Henri's truck pulled up. "Here comes Grandma Henri." He gave her a wave and she beeped the horn. "Your lunch at the house may be delayed. She and Cleo are bonkers about each other."

"I gathered that from all the preparations for the birthday party."

"Did she and Ben get that pony?"

"I'm not allowed to say."

He laughed. "They did. I knew it. It's a ridiculous expense, but what the hell."

"I heard that." Henri came to join them. "Did Penny spill the beans?"

"She did not. I just know how you operate."

"It's not that expensive. And the Babes chipped in, so it's from all of us." She gazed at Sky cavorting with Cleo Marie. "Did you tell him she loves piggyback rides?"

"No, ma'am. It was his idea."

"Clearly he has experience with kids."

"From helping with his brothers and sister, I expect," CJ said.

"I suppose so." She smiled as Sky spun in a circle while the little girl giggled and tugged on his hair. "I love having him here, but... why didn't he come earlier? Wagon Train's not that far away."

CJ put an arm around her shoulders. "Guess you'll have to ask him."

"I will. That's one of the reasons for this lunch. I want a chance to talk with him before things get crazy."

"Which brings up something else," Penny spoke quickly, because Sky had spotted them and was heading their way. "You'd probably like to talk with him privately. After lunch I'll excuse myself and—"

"Please don't. You're the most impartial person on this ranch."

"I'm not sure about that."

"You are. You help me see both sides."

"Okay, then."

Henri glanced toward Sky and raised her voice. "Nice job, son."

"Thanks." He was breathing fast. "I think she could do this forever."

CJ laughed. "Or at least until Grandma Henri arrives."

"Glad to be of service. Come here, munchkin." Henri held out her arms and Cleo Marie switched allegiances immediately. She couldn't get to Henri fast enough, snuggling in, patting Henri's cheeks and giving her kisses. Henri returned those kisses and added more for good measure.

Penny watched the scene with new eyes after hearing Henri's confession last night about longing to have children of her own.

"See you guys in a little while." Henri propped the little girl on her hip. "Good thing I brought carrots. Cleo and I have critters to feed." She carried the cooing little girl over to the pasture gate.

Several horses had gathered there. Clearly this was a special routine for them, too. Henri pulled carrot chunks from her coat pocket.

Sky gestured toward Henri and Cleo. "No question who's the favorite around here. Piggyback rides will only take me so far."

"Don't feel bad," CJ said. "She likes Henri more than anyone, and that includes Isabel and me."

"Henri must give awesome piggyback rides."

"She doesn't give any. She just surrounds that baby girl with her Henri-ness and Cleo falls under her spell. It's the damnedest thing."

"My mom has that same effect on kids. She loves them and they sense it. I've seen it happen with perfect strangers in restaurants. A toddler will just walk over and crawl in my mother's lap. My mom eats it up."

CJ lowered his voice. "Don't tell Henri that. If you know what I mean."

"I do. I don't want to add fuel to that rivalry fire if I can help it." He glanced at Penny. "Feel free to give me a nudge if I start going off the rails about my mom while we're up at the house."

"I'll do that." Interesting position she'd gotten herself into, the diplomat tasked with keeping everything congenial.

"Looks like Henri and Cleo are on their way back." CJ tugged his hat down. "Now comes the challenging part, prying my daughter away from Grandma."

Sky turned to him. "Has she had lunch?"

"Not yet."

"Does she like French fries?"

"Loves them, especially if I take her into town and pick them up from the drive-through window. Good idea." He clapped him on the shoulder. "I'm glad we ran into each other so you had a chance to meet my kid before the big party tomorrow."

"Me, too. She's terrific."

"Just be prepared that every time she sees you, she'll expect a piggyback ride."

"That's fine. It's good exercise."

"And the Brotherhood can rest easy now."

"Why?"

"Since you passed the Cleo Marie test, I can let them know you're not radioactive."

19

Sky held the door for Penny as they followed Henri into the house. Less than twenty-four hours ago, he'd stood in the entryway and glimpsed Penny coming down the stairs. Her gray eyes had widened, no doubt because of his startling likeness to the pictures she'd seen of Charley.

But her eyes had also flashed with interest. And his breath had caught. Unusual for him. Instant attractions weren't his thing. Taking a woman to bed after such a short acquaintance wasn't his style, either.

But he didn't regret a minute of the time he'd spent with her, didn't question whether he was making a colossal mistake. He wanted to be with Penny. If that privilege only lasted until the twenty-ninth, so be it.

"I need to warm up the chili." Henri hung up her coat and hat. "The salad's made. If either of you want cornbread—"

"I'm a fan." Sky helped Penny take off her coat. The last time he'd done that... nope, better not go there. "I can make it."

"Then the job's yours. That'll give me time to return a call from Ed."

"I'll be your helper," Penny said. "I've never made cornbread, but I'm a whiz at measuring stuff."

"Sounds like a plan." Henri went into the kitchen and pulled out ingredients, a couple of bowls and a baking pan. "Have at it, kids. I'll go talk to Ed. She's trying to decide on ribbon colors for the pony's mane and tail."

Sky chuckled. "This'll be fun to watch."

"He and Isabel tried to talk us out of it, but it's not as crazy as it sounds. Cleo will outgrow him, but guaranteed there will be more toddlers around here."

"My sister got a Shetland and she loves that little guy."

"You still have him?"

"We do. He's twenty-eight. Angelique dotes on him. So does my... family." He'd have to watch himself. References to his mom came too easily.

"What color?"

"Silver dapple."

"That's what we got Cleo! That silver mane and tail with the gray coat is stunning."

"It's a little girl's dream horse. On the other hand, if they're not well-trained, they—"

"Oh, this boy's trained within an inch of his life. Ed's been working with him since July. She's not letting that child near a misbehaving horse." She switched on the oven. "Do you need a recipe?"

"Got it in my head."

Her expression grew wistful. "Charley used to memorize recipes. He loved to cook."

"Cornbread?"

"No, that's my specialty."

"Uh-oh. Maybe I should wait and let you supervise."

"If you've memorized the recipe you clearly know what you're doing. See you guys later. Oh, and stir the chili, please." She left the room.

"I'll take care of the chili." Penny grabbed a long-handled wooden spoon from a crock on the counter and lifted the chili pot lid.

"Didn't expect to be alone with you."

She glanced up. "Not for long."

"And we have to get the cornbread in the oven."

Replacing the lid, she laid the spoon in the holder on the stove. Her saucy gaze met his. "Chili's in good shape. Tell me what to do."

He laughed. "Stop looking at me like that."

"Can't help it." She moved closer. "You were adorable giving Cleo Marie piggyback rides. I'm still thinking about you running around with that little girl clinging to your back."

"I love kids." Although she was within touching distance, he kept his hands to himself. "I get that from my mom."

"You almost mentioned her when you were talking about that Shetland, didn't you?"

"Almost. She babies that pony something terrible. It's a wonder he's not spoiled, but he's had a sweet disposition from the get-go."

"Like you." She lifted her hand as if to stroke his cheek. Then she sighed and stepped back. "We'd better start on that cornbread."

"Right." He forced himself to pick up the measuring cup instead of reaching for her. "I need a cup of flour, a cup of cornmeal and two-thirds cup of sugar in that bowl, please."

"Yes, sir."

"And I need a kiss, but we both know what will happen if we get started." He used a paper towel to grease the pan with butter.

"Good things will happen." She measured the ingredients and dumped them into the bowl.

"Inappropriate things."

"Nice things."

He groaned.

"What else do you need?"

"A teaspoon of salt, three and a half teaspoons of baking powder. And a hug." He found a small saucepan in the cupboard and melted the butter. "No, wait. A hug's too tame, I'd rather mix some honey into this butter, rub it all over you and lick you clean."

"Cool it." She sounded breathless. "Henri could show up any minute."

"I have another idea."

"Another impossible-to-execute idea that's guaranteed to stir us up?"

"This one's doable. Might stir you up, though. Does it for me." He cracked an egg into the bowl.

"Are you going to tell me or not?"

"Building the suspense."

"Sky."

"What if you stayed with me after the party tonight? I could bring you back here in the morning."

"On horseback?"

"Yeah, and simplify it by riding double on King, maybe even bareback. I'll check with Henri to see if that's okay, but he's built for it."

"It's obvious what you're built for, cowboy."

He glanced over. She was giving him a look hot enough to bake the cornbread. "Right backatcha, lady. Got those ingredients measured into the bowl?"

"I do."

"I need you to make a hole in the middle."

"Why?"

"So I can put the liquid in there."

She grinned. "You're making that up."

"No, ma'am." He gave her an innocent look. "That's just how it's done."

* * *

Henri came back as Sky slid the cornbread in the oven, which meant zero time to give Penny a quick kiss. He consoled himself with the excellent plan he'd dreamed up for later.

"Twenty-five minutes, right?" Henri glanced at the kitchen clock.

"Approximately."

"That's enough time to look at one of the albums." Crossing to the stove, she turned down the heat under the chili. "We can sit in the living room and soak up some Christmas tree ambiance."

"Sounds perfect." Sky rinsed the bowls and wiped out the saucepan before putting them in the dishwasher.

"A cook who cleans up after himself." She gave him a smile. "You're nice to have around, Sky."

"Thank you, ma'am."

Her smile wobbled. "Polite, too."

Normally he would have given his mom credit for that. "I appreciate the compliment." He dried his hands. "Let's take a look at those albums." He and Penny followed Henri into the living room.

"I especially want you to see the one with all the pictures of Charley and me on Prince and King."

"How long have you had those two?"

"Eleven years." She took the middle spot on the couch and picked up an album from the ones she'd stacked on the coffee table. "Prince was three and King was four when we got them."

Penny took a seat on Henri's left and he settled down on her right. So much for getting a nudge from Penny if he strayed into dangerous conversational territory.

Henri opened the album. "This picture is the one I told you about this morning. Where we're mounted up and holding hands. Don't we look a lot like you two?"

A chill went down his spine as he stared at the picture. Henri had been a blonde with long hair back then, and from a distance could be taken for an older version of Penny. Charley was an aged version of him. That's what he'd look like in his fifties. Crazy.

"Here we are in the Apple Grove Founders Day Parade. We led the Buckskin Ranch entry. Charley carried the Wyoming flag because he was born and raised here. I took the U.S. flag."

Penny leaned closer. "Look at you, all smiles."

"I'd never carried a flag in a parade before moving here and boy, did I love it. The parade ended at the arena outside of town. While everyone else headed back to the square for the mid-day barbeque, Charley and I would canter around the arena, flags flying. Just for the heck of it."

"I've heard about the Founders Day celebration from Leo," Penny said. "When is it?"

"The actual day is June sixteenth. We pick the closest weekend, so next year it'll start on the eighteenth."

"That could work out. I'll check to see when I'll be done with second semester."

He needed that reminder about her professorship at UCLA. He didn't like being reminded, but he couldn't forget about it, either. Six months from now he could see her again if he drove over. He wouldn't. Self-preservation.

Henri turned the page. "Oh, I love this one. We used to do this when we wanted to go for an evening jaunt around the property."

Sky's chest tightened at the sweetness of the picture. Charley and Henry rode bareback, tucked together on King like two halves of a whole. Her laughing face and Charley's wide grin spoke volumes about the life they'd created and the love they'd shared.

"Sometimes I'd take the front and steer," Henri said. "Sometimes Charley would. In this shot I was in charge."

Penny chuckled. "Very cute." She glanced over at Sky, a sparkle in her eyes. "Ever done that?"

"Yes, ma'am. It's fun."

"I can't remember who took this, probably Jake, because I'm cracking up. He used to tease us about being a couple of teenagers disguised as adults."

Sky wanted that snapshot. "Do you mind if I take a picture of it with my phone?"

"Go right ahead. I could try to make a copy but I doubt I have the negative anymore. You can probably do just as well with your phone."

"Let's see." He pulled it out, focused on the image and got a decent version. "That works." He showed it to Henri and Penny.

"It absolutely works," Henri said. "You could do the same thing with any of them."

"Thanks. I will. I just knew I had to have that one." His screen went dark. He refreshed it so he could gaze at the picture some more. Until now, he'd had no clear idea of how he wanted his future to look. *Like this.*

20

Was Henri playing matchmaker? Penny couldn't figure it out. Henri supported her academic career, so why would she foster a romance that would seriously mess with it?

Yet Henri continued through the album pointing out how much she and Charlie looked like Penny and Sky. Clearly she was fascinated by that fact. Was Sky fascinated by it, too?

Could be. He studied each picture as if it held some sort of secret code, although he didn't pull out his phone again. Maybe he was simply looking for clues about his father. That made sense. No need to get paranoid.

The stamp of Charley Fox's personality was on every page. He'd smiled a lot. He'd laughed even more. Clearly he'd loved Henri, their ranch, their horses and the young men they'd taken in. Mostly he'd loved life.

The deeper they got into the album, the more her throat tightened with grief for the loss of a man she'd never met. Leo had known him well, though. Charley had been more of a father to Leo than their dad. Thank goodness her brother's rebellious heart had led him here. He'd had ten years to soak up Charley's positive influence.

The oven timer dinged and Henri closed the album. "Time to eat." She rose from the couch.

Penny stood, too, but she didn't quite make the mental transition to the present. Although she went through the motions, setting the table and bringing the food into the dining room, she was still living in the pages of that album.

If Charley had been given a few more years, Sky would have met him this Christmas. Heck, she would have met him and discovered for herself what Leo had meant when he'd raved about Charley.

Maybe the Brotherhood wouldn't have been formed if Charley had lived. But she had no doubt those guys gladly would have traded the Brotherhood concept for more years with the man who was the father of their heart.

When the food was dished, they settled at one end of the long dining room table, Henri at the head, Sky and Penny on either side. Sky raved about the chili. Penny and Henri lavishly praised the cornbread.

Henri had made coffee, something Sky likely needed after his night with the Brotherhood. Penny didn't mind getting more caffeine in her system, either. If Sky's plan worked out, she might not get much sleep tonight.

"That album is my favorite." Henri scooped up a bite of chili. "Even more so than the wedding album. Our matching buckskins were such a delight. We felt like royalty when we rode them."

"They're beautiful animals." Sky helped himself to a second wedge of cornbread. "Very well trained."

"Thank you. King went through an adjustment period after Charley died." She grimaced. "Well, we all did, but I didn't figure on King becoming a handful. He wasn't too bad with me, but he acted up when any of the guys rode him."

"He didn't give me a bit of trouble this morning."

Maybe because he'd spent most of it tied to a tree? Penny quickly swallowed her mouthful of coffee before she spewed it.

"He's dropped his attitude," Henri said. "Ben rides him the most these days, but we still switch around so King won't get stuck in his ways like he was before."

"Is Ben able to come to the fire pit celebration tonight? I'd like to get to know him better."

"He'll be there. He likes to make sure the Moose is running the way it should during the holiday season so he's gone a lot. But he scheduled time off tonight."

"Great."

"He can tell you things about Charley… about your dad… that I don't even know. They were friends before I came on the scene."

Oh. Penny looked across the table at Sky. He was looking right back at her as if he'd just figured out what she had. Ben would have known Desiree.

"I see you've connected the dots. Ben and Charley were best friends, so of course he knew your mother. I asked him about her last night on the way to the Moose. Peppered him with questions is more like it. Poor man. I wanted to know what she was like back then. Smart? Personable? Beautiful?"

All those things, no doubt. Penny had been impressed with her last night. She would have had the same qualities at twenty-five.

"Ben was so diplomatic. He recalled that she was attractive. And nice. Now that I've met her, I'm fairly certain she was, and always has been, dynamite."

Sky cleared his throat. "Yes, ma'am."

Penny admired his restraint. And Henri's for that matter. She'd ended up with Charley, but now she was faced with his former lover, a beautiful woman who'd conceived a child with him, something she'd been unable to do. That had to hurt.

"In any case, Ben had no idea about the pregnancy. I gather nobody did."

"That's what she told me." Sky hesitated. "She moved away before she knew about it."

"Then she must have left soon after they broke up." Henri pushed aside her empty bowl of chili.

"That's how I understand it. She said until he met you, he was a confirmed bachelor out for a good time. Then he spent a week at a conference in Texas and came back engaged."

"You got engaged in a *week*?" Penny stared at Henri. That detail hadn't come up yesterday when they were going through the wedding album looking for shots of Charley.

"Yes, well..." Henri's cheeks turned pink, another unusual happening. "Like we told everyone back then, we bonded over buckskins."

Okay, a shared interest, but still. Getting engaged in a week was insane. "What kind of conference was it?"

"For breeders. Charley was already into it and I wanted to be. That first day we talked for hours. By the end of the week, we just... knew."

Penny struggled with what to say. Her brother had described Henri as a wise and thoughtful matriarch, the voice of reason. He'd laughingly told her that Ben had worked for more than a year to win her hand. Charley had only needed a week.

How did someone *just know* they'd met their future spouse? An instant attraction, like the one between her and Sky, was understandable. But agreeing to marry that person after only seven days? Crazy. "Clearly it worked out, but a week seems...."

"Reckless? My family accused me of that and more when I announced my plan to move to Montana and marry Charley. They predicted I'd regret it. I never had a moment's regret."

"There sure wasn't any regret in the album you just showed us," Sky said. "I've never seen two people look happier with their choice."

"We were. Every day, even the ones when we argued." She took a deep breath. "I didn't have the nerve to ask your mother this last night. It seemed too pointed. Do you know more precisely when she left town?"

"He broke up with her right after he came back from the convention. I get the impression she moved away about a week later."

"Then I doubt we crossed paths. I wondered if we had, but it took me almost three weeks to uproot my life in Indiana and make it out here. She was likely gone by then." Henri fell silent and stared into space. "He broke her heart, didn't he?"

Sky glanced at Penny. The answer to Henri's question shone in his troubled gaze, and she ached for him. She gave a subtle shake of her head. He didn't have to tell everything he knew.

"Never mind, son." Henri turned back to him. "I shouldn't ask you to reveal your mother's secrets."

"Thank you." Some of the tension left his expression.

"Maybe he didn't break her heart, but if she packed up and left that soon, her heart was at least bruised. I could tell that she was fond of Apple Grove. But staying would have meant constantly wondering when she'd come around a corner and see us together."

"Maybe, but she's tough. She probably just wanted a change of scenery."

"She might not have been that tough at twenty-five. Most of us aren't." She sighed. "I guess I can understand why she didn't want to tell Charley about you. It would have meant interacting with Charley... and me."

"She also might have thought she was doing you a favor."

Henri's posture stiffened and she pinned him with a laser-sharp stare. "If so, she was sadly mistaken. I loved Charley and I would have loved his child, no matter how that child came to be in this world. And I would have treated your mother with respect."

Sky didn't say anything.

"You don't believe me, but I would have. I'll admit to being angry about this sudden reveal, but that's mostly because Charley's gone and he was cheated out of the chance to meet you."

"That's partly on me. I could have come over on my own once I could drive."

"Why didn't you?" Her voice cracked. "Weren't you the least bit curious?"

A slight wince was the only sign that she'd landed a blow. Penny longed to be close enough to reassure him with a touch.

"I wish—" He paused to clear his throat. "I wish I had been curious. Now that I know more about him, I wish we could have met. And spent time together."

"He would have loved that, Sky."

"The thing is, I had no guarantee he'd welcome me. Or that you would. And it wasn't like I desperately needed him to fill a big hole in my life. I had my mom, my brothers, eventually a little sister. I had Buck and Mary Beth."

"Who?"

"The Weavers. Mom hired them when she bought the ranch twenty-five years ago. They're like grandparents to us."

"She's owned the ranch that long?"

"Yes, ma'am. Her books were making good money and the ranch was a fixer-upper. Still is, in a way. We're always changing things, making it more to our liking."

"I get that." Her voice had lost its hard edge. "The Buckskin is an ongoing project, too." She blew out a breath. "Doggone it, Sky, I still think you should have made the effort. Help me out here, Penny. Wouldn't you have tried to connect with the father you'd never met?"

"Probably." She gave Sky a quick glance that said *trust me*. "As a kid I immersed myself in fantasy because my reality was so boring. Unraveling the mystery of my unknown father would have been an adventure."

"See?" Henri gestured toward Sky. "An adventure."

"But that's my point. Sky was already living an adventure on a fixer-upper ranch with a bunch of brothers, a little sister, a pony who looks like a unicorn, a mother who writes books for a living. He didn't need more excitement in his life."

Henri met her gaze. "When you put it like that, it makes sense. But every time I look at Sky, I think about Charley." She turned to him. "He would have been so tickled about you. It's such a shame that he died without knowing you exist."

"Yes, ma'am. I regret that."

"It is a shame." Penny put a hand on Henri's arm. "I'm not saying I know how you feel. That would be presumptuous. But I was sad after looking at the album. Charley's missed out on a lot these last few years. Not just Sky."

"You're right. He'll never know Cleo Marie and he would have adored that munchkin."

"But then I got to thinking about the good part of this. Before Sky showed up, all you had were memories and photo albums. Now you have a whole lot more — his son who looks so much like him. When Sky smiles, I see Charley in his smile."

Henri's breath caught. "So... do I." Her voice was thick with tears. "Excuse me, guys." She bolted from the table.

Sky leaped up. "Henri—"

"Don't go after her." Penny pushed back her chair and stood.

"Why not? She—"

"She needs to be alone to gather herself. Remember last night when she left and went out to the barn?"

"Yes, but Ben was out there. He's not here for her, now. I could—"

"I doubt she's ready to let you see her cry. She doesn't know you well enough."

"Then maybe you should go."

"She doesn't know me well enough, either. Maybe one of the Brotherhood could comfort her, but they're not here. She's better off working through this on her own."

"Will she be back, do you think?"

"Of course. She invited us for lunch and she's a good hostess. She won't totally disappear."

"Okay." He didn't sound convinced. "That was nice, though, what you said, even if it made her cry."

"Crying's not always a bad thing."

"My mom says that, too, but..." He shrugged. "I like smiles better."

"Me, too." And she gave him one because she couldn't help it. He was so kind.

He gazed at her and slowly returned her smile. "You're wonderful, you know that?"

"So are you." She was in serious danger of kissing him. Bad idea. She'd rather not have Henri find them in a lip-lock. "Let's clean up the dishes. I predict she'll be back before we're finished. And I know she wants to show you more pictures."

"I'd like that." He stacked his dishes on top of Henri's and started for the kitchen. "Do you really think Rowdy Ranch sounds like fun?"

"Are you kidding? If it's anything like the Buckskin, it's the closest thing to a fantasy life the modern world offers." She followed him and handed over her dishes so he could rinse them.

"Then maybe you should come for a visit."

That stopped her in her tracks. "A visit?"

"Sure. See what you think of the place. Get a chance to spend more time with my mom, meet the rest of—"

"Sky, hold it. I thought... I thought we were on the same page."

"What do you mean?"

Her stomach churned. "Why would I visit your ranch?"

"Because you said it sounded like fun."

"And then what?"

"Well, I—"

"You'll come to L.A. to see me? We'll try to keep this thing going over hundreds of miles?"

"I honestly hadn't considered coming to L.A."

"Didn't think so." She took a shaky breath. "If it'll be too tough for you to say goodbye on the twenty-ninth, then maybe... I hate to say this, but maybe we should call it—"

"No. I don't want to end it now." A muscle worked in his jaw. "I get the picture. It's fine. Well, it's not fine. If I had some magic way we could spend time together without bankrupting ourselves buying plane tickets... but you're right. It's unworkable."

"We'll make this week special, something to remember the rest of our lives."

"That mission's already accomplished. I'll never forget you."

"I won't forget you, either." As she gazed into his eyes, CJ's comment came back to her. *When I hear it's temporary, I wonder if someone's fooling themselves.* Was Sky? Worse yet, was she?

<u>21</u>

Penny's response to his invitation didn't make Sky happy, but he couldn't argue with it. He'd wanted her to visit the ranch and fall in love with it. And him. Then what? Did he expect her to abandon the career she'd created with blood sweat and tears?

He didn't care to visit her in L.A. He wasn't prepared to leave Rowdy Ranch and look for a job in L.A. When he turned the situation around, he came off as an arrogant male who'd assumed she'd make the sacrifices. He'd better get his head out of his butt, accept the gift of this week and be grateful.

As Penny had predicted, Henri came back before they'd finished cleaning up the lunch dishes. The three of them spent the afternoon eating Christmas cookies and paging through albums until Jake texted Sky to offer a ride back to the bunkhouse.

"How did he know I wasn't there?"

Henri laughed. "Jungle drums."

"No, seriously. CJ knew I was coming to your house because we saw him at the barn, but—"

"Sky, you're an exotic addition to this year's Christmas celebration. Your association with Penny is of interest, too. The Brotherhood might have given you more free rein than they'd originally planned, but they've made it their job to keep track of you at all times of the day and night."

He patted his pockets. "Am I bugged?"

"That's not necessary with the number of wranglers on this ranch. I got a report from Jake that Prince and King spent the morning tied to a tree in front of the bunkhouse."

He'd been so proud of his stealthy moves. The heat rose to his cheeks. "That's unsettling."

"I find it comforting. And it wasn't like we couldn't guess why you chose to stay in the bunkhouse when you had the option to move back here."

"Um..."

"I appreciate your sensibilities. They're old-fashioned, but I like that in a young man."

"Thank you." Was now the right time to ask her about leaving Penny at the bunkhouse tonight? And bring her back on King? Or the worst time ever?

"I told Leo nothing would happen if we both ended up down the hall from each other," Penny said, "but they went ahead with their nutty plan, anyway."

"And it all worked out, didn't it? You two can enjoy your privacy down at the bunkhouse. On top of that, Ben and I won't have to worry that we'll shock you with our goings-on."

Sky smiled. The Buckskin was more like Rowdy Ranch than he'd figured on. That was a relief. His embarrassment faded.

But Penny wasn't used to living on a ranch. When the days were filled with shoveling horse poop and keeping randy stallions away from mares in heat, plain talk was the norm.

Henri grinned. "Penny, you should see your face."

"Well, of course you and Ben... I mean, you're newlyweds, actually, and it's your house, so you should feel free to do... whatever."

"But my old frame house has paper-thin walls and we're conscious of that when we have guests. Ben's planning to add extra insulation to our bedroom."

Penny took a quick breath. "Good idea. I mean, not that I've heard anything. I sleep like a rock, so I would never—"

"Relax, sweetheart. I'm just pulling your chain."

"So Ben's not adding insulation?"

"Oh, he is, but that's neither here nor there. I suspect you'll be spending your nights at the bunkhouse."

"I will?" Her eyes widened and she looked at Sky like *what now*?

Sky picked up his cue. "We've been hoping we could work that out, but—"

"I know the sticky wicket, as Jake would say. You're somewhat stranded there. Ranches are supposed to have spare trucks sitting around, but we use every one we have. We'll figure it out, though. Someone will give you a ride when you need it."

"Is King still up to carrying two people? Could be fun getting around that way. And simple if we ride him bareback."

"Did you think of it when I showed you the picture?"

"I'd thought of it before that." And Beau had pushed four-footed transportation from the get-go.

Henri smiled. "Enterprising young man, aren't you? To answer your question, King is as strong as ever. That could work sometimes, unless weather becomes an issue. Riding through a light snow is lovely, though."

"And clearly I've never ridden through snow at all," Penny said. "I hope we get some so I can experience it."

Sky glanced at her. "Ever had a white Christmas?"

"Never."

Henri looked surprised. "You never spent the holiday in snow country? I thought California folks loved doing that."

"Not mine. They both hate the cold. Once I was in college, I was too busy for winter trips. This is the first break I can remember where I made a conscious decision not to do any work."

"Sounds like it's about time," Henri said. "And I hope you get a white Christmas, although I'd appreciate very much if the snow doesn't start until after the birthday party tomorrow. The pony needs to be presented to Cleo Marie in my backyard."

Sky checked the weather app on his phone. "No snow predicted for tomorrow. Or Christmas Day, I'm afraid." He looked over at Penny. "Sorry."

"A weather app can be wrong, you know."

"Let's hope it is. A white Christmas is—" He paused as a truck engine rumbled outside. "Might be Jake."

"It is Jake," Henri said. "That's the sound of his truck. Fair warning, he may rope you into helping with the chuck wagon stew tonight."

"He already asked me during the poker game last night. I'm planning on it."

"How late did that game last?"

"We broke up around four."

"Yikes. I should have asked about that before I shoved more picture albums at you. You could have taken a nap, instead."

"I'm fine."

"Yeah, well, Charley used to say that, too, and then he'd fall asleep in the middle of whatever was going on. Maybe instead of making chuck wagon stew with the guys, you should grab a power nap on your bunk."

"I'll consider it."

She smiled. "No, you won't. I can tell you're plagued with Fear of Missing Out, just like he was. I used to get the same response from him whenever I suggested he should rest up before a big night. He would..." Her eyes widened. "Oh, you guys, that's part of it."

"Part of what?" If she dashed off to cry again, he'd go after her this time.

She closed the album. "Ever since Charley died, whenever something major happened around here, especially if it was something good, I'd have a sick feeling in my stomach. Now I know why. I was imagining how disappointed he would be because he missed it." She gazed at Sky. "Your arrival is the granddaddy of missing out."

"Makes sense."

She patted his knee. "You look worried. I promise I'm not about to rush out of the room again. I know that upsets you."

"Yes, ma'am."

"Figuring this out doesn't make me sad. I feel liberated. They say naming a thing goes a long way to being able to handle it. I—" She paused as the front door opened. "Hey, Jake."

"Hey, everybody." He strolled into the living room and took off his hat. "Skyler McLintock, your chauffeur has arrived. Oh, look! Christmas cookies." He walked over and picked up one of the two left on the plate.

Henri stood. "Jake Lassiter, you should be ashamed of yourself, keeping this poor man up until four in the morning. What were you thinking?"

"I was thinking that we needed to find out what he's made of. It's standard procedure to test out a new guy's endurance at the poker table. We did the same with Garrett and Zeke. You just didn't know about it." He bit the star off the top of a green-frosted Christmas tree.

"Because you knew I'd disapprove."

"I don't mind being tested." Sky moved away from the couch so Henri could get out. "Matter of fact, I'm flattered that they bothered to put me through it." He looked at Jake. "Did I pass?"

"You passed." Jake finished off the cookie. "If you hadn't, I wouldn't have asked you to help make the stew."

Henri rolled her eyes. "You keep him up for all hours so he's exhausted, and his reward is slaving away in the kitchen?"

"Awesome program, isn't it? Any guy who makes it through that without slicing off a finger chopping onions is aces in my book." He looked at Sky. "Ready to go chop some stuff?"

"Absolutely." He turned to Henri and Penny. "Thanks for the lunch and the albums. I'll see you at the bunkhouse."

Penny smiled. "With all your fingers, I hope?"

"I'm a careful chopper."

Jake glanced at the cookie plate. "Okay if I take the last—"

"Go ahead, you crazy man. How's everything coming along?"

"Like clockwork, ma'am. I love Christmas." Munching on a snowman, he put on his hat and headed toward the front door.

Sky followed him to the entryway, shrugged into his jacket and grabbed his hat before going out the door.

"I was kidding about the onions." Jake took the steps two at a time. "We'll give you a job that doesn't involve sharp knives. You must be dead on your feet."

"Nope. I'm on an adrenaline rush. And it seems I inherited FOMO from my dad, so bring it, buddy."

"I see."

Rounding the front of Jake's truck, Sky crammed his hat on and climbed into the passenger seat. He had the door closed by the time Jake started the engine, but he was still buckling up as they drove away. "I take it we're in a hurry?"

"Got some decorating to do before we start cooking."

"Decorating?"

"Millie seems to think the bunkhouse isn't festive enough."

"For the party?"

"The party's outside, so we decorate the fire pit area and leave it at that. This bunkhouse plan is to benefit whatever you and Penny have going, the thing that's fueling your adrenaline rush and your FOMO."

"You're decorating the bunkhouse for us?"

"We're decorating it *with* you, dude. You're helping. CJ and Garrett said they'd figure out where the tree will go. You can't put it anywhere near the wood stove, and if it's in the kitchen, you won't—"

"A tree? There's no room for a tree in there. What the hell, Jake?"

"Since Penny's spending her nights at the bunkhouse, Millie wants it to be more Christmasy."

"How does Millie know Penny's spending her nights with me? For that matter, how do you know? That was decided ten minutes ago!"

"No, you found out ten minutes ago. It was decided this morning after I told Henri you two were shacked up there. She saw no point in you two burning valuable daylight hours in that activity when Penny could simply spend her nights with you and take care of business at that time, like couples normally do."

"So this is about time management?"

"Isn't it?"

"I suppose, but you didn't have to get us a tree."

"Millie said I did. She sent me out to cut one for you. It's in the back, along with a stand and some lights. I found you a nice one. It has a pretty shape."

"I don't know what to say."

"Say thank you. There's nothing like making love with a Christmas tree in the room. The smell of pine, the glow of the lights... the ladies go for it. Truth be told, I like it, too."

"Well, thank you, although there's no way you can get a tree in that space. And twenty-four hours ago, you were determined to keep me away from Penny. Now you're helping me decorate a holiday love nest?"

"Yes sir, that's about the size of it."

"What's the catch?"

"No catch. The women showed us the error of our ways. Or more precisely, they threatened to cut us off if we didn't reverse our decision."

"Oh." Sky glanced out the side window to hide his grin.

"Needless to say, we were highly motivated to change our minds, but we didn't want you to know that. And we weren't gonna simply roll over without giving you the poker-night test. Fortunately, you passed."

"Fortunately for everyone, it sounds like."

"It was. Conjugal relations have been restored in our various households."

"Glad to hear it."

"That said, if you cause Penny any distress whatsoever, the Brotherhood will be coming for you."

"Understood."

22

From the backseat of Ben's big red truck, Penny didn't have a good view of the bunkhouse. But the minute she climbed out, overnight satchel in hand, she spotted the Christmas tree through the front window. How in the heck had someone managed that when the bunks filled so much of the space?

Henri took one look at the tree in the window and laughed. "Good for them. Let's go see how they did it."

"Only one way they could," Ben said. "I just hope it's stable."

"If Jake and Garrett are involved, it'll be stable."

Penny hooked the strap of her bag over her shoulder as she walked with Ben and Henri to the front door. Her bag was only slightly bigger than a large purse. With luck, she'd be able to slip inside and leave it on Sky's bunk. She'd rather not make a big production of this sleepover plan.

As Ben opened the screen door, Jake flung back the wooden one. "Ho, ho, ho. Come in, folks." He beamed at them. "The elves have been hard at work. Here, Penny, let me take that."

"Um, okay." She handed it to him and he slung it over his shoulder. Her flowered tote on the shoulder of that brawny cowboy shone a spotlight right on the thing. Great.

"Feels light, like there's not much in there. Are you sure you brought enough?"

"I'm sure." She stepped inside a room fragrant with the scent of fresh pine. Boughs of it tied with wide red ribbon hung on the vacant hooks over the bunks on the far wall. "The place looks wonderful, Jake."

"Thanks. Listen, if you need anything while you're here, there's extra shampoo in a cupboard in the shower room, and we have lots of towels if you—"

"I'll be *fine*." She sent him a quelling glance. Time to drop the subject.

"Oh, okay. Just checking. What do you think of the tree?"

She turned and her breath hitched. "Oh, that's really pretty, Jake. Clever use of space, too." The guys had anchored it in a sturdy stand and set it on the bed slats inside the bunk frame. The mattress lay on the next bunk over. Multi-colored lights nestled in the dark green branches added a soft glow. "The shape is perfect."

"I know, right? I measured it a while ago and it's seven feet, five inches. Tall enough to look good, but not so tall it's hard to get in and out of here."

"It's beautiful," Henri said.

Ben nodded. "Great job."

"We still need to scare up some ornaments, but we can do that later."

Penny gazed at the tree. "I think it looks better without them. It fits the idea of bunkhouse simplicity."

"You've heard about that, have you?"

"I have and I'm a fan. A lovely scent and pretty lights is all you need for that tree. What a great idea to put it up for the party."

"Yes, ma'am, except it's not exactly for the party."

She stared at Jake in confusion. "Then what—"

"It's for us." Sky walked in from the kitchen, a towel thrown over one broad shoulder, a hot pad in one hand.

"I cut the tree and brought it here," Jake said. "But it was Millie's idea to do it. She gets the credit."

"Millie?" She glanced at Sky. "Did you know about this decorating scheme?"

"Not until I got in the truck with Jake this afternoon. I'll explain later. Just so you like it."

"I do. It's lovely."

"Good." He gave her a smile and returned to the kitchen.

She glanced at Jake. "Thank you." Talk about an overcorrection. Last night she was arguing with Leo about the Brotherhood's obnoxious plan. Tonight Jake was knocking himself out to make sure she had a comfortable stay.

"You're welcome."

"And thank Millie for me."

"You can thank her yourself when you get to the fire pit. She's already out there setting the table."

"Then we should go help."

"I'll walk out with you," Jake said. "The guys don't need me getting in their way."

"Stew smells good," Ben said. "I'm still waiting for the recipe, Jake."

Jake grinned. "It'll be a long wait, Ben." He started toward the kitchen.

"Jake? My bag?"

"Oh, yeah. It's so light I completely forgot I had it." He walked back and gently laid it on Sky's bunk. "If you get cold in the night, there are extra blankets in the—"

"Thanks, Jake."

"Right. Off we go."

"Don't you need a coat?"

"I left it on a chair in the kitchen."

Penny followed him, passing Sky, CJ and Garrett standing side-by-side efficiently putting the finishing touches on the meal. CJ and Garrett chopped cabbage and carrots for a huge bowl of coleslaw while Sky popped hot rolls out of muffin tins into napkin-lined baskets.

"See you out there, guys."

All three gave her a *yes, ma'am*. Sky added a wink. That wink warmed her so thoroughly she barely felt the cold when she walked out the back door.

Jake turned at the bottom of the steps and offered his hand to guide her down.

"Jake, you're such a gentleman."

"That's how Henri and Charley raised us."

"They did a fabulous job." She descended the last step and took in the scene in front of her with a sigh of happiness. "I'd forgotten how much I love this setting."

"Don't mean to rush you," Henri said. "But you're kinda blocking the way, toots."

"Sorry." She started down the lantern-lit path. "My phone won't capture it so I was just taking a mental picture. Who dreamed up the idea of projecting lights into the trees?"

Jake fell into step beside her. "Your brother."

"No kidding? He didn't tell me that back in October."

"Probably didn't tell you he contributed his sound system, either."

"Nope."

"Prior to that, if CJ didn't play, all we had was a cranky old boom box."

"I'm not surprised on either count. He's loved light displays since he was a kid and he's an audiophile, so the boom box wouldn't do it for him. What's this about the stew recipe?"

"Thanks for asking," Ben chimed in from behind them. "I've tried for years to pry it out of him so I can serve it at the Moose."

"And if I let you have it," Jake said, glancing over his shoulder, "Ezra will mess with it. I know that ol' boy. He won't be able to resist. It'll still say Jake's Buckskin Ranch Stew on the menu long after it no longer resembles my stew. I'm protecting the brand."

Ben laughed. "And I admire you for it. But I've promised Ezra I'll keep asking, so I just did. Gotta keep Ezra happy. He's a terrific cook."

"I'll grant you that, but—oh, hey, Claire." He glanced down as his energetic nine-year-old niece rushed toward him and grabbed him around the waist.

She gazed up at him, a purple stocking cap covering her blonde hair except for the long braid hanging down her back. "I've been waiting and waiting and *waiting* for Uncle Sky to come out. Where is he? Nobody tells me *anything*."

"I have an idea, sweetheart." Jake scooped her up in his arms. "Since you're the last one to meet him and he's almost finished fixing dinner, let's go see him right now."

"I'm not the only last one. Georgie hasn't seen him, either. We need to go get Georgie. He's right over there with Aunt Anna." She glanced at Henri. "It would be good if you came, too, Gramma Henri. Georgie's still shy when he meets someone new, especially a man."

"Sure, I'll go with you."

"Alrighty, then." Jake shifted his hold on Claire. "If you folks will excuse us, we'll collect Georgie and seek an audience with Uncle Sky."

"Go for it," Ben said. "Penny and I will mosey over and get some of Ed's pricey champagne." He offered his arm.

She slid her hand through his crooked elbow as they continued down the path toward the blazing fire and Ed's bubbly. "You are one classy dude, Ben."

"Thank you, ma'am."

"If Claire thinks of Henri as her grandma, what does she call you?"

"Before Henri and I got married, I was *Mister* Ben, but that ceremony convinced her I was here to stay. She approached me at the reception and asked if she could call me *Grandpa* Ben. Which I love, of course."

"That's very cool."

"You have no idea how cool. Long ago I abandoned the dream of having a big family. But now...."

"I have a feeling you'll end up with a whole passel of kids who call you grandpa."

"That would make me very happy."

"Listen, before we plunge into the crowd, can I ask you something? Privately?"

"Sure." He changed course and moved away from the fire pit. "Shoot."

"Do you think there's any chance Henri wishes I'd end up with Sky?"

He hesitated. "Have you asked her?"

"Not yet."

"Are you planning to?"

"Yes."

"Then her answer's more important than mine."

She smiled. "Nicely put. Henri's lucky to have such a diplomatic partner."

"I'm lucky to have her. I don't take that honor lightly."

"Which means you'd rather not speculate about her motives."

"Right."

"Then I'll talk with her and make sure she knows that Sky and I have no intention of a long-term relationship. Neither one of us wants to move."

"Wouldn't hurt to spell that out. Especially since she upended her life to be with Charley."

"And after only knowing him a week. That's still hard for me to believe. It seems out of character."

"I think it was. Those three weeks before she showed up in Apple Grove were hell for Charley. He kept expecting her to call it off. But she didn't. She took a leap of faith."

"And it was the right move."

"Definitely the right move. Charley was her soulmate. I knew it then and I know it now."

Her chest tightened. That had to be hard for him to admit. "Does it bother you?"

"I'd be a fool to let it bother me. He's gone and I have her for as many years as I'm able to walk this earth. Does she love me as much as she did Charley? I don't ask myself that question."

"Ben, I adore you."

He smiled. "I'm very fond of you, too. Which is why I'm telling you this next part. Henri has figured out that if she hadn't agreed to marry Charley while they were in Texas, she would have lost him."

"Seriously?"

"Charley was a great guy, but he was human. He called it quits with Desiree because he was an engaged man. But if Henri had waffled, if he'd come home not knowing whether she wanted him or not...."

"He would have continued to see Desiree?"

"No question. She was gorgeous. She could have had any man in town, me included. She picked Charley. If their relationship had continued, she would've told him she was pregnant. He would have married her."

"She might have turned him down. I get the impression she's anti-marriage."

"She wouldn't have turned him down."

"How do you know?"

"I met her for drinks the night after they broke up. She needed a shoulder to cry on."

"Ah."

"She spilled her guts to me that night. She was crazy about Charley and assumed it was mutual. When he said he had something important to discuss, she was convinced he was going to declare his love and propose. She'd planned to say yes."

"Oh, dear."

"Anyway, that's where Henri's head is right now. She came within a hair's breadth of missing out on the love of her life. And because she took that leap of faith, she got Charley."

"That's good to know before I talk with her. I hope she'll understand that the situation with Sky and me is very different."

"I think she will. She's a smart lady."

"Yes, she is." But a smart lady who'd recently been put through an emotional wind tunnel could lose her sense of direction.

23

Sky's brash comments to Jake about his invincibility came back to haunt him as the evening picked up speed. Maybe a couple of hours of sleep weren't enough to carry him through this party, after all.

Under the circumstances, one glass of champagne was more than enough. He'd cut himself off. He'd engineered having Penny in his bed tonight and he would by God stay awake long enough to enjoy that privilege.

The food helped. Jake had a winner in that chuck wagon stew he'd created. Sky had tasted a bite in the kitchen and raved, expecting to be offered the recipe.

Didn't happen, so he'd asked Garrett, only to discover it wasn't written down and never would be. Evidently the recipe was a secret more carefully guarded than the nuclear codes.

He'd taken note of the ingredients while he'd helped make it, though. Normally he'd have the info filed away so he could reproduce the stew once he was back at Rowdy Ranch.

But brain fog had set in and he wouldn't be able to remember how to make that stew if his life depended on it. Oh, well. Didn't matter. Penny mattered, though, and somehow he hadn't ended up next to her for the meal.

The large crowd had gathered at three long picnic tables pushed end-to-end. In his current befuddled state, he hadn't had the presence of mind to seek her out during the seating process. He couldn't even see her from this angle. Instead he'd found himself surrounded by the Babes.

Four of the seven had husbands in attendance, but those guys were involved in their own gab fest at the far end of the table. Looked like the Babes might have planned it so they'd have him all to themselves during dinner.

He couldn't very well change up the arrangement once it was in place. Anyway, they were a fun bunch. They sure loved their champagne, too. They also held it well. They got more animated as the meal wore on, but there was no slurring of words as they lobbed questions at him.

At first it was the usual — his preference about food, movies, games, horses. They wanted a rundown on the Rowdy Ranch stable. Any buckskins? No, but after riding King, he was a fan. Might look into getting one.

Josette, a French lady who was sitting across from him, asked how many siblings he had. He told her.

"Oo, la-la." She blinked. "A baseball team, no?"

"As a matter of fact, we built a diamond in one of the pastures. Made a backstop for it, too. When the weather's good and we can round up enough friends, we play a few innings. Mom umpires." Maybe he shouldn't have volunteered that last bit. He flicked a glance at Henri, who was next to Josette.

She gave him a smile. "Sounds like fun."

"It is." Could be the champagne had mellowed her out regarding his mother. He waited for questions about who'd fathered those baseball-playing kids. No questions came. Bonus.

Instead the lady on his right, a redhead with a holly wreath in her hair, asked if any of his siblings had children.

"No, ma'am."

"My name's Red, sweetheart. Feel free to call me that."

"Yes, ma'am... Red."

"Are any of your siblings married, *cherie*?" Josette had called him that a lot tonight.

"No, ma'am."

"Engaged?"

"Not at the present time." Aha. Now they'd get down to the nitty-gritty of his status. They'd clearly been edging toward it from the beginning of the conversation.

Ed, the spriest eighty-something woman he'd ever met, had claimed the seat to his left. "I'll bet you've been engaged, though, cutie-pie."

"I've never been engaged, never proposed to anyone, either."

"My goodness. At your age, I'd already been married and divorced. And remarried, come to think of it."

Josette came at the topic from a different angle. "Has a woman ever proposed to you, *cherie*?"

"Twice."

"*Deux*? *The* same one both times?"

"Two different ladies."

Red sighed dramatically. "And you refused them both."

"Obviously, Red." The Babe with long, wavy brown hair rolled her eyes. "He just said he's never been—"

"I know that, Peggy. I just feel sorry for them, working up their courage and then... denied."

"But you can't marry someone because you feel sorry for them." Peggy turned to the woman beside her, who had sparkles in her short dark hair. "Right, Pam?"

"Well, you *can*. But you get a sucky marriage out of the deal. Ed can attest to that."

"Sadly, I can."

Henri glanced around at her friends. "Maybe Sky doesn't want to get hitched, ladies. The Buckskin has been Marriage City the past couple of years, but not everyone's into the concept. I don't think his mother's big on marriage."

And now he finally knew why. "I'd like to get married. Someday."

"I loved *getting* married." Ed had placed her ice chest full of champagne bottles behind her seat and she reached back to pull out a new one. "But I have a devil of a time *staying* married." She opened the bottle with the efficiency of a pro and handed it across the table.

Josette poured herself another glass and offered the bottle to Henri. "I believe we have a one-woman *monsieur* among us, ladies. Skyler's searching for Miss Right and he hasn't found her, yet. *C'est vrai?*"

He nodded. "Yes, ma'am. That's it, exactly." He braced himself for subtle or maybe not-so-subtle comments about Penny.

"Sometimes that person is right under your nose." Ed took the bottle Josette handed back.

"Yes, ma'am." Yep. Talking about Penny.

Ed motioned to his empty glass. "Are you sure you don't want more of this? It's primo stuff, y'know."

"No, thank you. It's great champagne, but I'll take a pass."

"Son, you're way too young to be this sensible. Go for the gusto. Know what I mean?"

"I think I do."

"I agree with her." Red topped off her glass. "Life's a feast. Take big bites."

"In all things, *cherie.*" Josette gave him a sly look.

Any minute now, the hints would get more pointed. They might have, except CJ stood and announced he'd start playing in ten minutes.

A flurry of activity followed as dishes were cleared and carried back to the kitchen. A couple of benches were moved over by the fire pit to add seating for those who wouldn't be dancing.

Who would that be? Sitting still instead of moving around with a warm partner in your arms made no sense. He would be dancing. Preferably with Penny.

At Ed's request, he carried her cooler of champagne closer to the dance area.

"Thank you, son. You've never heard CJ play, but you're in for a treat. I'm just sad Teague isn't here to add his harmonica to the mix."

"Teague?"

"Oh, right. You look so much like Charley that I forget you just got here. Teague is my wrangler, the only one I have since I reduced the size of my stable."

"Now that you say that, I think someone mentioned him last night during the poker game."

"Probably. He's like an honorary member of the Brotherhood. Anyway, he and his fiancée Val are in Oregon visiting his mother over Christmas. His mom wanted them to meet the guy she's dating. Teague will be sorry he missed you, though."

"I'm sure I'll be back."

"Make it soon, okay?" She patted his arm.

"I will." But next time he drove over, Penny would be in L.A. He glanced around the area, needing to see her, needing to hold her. Time was going fast. Too fast.

There she was. He excused himself from the conversation with Ed and walked over to where she stood talking with Fiona.

She turned with a smile. "Hi, there, stranger. Looked like the Babes had you surrounded."

"They put me through my paces."

Fiona laughed. "I'm sure they did. They have a vested interest."

"I can tell, but I'm not sure exactly what it is."

"They're mostly protective of Henri. You're a blessing, but..." She shrugged.

"A mixed blessing," Penny said.

"Because of my mom."

"Bingo. Fiona and I were just talking about it. She looks at you and sees Charley... but also thinks of Desiree."

He sighed. "Can't do much about that. She's part of the story."

"For what it's worth," Fiona said, "I liked her a whole lot. I'm rooting for her to become friends with Henri because then she'd feel comfortable coming over here. She's interesting to talk with."

"I hope it works out."

"I love what she said last night. I don't raise children. I raise heroes."

"Can't tell you how many times I've heard her say that, sometimes after one of us screwed up in a most unheroic way. I don't suppose Henri was around when she said it."

"No, she wasn't. Why?"

"I'll bet Henri and my mom think alike on parenting. I wonder if they'll ever find that out?"

"I hope so," Penny said. "Fi's right. If those two became friends, everybody wins."

"I'll be working on it, that's for sure." He glanced at her. "CJ's tuning up his guitar. Could I interest you in a dance?"

"Absolutely."

Fiona chuckled. "Sky, you haven't lived until you've two-stepped on bumpy ground while trying to keep stray sparks from lighting you on fire."

"Nobody catches on fire," Penny said. "I was here in October, remember?"

"I was kidding. Mostly. They've let it burn down so it won't be throwing off sparks. But stay alert."

"Don't worry. I will." Just being close to Penny had recharged his batteries. Wrapping an arm around her waist, he walked toward an area between the semi-circle formed with Adirondack chairs and picnic benches and the fire pit. "Are we dancing with our jackets on?"

"Unless it's a slow one. Then couples unbutton their jackets so they can snuggle."

"I like the sound of that." He didn't care for the image of Penny dancing with Barry that way, though. "Does it work? Do you stay warm?"

"I don't know if the slow dance thing keeps you warm. Barry refused to dance at all. Said it was a ridiculous excuse for a dance floor. Fast numbers definitely work, though."

"How do you know?"

"The Brotherhood made sure I got out there for those."

"So will I." He swung her into his arms as CJ belted out the lyrics to Vince Gill's *Liza Jane.* It was a peppy tune and CJ didn't slow it down. Sky laughed as he stumbled over an uneven part of the ground.

"You okay?"

"Never better. Music's terrific." He executed a decent twirl. "And I love a challenge."

"Because your momma raised you to be a hero?"

"You've got it." He wanted to be Penny's hero. Too bad it meant giving her up.

24

Dancing with Sky at the Moose didn't hold a candle to the rambunctious experience of fire pit dancing with him in the cold night air to CJ's mad talents with his guitar. The chilly weather encouraged whirling dervish syndrome.

Churning in a ragged circular pattern, the couples sometimes smacked into each other. But like bumper cars at the county fair, they were all well-padded. Thanks to sheepskin jackets and down-filled parkas, they bounced off each other and danced on.

By the time the tune ended, Penny was laughing so hard she couldn't talk.

Sky grinned. "I take it that was a hit."

That set her off again. "Lots... of... hits."

"Looks like CJ's giving us a change of pace." He unbuttoned his jacket as CJ played the intro to Tracy Byrd's *Keeper of the Stars.*

Her laughter faded. Wouldn't you know? A sweet song of fated lovers. Had CJ chosen that one on purpose? He couldn't know she loved the tune, although they'd had a conversation today about this very thing.

"Need some help with your buttons?"

She held his smiling gaze as the lyrics swirled around her. "I've got it." Quickly unfastening the buttons holding her coat closed, she moved into his arms. "Did you request this?"

"No, ma'am." He slipped both hands inside her coat and drew her close.

"Then CJ picked it. Probably for Isabel." She wrapped her arms around his solid body and settled in. Heaven.

Slowly he moved to the steady beat of the music. "Wish I'd thought of requesting it. One of my favorites."

She lifted her gaze to his. "Mine, too."

"Great lyrics."

"Uh-huh."

He tugged her closer as they moved slowly over the frozen ground. "Did the Keeper of the Stars bring us together?"

"Maybe."

"Maybe?" His eyebrows rose. "From someone who loves *Lord of the Rings*?"

"Okay, yes, I believe we were destined to meet."

"Why?"

"You ask tough questions."

"Seems like the right time. When we're alone I'm too distracted to ask questions. And I want to know what you think." He slid his hands into the back pockets of her jeans.

"That's a sexy move, cowboy."

"Like it?"

She melted against him. "Yes."

"Why did we meet, Penny?" His voice grew husky. "Just for this?"

She sucked in a breath. Granted, their chemistry was off the charts, but... "It's more than that. It's about spending time together sharing the holiday, the beauty of the ranch decorated for Christmas, the company of these wonderful people. The whole experience."

He nodded. "Sounds right."

"The attraction between us is like the secret sauce that makes everything better."

"I just wish it wasn't going by so fast. I'm starting to miss you already."

"Which means you're not living in the moment." She held his gaze. "Concentrate on what we're doing right now — slow dancing while CJ sings *Keeper of the Stars.*"

"He does it well."

"Yep."

"And you're warm and soft in my arms, and you smell like cinnamon."

"And you have that look on your face like you want to kiss me."

"Because I do. I bet you'd taste like cinnamon. You had some of that apple pie, I hope?"

"Delicious pie. We'd both taste like cinnamon."

"But I won't kiss you. I can wait. We have all night."

She smiled. "We'll have to spend some of it sleeping."

"But we'll be together. That's the main thing."

"Very close together."

"That was fun squeezing into my bunk this morning, but once we have the place to ourselves, I plan to make some modifications. I want room to maneuver."

"Oh, really? There's a comment guaranteed to fire up my imagination."

He grinned. "Easy does it, Penny. Stay in the moment."

* * *

CJ alternated between fast tunes and slow ones. Penny's mood shifted each time, from the hilarity of the fast numbers to the seductive tug of the slow ones. Predictably, CJ ended the evening with a slow one, leaving her extremely ready to be alone with Sky.

Fortunately, the party broke up quickly after CJ stopped playing. Sky volunteered to carry Ed's mostly empty champagne cooler out to her truck. Penny joined everyone else in the cleanup while Matt and Rafe smothered the fire.

The steady stream of folks into the kitchen and then out the front door eventually ended, leaving only Penny, Jake and Millie. Jake finished loading the dishwasher while Penny and Millie wiped down the counters.

Millie had left her bright red curls loose tonight. Combing her hair back from her face, she glanced toward the front door. "Is Sky still out there with Ed?"

Jake laughed. "Must be. No doubt she's trying to give him a couple bottles of champagne for the duration and he's determined to politely refuse them. Poor boy doesn't understand this is Ed's thing."

"I guess I didn't know it, either," Penny said. "I remember she provided the champagne for the wedding reception, but I hadn't heard that she likes giving bottles out randomly, too."

"There's nothing random about it." Millie finished wiping around the sink, squeezed out the sponge and left it in the holder. "She offers champagne to couples she approves of, hoping to give them a boost in the right direction."

"I'm afraid to ask which direction that is."

"Don't worry." Millie picked up her coat from the back of a kitchen chair and Jake's from the one next to it. "She won't follow you to L.A. and drag you back here."

Penny winced at that image. "But will I be in trouble with her the next time I come for a visit in June?"

"You'll never be in trouble with her. She's not like that. If you've held out six months without taking the plunge with Sky, she'll abandon her hopes for you two. She likes and admires you. That won't change."

"That's a relief, because I like and admire her, too." She hesitated. "So Henri and Ed want us to get together. Who else?"

"Pretty much everybody."

She groaned. "I should have seen this coming. You guys don't believe in ships that pass in the night, do you?"

"No, ma'am." Jake took his coat from Millie and helped her put hers on. "We believe in ships that sail into the Buckskin harbor, tie up there and get chummy."

"Then why did you block the harbor when Sky arrived?"

"Some of us—"

"The male contingent," Millie said.

"Some of us thought we needed to check the ship's manifest before letting him dock here, so to speak."

Millie heaved a sigh. "We're not getting into docking metaphors, Jacob. Time to go."

"Before you do," Penny said, "I haven't had a chance to mention the fabulous decorating job. The bunkhouse looks wonderful. Thank you, Millie."

"I'm glad you like it."

"I love it."

"FYI, that decorating comes with no strings attached. While you and Sky make an adorable couple and I would love to see it work out, I understand about your attachment to UCLA."

"Me, too," Jake said. "Leo kept us in the loop from the bachelor's all the way to your doctorate and your teaching appointment. You're a star, Penny. We don't seriously expect you to throw it all away."

"Good."

"We have some magical thinking going on." Millie buttoned her coat. "Probably because Sky looks so much like Charley. Henri and Charley's story was like a fairytale, so we're looking for another one. We—"

The front door opened and Sky walked in with a bottle of champagne in each hand. "Here I am, with several hundred dollars-worth of champagne. I couldn't talk her out of it."

"You were in a losing battle right there, buddy. She wouldn't have left until you agreed to take it."

"I figured that out." He held up the bottles. "I don't even know when we're supposed to drink it. There's Ed's Christmas Eve deal tomorrow night and Christmas dinner at Henri's. You guys should take at least one of them."

"Oh, no." Millie waved both hands. "She meant those for you two. I'm not messing with that. It's bad juju to second-guess the will of Edna Jane Vidal."

"She's right." Jake tugged on his hat brim. "Do whatever you want with that champagne. Pour it down the sink if necessary, but it stays with you."

"Pour it down the *sink*?" Penny walked over and took charge of the bottles. "This is a gift of abundance. I'll stick them in the fridge for now, but we will drink this champagne, Sky." She cradled one in each arm.

He looked startled. "Okay."

"On that note," Jake said. "We'll be shoving off." He turned to Penny. "Like I said, if you don't see anything you need, go through the cupboards in the bathroom. Chances are we have—"

"You're delusional, sweetheart." Millie gave him an indulgent smile. "I've looked in those cupboards. I found some kind of he-man deodorant, shampoo that smells like saddle soap and a can of jock itch powder."

Penny grinned. "No worries. I brought my own stuff."

"Good girl. Come on, Jake. These two want to be alone."

"Yes, ma'am." Jake ushered her out the door, but turned at the last minute. "Like I said, extra towels are in the—"

"Jake!" Millie tugged on him so hard he almost lost his balance.

"'Bye." He glanced at Sky. "Good luck." He closed the door.

"Why did he wish you good luck? I mean, you have me in residence, so it's not like you need luck to—"

"He's worried that I haven't had enough sleep and I'll conk out on you."

She smiled. "You do look a bit ragged around the edges, cowboy."

"Oh, I do, do I?" He lifted the champagne bottles from her grasp and set them on the floor. "We'll see about that." And he proceeded to kiss her senseless. Lifting his head, he gazed at her, his blue eyes sparking fire. "You were saying?"

She dragged in a breath. "Let's go to bed."

"Yes, ma'am."

25

Wrangling with Ed about the champagne had nearly tipped Sky over the edge into exhaustion. But once the door closed behind Jake, once Penny gave him that saucy look, his libido kicked in full force. Picking up the bottles, he handed them to her. "If you'd be so kind as to put these in the fridge, I'll set us up in here."

Her eyes brightened with eagerness. "The modifications?"

"Exactly." He stripped off his jacket, walked to the door and twisted the lock. Leaning against the door, he pulled off his boots and tossed them aside. "We're in for the night."

"I like the sound of that." She held his gaze for a sizzling moment before turning toward the kitchen.

By the time she came back, he'd laid his mattress and the one across the aisle in the area between the front door and the wood stove. By pushing them up against the door, he wedged them in the entryway created by the bunk frame and the kitchen wall. Perfect fit.

Standing in the kitchen doorway, now blocked by a mattress, she flashed him a grin. "Barricaded us in, have you?"

He stood on his side of the makeshift bed. "Any objections?"

"None." Reaching around the doorframe, she doused the kitchen light. "After I stuck the champagne in the fridge, I put the chain on the back door. Not that anyone would intentionally barge in, but...."

"They might out of habit. This is a way station for the Brotherhood. I can't block the door except at night." Without the overhead on in the kitchen, the Christmas tree and the embers glowing in the wood stove provided the only light. The sexy factor just shot up.

"But we can recreate this tomorrow night."

"And every night. Until I leave." He sucked in a breath. "Sorry. Didn't mean to bring up the leaving part."

"I didn't hear a thing." She toed off her boots. "Are you done? It's a little Spartan, but I—"

"I'm not done. We need sheets." He grabbed the ones he'd pulled off his bunk and dropped them on the mattresses. "It'll go faster if we work together." Crouching down, he shook out one of the sheets, flipping it so it lay over the top half.

"If I help make my bed, can I lie in it?"

"I had something more aerobic in mind, but if you're sleepy...."

"Not sleepy. Warm, though. The stove puts out a lot of heat." She unbuttoned her silky red shirt and took it off, revealing a black confection of a bra hugging her full breasts and her taut nipples.

He swallowed. "Nice." Rising to his feet, he winced as his jeans pinched his privates. "If you'll toss that over, I'll hang it up for you."

"Thanks." She flung the shirt in his direction, sending a wave of her scent with it.

"Cinnamon."

"Hm?" She unfastened her jeans and glanced up.

"Your perfume. It smells like cinnamon rolls baking."

"Like it?" She went back to her task, pulling down the zipper, but not in a striptease way.

"I do."

"Good. It's new. I decided... well, never mind what I decided." She shoved her jeans over her hips, giving him a glimpse of her black lace panties.

He cleared the lust from his throat. "Are you planning to strip off everything?"

"Not everything." She looked over at him. "Weren't you going to hang that up for me?"

"Yes. Yes, I was." He turned toward his bunk and made use of an empty hook.

"Might as well take these, too." She stepped out of her jeans, picked them up and lobbed them at him.

Pivoting, he made the catch without looking. Penny had his complete attention. Black lace hugged her curves as a rainbow of Christmas lights bathed her creamy skin and the shimmering curtain of her hair. He forgot to breathe.

A smile tilted the corners of her full lips. "I guess it works."

He blinked. "What?"

"Sexy underwear. It always seemed pointless, since it comes off so quick. But when you said we still needed to put on sheets, that meant I had time to—"

"Drive me crazy?"

"That's the idea."

He groaned and unsnapped the cuffs of his shirt. "Forget about the sheets. We'll just—"

"But I don't want to forget about the sheets."

He paused. "You don't?"

"If we make the bed while I'm still wearing this set of undies, I'll get my money's worth. And you'll build up a head of steam."

"Steam's already coming out of my ears, lady." Snaps popped as he yanked open his shirt.

"Are you saying you couldn't hold off long enough to put on these sheets?" The light was dim, but not dim enough to mute the devilish gleam in her eyes.

"I think I just heard a gauntlet hit the ground."

"You said you loved a challenge."

"You're on. We'll see who cracks first." He took his time peeling off his shirt and hanging it on the wall. Unbuckling his belt, he pulled it slowly through the loops as he held her gaze.

The pink flush on her cheeks had nothing to do with Christmas lights. Her glance dropped to the button on his jeans.

Leaving his jeans fastened, he hung up his belt. "If we tuck one sheet around the top half and the second one around the bottom half, it should hold together."

"At least in the beginning." She dropped to her knees and set to work, treating him to an eyeful of tempting cleavage.

"And after that we won't care." He crouched on the opposite side of the makeshift bed and sent an apology to his tortured package.

She shoved the end of the sheet under the mattress on her side. "Fresh sheets?"

"Yes, ma'am. Almost didn't change 'em. I liked breathing in the scent of you on those sheets. Reminded me of being deep inside you."

"Hm." Her color was even higher as she concentrated on her task.

"But you might prefer clean ones."

She cleared her throat. "Either way is fine."

"There's a cupboard full of extra sheets. In the morning we can decide if we need to change these. Depending on how many times we—"

"Right." The word came out a little breathy.

He was getting to her. But he was getting to himself, too. Good thing the bed was nearly ready. He pulled the sheet taut on the bottom half and anchored it under the mattress. "How many pillows do you want?" He got to his feet and swallowed a whimper of distress.

"I guess we just need two." She glanced at his fly. "How're you doing?"

"Just dandy." He picked up one pillow from his bedframe and one from the one opposite his. Tossing them toward the head of the bed, he got them approximately where they needed to go. Then he undid the button on his jeans.

Her breath hitched.

Aha, she'd noticed that move. Time to interrupt the action and build up a bigger head of steam in that saucy lady. "You know what? I'd like more than two."

"Two what?"

"Pillows." He walked down the aisle between the beds and snagged a couple more. "Extra pillows can come in handy for certain positions."

"You're so right. Great idea."

Her husky tone should have warned him that she was up to something. When he turned around, she'd stretched out on the bed, lying on her side facing him.

Propping her head up with one hand, she used the other to toy with the front catch of her bra. "A strategically placed pillow can make all the difference."

His pace quickened of its own accord. He forced himself to amble the rest of the way. "Better access."

"Deeper penetration." She flipped the clasp on her bra and cupped her breast.

He sucked in a breath. "You win." Leaving the extra pillows within easy reach, he unzipped his jeans.

"*Finally.*" She sat up and shrugged out of her bra. Then she reached for the elastic of her panties.

"Stop."

"I don't want to stop. I want—"

"And you'll get. But after all this, I'm taking those black lace panties off with my teeth." He pushed his jeans and briefs to the floor, stepped out of them and wrenched off his socks.

"Oh." She pulled her panties back on, her breath coming fast as her gaze locked onto his package. "That sounds... interesting."

"Interesting?" Scooping up a handful of condoms from the drawer under his bunk, he dropped them on the floor next to the bed. "By the time I'm finished, you're gonna need a better adjective than that."

She grinned. "Grammar? Really?"

"You may be an English major, lady." He dropped to his knees and crawled in next to her. "But you're dealing with the son of a best-selling author. I know my parts of speech."

26

Heart thrumming, Penny bunched a pillow under her head so she could keep track of the action. "Grammar talk turns me on."

"Figured it might." Nudging her knees apart, Sky braced himself above her with a hand planted on either side of her hips. "I've been waiting to use that line since I was fourteen."

"Great line." She shivered with anticipation. "Limited, though."

"It served its purpose." His hungry gaze swept over her, lingering on her breasts before zeroing in on the skimpy triangle of lace that barely covered the subject. "If you're a good girl, I'll diagram a sentence for you."

"Be still, my heart."

"I don't want your heart to be still." His biceps flexed as he lowered his torso. "I want it to beat like the hooves of a runaway horse."

"Now you're showing off." She trembled as his warm breath encountered damp lace.

"That's not showing off. *This* is showing off." Taking hold of the lacy triangle with his teeth, he tugged hard, scooted back and pulled the scrap of material to her knees.

One more pull, and it was down around her ankles. And then gone... somewhere. She no longer cared because he'd grabbed a pillow, slipped it under her hips and settled in, his mouth doing special things... incredible things... unbelievable things....

She cried out as a spectacular orgasm arrived, blotting out her surroundings. There was only pleasure. So much pleasure. Produced by a gifted lover.

Sky. She tried to say his name but could only produce a moan of gratitude. Sky... magic maker, the artist creating miracles in her quivering body. And doing it *again.* She gasped as he sent her flying, soaring and swooping, giddy and breathless.

Gradually he slowed the pace, bringing her down easy, kissing all her tender parts before nibbling his way slowly up to her mouth. "You're amazing."

"I... I..." She had no words.

His chuckle was low and intimate. "Just the reaction I was looking for." Settling down on his forearms, he pressed her to the mattress and captured her mouth in a passion-flavored kiss.

With the first thrust of his tongue, her last protective barrier crumbled. He'd breached her walls and discovered a soul-deep sensuality she'd never let anyone see. Only two days, and he knew her as no one else did.

Tucking his thumb into the corner of her mouth, he coaxed her to open even more. She abandoned herself to the voluptuous moment, savoring his weight bearing down on her, the rapid beat of his heart, the heady scent of musk, the solid ridge of his cock caught between his body and hers.

His breathing roughened and his kiss grew more urgent. Cool air wafted over her heated body as he moved away. Eyes closed, she held onto the mood.

Just as a chill began creeping over her damp skin, he returned, bringing the warmth of his lightly furred chest, the brush of his thighs against hers, and... ah, *yes.*

The invasion was gentle, and all the more erotic because he was unhurried. He'd created a foundation. All he had to do was build on it. And build he did. With easy friction. A deceptively casual rhythm.

Highly effective. Her core tightened.

He hummed low in his throat. "Felt that."

She opened her eyes.

His intense gaze met hers. "I love making love to you."

"You've melted me."

"Too much?"

"No." She dragged in a breath and slid her arms around him. "Not too much."

"That's good news." He kept up the steady pace.

"You're so... calm."

He smiled. "Think so?"

"You're not?"

"No, ma'am. But I'm reining myself in. Need to make this last."

She stroked his sweaty back. "Because this might be it for the night?"

"I don't want it to be."

"I do."

He chuckled. "Sick of me already?"

"On the contrary. I'm already looking forward to tomorrow night."

"But tonight isn't over."

"Yes, it is. If I have anything to say about it." She wound her legs around his and clenched her core muscles.

He sucked in a breath. "Felt *that.*"

"Evidently I do have something to say about it. Hold still."

"But I—"

"Hold still, please." She cupped his buns and held him immobile. "Let's see if I can make you come."

"Let's not. I can last a while longer and I want to make sure you—"

"Don't worry. I will." She squeezed again.

He moaned. "Guaranteed I will if you keep that up."

"I'm keeping it up. I want to."

He gave a nod of surrender.

That nod earned him a million points. He could let go of control. He could allow himself to be vulnerable. Holding his gaze, she tightened her core muscles around his considerable girth.

His breath hitched and his eyes darkened.

When she did it again, she was rewarded with a slight twitch. Another squeeze brought a stronger twitch, and one more....

He erupted, pushing deep with a groan as his cock pulsed within her.

Right on cue, she responded in kind. She arched upward with a cry of triumph, her body curving to meet his.

Sliding one arm under her back, he pulled her closer, strong emotion shimmering in his eyes. And just like that, he stole a piece of her heart.

* * *

When Penny woke, the bunkhouse was dark except for a soft glow from the Christmas tree. Cozy and warm under a sheet and a couple of army blankets, she stretched and turned over. No Sky.

A thump in the kitchen was followed by a soft oath.

"Sky? Are you in there?"

"Go back to sleep, Penny."

"Not doing that." Throwing back the covers, she sat up, grabbed the doorframe and pulled herself to her feet. "Did you hurt yourself?" She took two steps into the kitchen and smacked into his broad, naked chest. "So there you are."

His arms came around her. "And there you are." Amusement tinged his voice. "You don't like taking direction, do you?"

"No, I don't." She nestled closer and discovered he'd put on his jeans, darn it. "When I was a toddler, Leo thought he could be the boss of me. It didn't go well." She glanced up and could barely make out his face. "What's up?"

"Me, in more ways than one now that I have a naked woman in my arms. But sadly, I can't do anything about that latest development. I need to take a quick shower and go help Rafe feed. I wanted to leave you a pot of coffee, though."

"You can make coffee in the dark?"

"Apparently not. I haven't located the coffee and I managed to hit my head on the cupboard."

"Poor baby." She cupped his face in both hands. "What part of your head?"

"Doesn't matter. It's better, now." He tugged her closer. "You've given me other things to think about."

"Tell you what. Go take your shower and I'll make some coffee."

"Do you know where it is?"

"No, but thanks to Thomas Edison, I should be able to find it. Close your eyes."

"Gonna kiss me?"

"Yes, right after I give us some light." Reaching behind her, she flipped the wall switch. She turned back to find Sky with his eyes obediently closed, a reddish spot on his forehead, a bit of scruff darkening his jaw, and a cute little smile on his kissable lips. "You're adorable." She gently pulled his head down and touched her mouth to his.

"Mm." He slid both hands over her bare back and cupped her tush.

Her breath caught as lust shot through her veins. In no time, she was kissing him for all she was worth. Never mind that his beard was a little scratchy. Never mind that he had to leave in a few minutes.

He gave it right back, delving into her mouth and tucking her against the stiff denim of his fly. His breathing roughened and he picked her up. Next thing she knew, she was lying crossways on the double mattress.

He continued to kiss her as he fumbled on the far side of the bed. Foil crinkled, a zipper buzzed and seconds later he'd buried his cock in her very willing body.

Lifting his head, he gazed down at her. "Hope you don't mind."

"Not a bit."

"Good." He didn't waste any time, thrusting with firm intent.

She came fast and he followed right after, eyes glowing with pleasure as he gasped out a heartfelt *hell, yeah.*

She grinned.

He grinned back. "Great way to start the day."

"Hell, yeah."

27

Sky figured that if the members of the Brotherhood were anything like his brothers, at least one of them would still have Christmas shopping to do on the twenty-fourth. Turned out Rafe did. He agreed to pick up Sky at the bunkhouse around ten for a quick trip to town.

They fed King first so he'd be finished with his breakfast by the time Sky was ready to ride him over to the bunkhouse. After they'd delivered hay flakes to the rest of the herd, King had polished off his meal.

"Okay, big guy, time for a trip down memory lane." Sky tacked him up with his halter and bridle before leading him out of the barn.

Rafe followed him out. "Mind if I get a shot of you riding him bareback?"

"That'd be great. If you'll send it to me, I can text it to Beau." *Beau.* He'd promised to stay in touch. Whoops. He'd call on his way to the bunkhouse.

Grabbing a handful of King's black mane, he vaulted onto the gelding's broad back.

Rafe snapped off a few shots. "Sure puts me in mind of Charley. He loved riding bareback, especially on King. I never did see the appeal. A saddle suits my ass way better than a horse's backbone."

"Did you get to ride when you were a kid?"

"No. Wish I had."

"That's when I learned how easy this was. Just grab a bridle, catch a horse and off you go."

"Guess so." He laughed. "I'm not convinced I could do that vault thing, though."

"Sure, you could. Just takes practice."

"I dunno. There's a lot of me. If I went sailing up there and came down wrong, I could do some damage."

"So you practice on a dummy."

"It's not just the horse I'm worried about."

"You got bad knees?"

"My knees are fine. But I gotta protect my boys."

Sky grinned. "Then tie a pillow to the dummy."

"Not worth getting Kate riled up. Sure as the world, she'd catch me at it, or somebody would tell her. She's already worried about sperm count and motility since I've passed the big three-oh. If she heard I was vaulting onto a horse like a Hollywood cowboy she'd have something to say about it."

"Then I guess you'll have to give it a pass."

"I don't mind. You do a great job of it, though. Should impress the heck out of Penny."

"Which isn't a bad thing."

"No, sir." He stepped back and took several shots. "Okay, I'm texting you these right now."

"Thanks. And thanks for letting me tag along on your shopping trip."

"I'm glad for the company. I sweat bullets trying to pick out the right thing."

"Then we'll sweat it out together. See you soon." Sky touched two fingers to his hat and nudged King with his heels. Rafe was good people. They all were. He'd be forever grateful to his mom for dragging him over here.

Once he'd directed King over to the path leading to the bunkhouse, the gelding turned into a self-driving horse. King knew the way better than he did.

Pulling out his phone, he texted Penny to let her know he'd arrive in a few minutes. Then he called Beau. No surprise, his brother didn't pick up. The guy was notorious for last-minute shopping.

No sooner had he left a message than his phone chimed with Beau's call-back. Smiling, he answered. "Out shopping, bro?"

"What else? But enough about me. Did you go through with it?"

"No, but—"

"Aw, you chickened out. That's why you didn't call. You couldn't bring yourself to admit—"

"That's not why. I haven't had a free second. Penny's spending her nights at the bunkhouse with me."

"She *is*? But you said you didn't work the plan."

"Didn't have to. The Brotherhood gave us their blessing."

"No shit."

"Mostly. They're still keeping an eye on me."

"I'm sure, but hey, congrats on winning them over."

"It wasn't me. The women took a stand and that did the trick."

He laughed. "I had a hunch that's where the real seat of power was over there. Anyway, you and Penny... how's that working out?"

"She's the woman of my dreams, Beau."

"Are you the man of her dreams?"

"Seems like it. At least until December twenty-ninth."

"Hm. I don't like the sound of that."

"I'm not a fan, either, but that's the deal. I can take it or leave it. I'm taking it."

Beau sighed. "I'd do the same in your shoes, bro. Just remember, it's not over 'til it's over."

"I'm holding onto that. How's the shopping going? Got something for Mom, yet?"

"Sure do. I'm giving her what you got her."

"The hell you are."

"I do believe I am. I just changed the tag and made it from me."

"Damn it, Beau! You—"

"I'm doing you a favor, bro. She'll be way happier with a bathrobe from the Apple Grove Hotel than those riding gloves. I'll pay you for 'em."

"That's not the point." But something from the town where she'd conceived him would be a better gift. His brother was right about that. "You think she'd like a hotel bathrobe?"

"I know she would. She almost bought one for herself but decided it was silly. You know, saying she didn't need one, that she had a perfectly good one, all that garbage. I couldn't buy it without her catching me. So I'm letting you get her one. Better coming from you, anyway."

"Okay. I'll pick one up today."

"You're welcome."

He rolled his eyes. Only Beau could pull a fast one and turn it around so he came out looking like a hero. "Thanks, bro."

"Anytime. Listen, I have to get going. I need a gift for a certain lady."

"Jessica?"

"Yep."

"Things must be working out for you two."

"Definitely. Jess and I— well, never mind. I'll tell you on the drive back next week."

"Okay. I'll call tomorrow and talk to everyone."

"You'd better or your ass is grass."

He laughed. "I'll call. Merry Christmas, bro."

"Same to you, loser."

"Yeah, I miss you, too. 'Bye." He disconnected and sighed. He wanted to be here with Penny. Didn't mean he wasn't homesick.

He smelled bacon frying as he tied King to the same tree they'd used the previous morning. Penny had offered to have breakfast ready when he rode back from the barn. Sweet gesture. Then she'd warned him she wasn't the best of cooks.

Talk about a domestic setting. The woman he'd made love to last night and again this morning

221 Vicki Lewis Thompson

was inside bravely cooking up bacon and eggs for a shared breakfast. Giving it a shot even though it wasn't her strong suit.

He couldn't wait to see her smile and kiss her hello. He'd rave about the meal she'd prepared even if it tasted like crap. He'd tell her about Beau's maneuver. She'd get a kick out of it.

Had she moved the mattresses he'd told her to leave for him to handle? He'd find out if he tried the front door instead of going around to the back.

He smiled as he approached the door, ninety-nine percent sure the mattresses would be back where they belonged and he'd be able to walk right in. This was Penny, the feisty lady who wasn't good at taking direction. One of her many endearing traits.

It isn't over 'til it's over. Yeah, he'd hold onto that with both hands.

28

Since Penny was concentrating on food prep and Sky arrived on King instead of driving a vehicle, she didn't hear him come back until he opened the front door.

"I see you moved the mattresses I told you not to bother with," he called out.

"Of course." Putting down a spatula, she left the kitchen. "You knew I would."

He hung up his coat and hat. "In other words, I could have saved my breath." He turned just as she reached him and gathered her close.

"Now you're getting the idea." She wound her arms around his neck and gazed up into his laughing blue eyes. "Missed you." Ridiculous as that might sound, it was true. She didn't look forward to spending the morning apart, but it was necessary. He had Christmas shopping to do and she'd promised to help Henri with birthday party prep.

"I missed you, too." He kissed her full on the mouth.

How was she supposed to keep her cool when he had the most seductive kiss ever? In seconds she was all in, aroused and ready to forget about breakfast.

He lifted his head. "Bacon's burning."

"Dammit!" She wiggled out of his arms and raced for the kitchen. "Oh, well. Only on one side." Grabbing the spatula, she flipped each strip to the uncooked side. They hit the pan hissing and popping. She jumped back and bumped into him.

"Might need to turn it down."

She laughed. "You think?" She lowered the heat and the popping eased up. Moving aside, she gestured toward the bacon. "Is that top part too burned for you?"

"Looks perfectly fine."

"I'm used to a microwave. I looked all over, but I don't think they have one."

"Not that I saw last night." He glanced at her. "Want some help?"

She heaved a sigh. "Yes, please. I'll monitor the bacon if you'll cook the eggs."

"Sure thing." Walking over to the sink, he rolled up his sleeves and washed his hands, rubbing the suds up past his wrists and over his muscled forearms.

Warmth stirred in her lady parts. "When you wash up, you really go for it."

He flashed her a smile. "After years of coming in from barn chores, it's an ingrained habit."

"You have nice habits."

"Just what a guy longs to hear from a lady he's trying to impress." He dried his hands and pulled a frying pan out of a bottom cupboard. "Ranks right up there with complimenting my penmanship."

"Do you have good penmanship?"

"No, ma'am. Nobody can read my writing. Not even me." He opened the carton of eggs. "Scrambled?"

"That's all I know how to make. When Leo was home he used to do the over-easy kind and I liked that. I was going to have him teach me and then he left."

"Over-easy, then?"

"That would be lovely. Especially now that I'm not mad at him anymore. For years I couldn't even order them in a restaurant because it would make me sad."

"Then over-easy it is." He melted butter in the pan.

Cozy, standing next to Sky, cooking with him. "Are you trying to impress me?"

"Every chance I get. How am I doing?"

"Not bad. Sounds like you need to work on your handwriting, though."

"I'll get right on it." He cracked the eggs into the pan.

She eyed the progress of the eggs. Yep, exactly how Leo used to do it. She used the spatula to lift a piece of bacon. "It's not cooking very fast."

"You can turn the heat up a little. Just not as high as you had it."

"I was trying to hurry things along." She goosed up the heat and the bacon responded with a gratifying sizzle. "I had this image of doing it all myself, but I assumed they'd have a microwave. Doesn't everybody have one?"

"We ditched ours because we hardly ever used it."

"I couldn't live without mine. And it's so fast. My plan was to make the bacon first and then the scrambled eggs. You can do it in no time if you have a microwave. Now we're running behind."

"We'll be fine." He glanced at the kitchen clock. "We just need to keep moving."

"I'll make the toast. I'm good with toast."

"And coffee. Don't forget you took over the coffee detail for me this morning."

"I could never forget *making the coffee*." She nudged his hip with hers. "That was unprecedented."

"Best eye-opener ever." He returned her hip bump. "I'd be up for a replay tomorrow morning. Or now, if time permitted."

What a nice buzz she had going. "You'll have to save that plan for after Ed's party tonight."

"That's a lot of hours to hold onto a plan."

"We'll appreciate the experience that much more when we have to wait for it."

"Speaking for myself, my appreciation is already the size of Montana."

"You're exaggerating a bit there, cowboy." She glanced at his crotch. "Currently it's more like the size of Rhode Island. No, maybe Vermont. You might want to aspire to Florida, though. I've always thought—"

"Having fun?"

"Sure am."

"I need your spatula."

"Oh?" She batted her eyes at him. "Is that your code word for my—"

"I need to flip my eggs."

"I'd be happy to flip your eggs, but we're running out of time."

He grinned. "If I didn't hate to waste food, we'd be in that bunkroom right now, Miss Saucy Mouth."

"But we're not going to waste this food the Brotherhood left for us and we worked so hard to cook."

He met her gaze, heat flickering in his blue eyes. "No, we're not. I'll dish up while you—"

"Toast your bread?"

"I swear, you'll pay for this tonight."

"I certainly hope so." Best cooking session ever.

* * *

By paying attention to the excellence of the over-easy eggs, she managed to keep from jumping his bones during breakfast. They talked about Cleo's party, Beau's Christmas gift switch, the Shetland pony — everything but the constant hum of sexual tension that colored every word, every glance, every moment they sat across the table from each other. Delicious.

When they finished the meal, he took a deep breath and stood, as if he'd just met and conquered a challenge. "We need to clean up the kitchen and make the beds. If we each take one of those, we have a chance of getting out of here without—"

"I'll make the beds." She got up, too.

"Then I'll clean the kitchen."

"I promise to keep away from the kitchen if you promise to stay away from the beds."

"Deal." He took another breath. "We still have the ride to Henri's on King. Think about whether you want to be in front or behind me."

"Doesn't matter. Either way will get me hot."

"You could ride and I'll walk."

"That'll take too long."

He consulted the kitchen clock again. "True. Meet me outside in ten minutes and we'll decide then. And please turn off the Christmas tree lights."

"I will. I just left them on to welcome you home." Her breath hitched. "I mean *back*, welcome you *back*."

He held her gaze. "You said it right the first time."

"I'll be outside in ten minutes." She turned and fled.

Ten minutes later, she unplugged the tree lights, put on her coat and walked out of the bunkhouse. She could use some air.

Cramming on her hat, she walked over to King, who swung his head around to check her out. "Sorry, big guy. I didn't bring treats."

His velvet ears flicked forward and he blew air through his nostrils. The winter sun had warmed the air enough that his breath didn't create clouds of vapor.

"See, nothing in my hand." She let him smell it and then she stroked his nose. "Having you right outside the door ready to take us somewhere is kind of cool. I used to pretend my bike was a horse, but having an actual horse is five-hundred times better."

"Only five hundred?" Sky closed the screen door and started toward her, his strides making short work of the distance. "I rode a friend's bike once. I'd put the difference between that experience and riding a horse in the thousands, at least."

"You never had a bike of your own?"

"Why would I? I've always had access to a horse, and in Wagon Train you can ride them in town. Some of the businesses even have hitching posts. If we were respectful of the privilege, we could take those horses to town anytime we wanted."

"At what age?"

"Ten. And we could take along one of the younger ones after we turned twelve. I was hauling Angelique into town when she was only four."

"It sounds magical."

"It was. Still is. Ready to mount up?"

"Once I figure out how."

"Easy." He cupped both hands. "Put your foot in here, grab his mane and swing on up."

"What about you?"

"I'll hop on him once you're settled. Do you want to steer of have me do it?"

"I want to steer." Placing her boot in his hands, she clutched King's mane as Sky boosted her aboard. She settled herself on the horse's broad back. "Funky."

"You'll get used to it." He unclipped the lead rope and looped it over the branch. "I'll fetch this later. Scoot forward a bit. There, that's good."

Grasping a fistful of mane, he vaulted up behind her.

His athletic prowess stole her breath. His warm crotch pressed against her backside sent her libido into overdrive.

"Penny? You okay?"

"I might have miscalculated. This is intense."

"Want to switch?"

"No. We have to get going."

He rested his hands lightly on her thighs. "You sound like you're hyperventilating."

"I am." She turned King around and started across the parking lot to the road that would take them to Henri's. "I knew this would be suggestive but it's way more than I expected."

"Only because you're already hyped up."

"And so are you. You can't hide anything from me when we're smooshed together like this."

"Have I achieved Florida?"

"And then some."

He lifted his hands from her thighs and scooted toward King's rump. "Better?"

"No. Now I feel as if I might slide off. I like it when we're tucked together. I feel safer. It's just... damned arousing."

He chuckled. "So you can feel safe and aroused or wobbly and platonic. Take your pick."

"Safe and aroused."

"Good choice." He scooted closer and wound his arms around her waist.

"Do you suppose Charley and Henri got a buzz when they rode bareback together?"

"I wouldn't be surprised. That could be the reason they loved doing it." His breath tickled the side of her neck. "They'd take King out for an evening ride around the property, go home and make love."

"That sounds nice."

He sighed. "Yes, ma'am."

"Think we could make that happen?"

"I'll do my best to see that it does."

29

"Does that robe for your mom take care of it?" Rafe backed out of a parking space in front of the Apple Grove Hotel.

"Sure does." He set the festive bag down by his feet. The back seat of Rafe's four-door pickup was already stuffed. "Thanks for letting me be part of your shopping trip."

"Like I said, I appreciate the company. If you hadn't come along, I'd still be in that antique shop trying to decide which display case to buy for Kate's teacups."

"I think she'll like it. My mom loves antiques and she would've bought that one."

"That's good enough for me."

"You're sure you don't mind hauling my gifts up to Henri's tomorrow?"

"No worries. "It's not like I have to go far."

"Do we have time to stop by the bunkhouse before the party? I'd like to leave this robe and Penny's present there."

"Sure thing." Rafe cruised through town and turned onto the two-lane leading to the Buckskin. "Do you think Penny will stick to her guns?"

"Probably." Sky took off his hat and leaned back against the headrest.

"Is that okay with you?"

Sky glanced over at him. "What do you think?"

"I saw you dithering over that gift. I'd say you're in up to your neck."

"Yes, sir."

"Now that I know you better, I think you two might be a good match."

"I think so, too, but I can't ask her to move and I'm not leaving Rowdy Ranch."

"She seems to love Montana, though."

"And ranch life. Everything she says, everything she does, tells me she'd thrive out here, but...."

"There's no university in Wagon Wheel."

"That's part of it. She'd have to commute almost fifty miles to UM in Missoula."

"Have you mentioned that option?"

"No, and I won't. It's a good school, but it's not right next door to the ranch and it's certainly not UCLA."

"Still, it's something to consider. Might be enough to change her mind."

"Maybe, but there's the broken engagement."

Rafe snorted. "He was a dick."

"Maybe so, but she doesn't trust herself to make another commitment this soon, especially to a guy she's known less than a week."

"Henri did."

"Henri wasn't fresh from a breakup. And she met Charley at a conference about buckskins. They had a common interest."

"You guys have a common interest."

"Sex isn't enough to—"

"Just hold your horses, there, pilgrim. I'm talking about your mom. And her books. Penny's into that. She'd have a chance to live on the same ranch as a person who writes the books she's studying. That's a golden opportunity."

"I hadn't thought of it that way."

"Could you casually work it into a conversation?"

"I could but I won't. Giving her a bunch of reasons why she should be with me — that's just wrong. She set the ground rules. She's the only one who can break 'em."

"Good point." Rafe sighed. "Made that mistake with Kate."

"You must've fixed it, then."

"I didn't fix anything. Her crazy aunt put her in a bind and she needed a husband ASAP. Turned out she didn't mind being married to me, once she got used to the idea."

"Looking at you two now, I'd never guess you went through that kind of drama."

"All's well that ends well."

"And she did end up coming to you, even if it was a last resort."

"Yep."

"That's how it would have to be with Penny. She's gotta decide I'm worth it, that we're worth it. Looking at the odds, I don't see it happening."

* * *

Sky hadn't been to a kid's birthday party since Angelique was little. The abundance of crepe paper streamers and balloons looked familiar. The portable heaters in the backyard did, too. Angelique's b-day was on Valentine's Day.

Cleo Marie had marked her one-year birthday by taking her first steps this morning. CJ was busy sharing the big news with anyone he came across.

With the help of the adults gathered in the backyard, Henri spread a tarp on the frozen ground and laid an old quilt on top of it. Isabel set her daughter in the middle, her red snowsuit bright against the faded material of the quilt. Sky helped Penny and Ben carry out the gifts and put them near Cleo.

Everyone wanted to take pictures, so Ben volunteered to hand her the gifts and help with the unwrapping if needed. Sky found a place next to Penny in the circle of adults and pulled out his phone.

Turned out Cleo didn't need help. Once Ben showed her the routine, she ripped into that paper with gusto, chortling and bouncing with glee. Setting the opened present aside, she held out her hands for the next one. And the next one.

Penny leaned toward Sky. "I don't think she cares about the gifts."

"That's about right for a one-year-old."

"Really?"

"Angelique only cared about the paper. Eventually tried to eat it. Lucky and Rance just wanted to throw it at each other. Gil decided to roll in it. He liked the crinkly sound."

"I'll bet you have more experience with kids than anybody here."

He shrugged. "Taking care of the younger ones comes with the position of being oldest."

When Cleo finished with the last present, she crawled over to the mound of crushed and torn paper, sat down and began mashing and shredding every bit she could reach.

"Hey, Cleo." Claire dropped to her hands and knees and crawled across the blanket. "Look at this cool thing you got." She picked up a set of stackable rings and began taking them apart while enthusiastically trying to sell Cleo on the concept. No dice.

Running the cute little train around the blanket and making train noises got no response, either. Cleo was all about the paper. Georgie joined them on the blanket and explained to Cleo how amazing the train was. He ended up playing with it by himself.

Looking around at the assembled adults, Claire got to her feet and let out a beleaguered sigh. "I give up. Next time just get her wrapping paper. It would be way cheaper."

"She'll play with the toys once she's back home and bored." Isabel began gathering her daughter's loot into a large cardboard box. "Thank you so much, everyone. I made a list and I promise to take pictures of her enjoying each of your gifts. I'll text them to you."

"Uh-oh," Henri said. "Now she's eating it."
Scooping Cleo into her arms, she gently coaxed her
to let go of the soggy wad of multi-colored paper.

Penny glanced at Sky. "You called it."

"See if you can distract her for a minute,"
CJ said. "I'll get rid of the paper."

Henri's gaze fell on Sky. "I have the perfect
distraction. Want a piggyback ride, Cleo?"

"I'll take charge of your hat, cowboy."
Penny flashed him a grin.

Leo held up his phone. "I'm so getting a
video of this."

As Sky circled the yard several times with
Cleo clinging to his neck and giggling, he endured a
fair share of ribbing and several critiques of his
piggyback performance. He cherished every word.
They wouldn't give him a hard time if they didn't
like him. His family was the same. Only good
friends got teased.

Henri reclaimed Cleo after the wrapping
paper was stuffed in a garbage bag. "Thank you."
She beamed at him as she propped the little girl on
her hip. "You'll be a great dad someday."

"Hope I get the chance."

"You will." She glanced over his shoulder.
"Here comes Penny with your reward. Cleo, let's go
wash your hands, sweetheart."

Sky turned as Penny walked toward him
with two steaming mugs. Smelled like cider. Her
golden hair glowed in the soft rays of the winter
sun. Her smile warmed him faster than Henri's
portable heaters. "I take it one of those is for me?"

"It is if you say the magic words."

"Making the coffee."

She laughed and handed him a mug. "You're good."

"I hope you realize that phrase is now permanently linked with you and what happened this morning."

"Ditto." Holding his gaze, she lifted the mug to her full lips and took a sip.

Her mouth would taste like warm cider. He couldn't experience that now, but once they were in the bunkhouse and locked in for the night, he would suggest heating a bottle of it and adding that to a holiday make-out session.

She swallowed and lowered the mug. "How was your shopping trip?"

"We got 'er done."

"I have a sneaky suspicion you bought me something, which is embarrassing because I have nothing for you."

"That's where you're wrong. You have everything for me."

"I'm not talking about—"

"I'm not either." He held her gaze. "*Making the coffee* is only part of it. Not even the biggest part."

Her gray eyes grew luminous. And a little bit sad? "I know."

In a perfect world, he'd draw her away from the crowd and find a private spot where he could kiss her. But he was here to celebrate a birthday that clearly meant a lot to CJ and Isabel, Henri and Ben, to the entire Buckskin gang, really. "How soon is the pony showing up?"

"Ed should be here any minute." She cocked her head. "That could be her truck coming up the drive."

"*Elle est ici!*" Josette hurried past them, followed by the rest of the Babes except Henri.

"Oh, I get it," Sky said. "Henri took Cleo inside because she knew Ed was almost here."

"Right. They want Henri to bring her back out when they're all set. They're gonna sing Happy Birthday and we're all supposed to join in."

"Too bad they can't wrap that pony."

Penny chuckled. "Yeah. How do you think Cleo will react?"

"Henri's taught her to enjoy horses, so I think she'll be excited to see one that's closer to her size. I've been wondering about Claire and Georgie. Will they be jealous?"

"I asked the same thing. Claire won't because of the buckskin Ed gave her this summer."

"Right. I'd forgotten Cinnamon is hers. Georgie's the perfect age for a Shetland, though."

"Except he's in love with Lucky Ducky. He's bonded with that old guy."

"That's cool."

"It's very cute. Georgie thinks he's all that and a bag of chips when he's on Lucky. A pony would be a comedown."

"That's good. When Angelique got her pony, my mom convinced my little brothers that they were way too grownup for a Shetland."

"Smart move. I—oh, my goodness." Penny sucked in a breath. "Here they come." She grabbed her phone and snapped off several shots. "Look at those ribbons! That dappled gray coat and white mane... he's... *beautiful.*"

Was that a catch in her voice? Sky glanced at her. Sure enough, she watched the women parading up the drive though a sheen of tears. "Did you want a pony?"

"Desperately." She thumbed the moisture from her eyes. "When I outgrew that phase, I began dreaming about having a hunter-jumper. I understood that was impractical, though. I was college-bound. A horse didn't match up with my career goals."

And you still want that horse. Would she trade the prestige of UCLA for the joy of having a horse of her own? He'd told Rafe he wouldn't try to talk her into anything. But damn, he was so tempted.

<u>30</u>

How stupid to get emotional over this pony. Penny blinked away the tears and took deep breaths. Maybe she'd get some comic relief from Cleo's reaction. That little girl had a mind of her own. No telling what she'd do when she caught sight of her spectacular birthday gift.

The Babes formed a semi-circle behind the extremely well-behaved Shetland, who stood, ground-tied, facing Henri's back porch. The rainbow of ribbons woven through his mane and tail fluttered in the breeze.

Isabel and CJ stood to one side of the porch giving each other nervous smiles. Several other members of the Buckskin gang gathered over there, too. Penny and Sky ended up on the opposite side with the rest of the group.

Ben mounted the porch steps and crossed to the door before giving it three quick raps. Then he went back down to join Isabel and CJ.

When Henri appeared with Cleo, the Babes began the song. Clearing her throat, Penny sang with the group. Darn it, even the song was getting to her. As if he sensed it, Sky threaded his fingers through hers and squeezed her hand. She swiped at her eyes and kept singing.

Cleo's eyes widened and her rosebud mouth formed a perfect O. Her blue gaze traveled around the assembled group and settled on the pony. She stretched out her arm and pointed at it.

Taking her cue from Cleo, Henri walked down the steps and within a couple yards of the Shetland. The song ended and Cleo wiggled to get down. Henri set her on her feet and kept a firm grip on her hand.

Taking wobbly steps, Cleo made soft cooing sounds as she led Henri up to the pony. The drama played out to a hushed crowd.

Crouching down, Henri pulled out a small piece of carrot from her coat pocket and handed it to the little girl. "This is your pony, Cleo. His name is Handsome Sam."

Sky leaned down and murmured in Penny's ear. "That'll change."

"Mm." He was probably right, although she liked the name. Reminded her of Samwise from *LOTR*. She also liked standing here close to Sky, her hand tucked into his, sharing this special moment.

Cleo balanced the piece of carrot in her pudgy palm and held it toward Handsome Sam. He took it like a gentleman. Turning, Cleo babbled something to Henri and patted her arm.

Henri produced another carrot chunk. That routine continued as everyone, Penny included, took countless pictures. Eventually the supply of carrots ran out. Henri informed Cleo the treats were all gone and the child nodded. They had this carrot routine down.

The pony lowered his head, clearly hoping for more goodies. Cleo pulled her hand from Henri's and wrapped both arms around as much of Handsome Sam's neck as she could reach.

As she hugged that beautiful Shetland, Penny gulped. Gripping Sky's hand, she moved away from the crowd, pulling him along with her. Chances were good everyone was so engrossed in the sweet tableau they wouldn't notice.

At the edge of the yard, she stopped and turned to Sky. "I don't know why that affected me, but—"

"You wanted a pony."

"I didn't know how much."

His warm gaze held hers. Then he folded her into his arms. And everything was okay. Because he didn't think she was a sentimental fool. He got it.

* * *

Penny had left her party clothes at Henri's, which had made sense to her at the time but meant she had to dress for Ed's Christmas Eve shindig in her room at Henri's. Jake and Millie took Sky back to the bunkhouse to freshen up.

She rode to Ed's palatial home with Henri and Ben, the proud grandparents who couldn't stop talking about Cleo Marie's first meeting with Handsome Sam.

"She's a natural." Ben glanced over at Henri. "Have you ever seen a one-year-old make that kind of connection with her first contact?"

"Never. It was like she knew that pony the moment she saw him. And he knew her. Did you see how he lowered his head so she could hug him?" She swiveled toward the backseat. "You saw that, right, Penny?"

"I did. Amazing." She kept a straight face even though inside she was giggling. Clearly when Henri was truly besotted, her sensible side went on vacay. That pony might have been okay with a hug, but more likely he'd lowered his head looking for another carrot.

Henri's quick decision to marry Charley wasn't a mystery anymore. She was the calm voice of reason until she was blinded by love.

Ben met Penny's gaze in the rearview mirror. "Wait until you see Ed's place decorated for Christmas."

"I can only imagine. It was spectacular in October."

"That was nothing compared to what you're about to see," Henri said. "We're almost there. I can't wait until the kids are old enough to come to these parties."

Ben laughed. "Claire thinks she's old enough, now."

"Maybe next year, when she's ten. I'll talk to Nell and Zeke about it."

Penny sat forward. "I can see a glow up ahead."

"That's her place," Ben said. "She has huge lighted wreaths at the entrance and lights on the evergreens lining the road going in."

"You're not kidding about huge." Penny gaped at the wreaths on twin pillars marking the entrance. "Those are almost bigger than me."

"Now watch the tree lights," Henri said. "When a vehicle passes the entrance, that trips the switch."

"And they change colors. I love it." She glanced back. "The ones behind us have gone back to white. No, they're changing again. Somebody else just drove in."

"Your brother and Fiona," Ben said. "I recognized the front grill on Leo's truck."

"Are they bringing Sky?" Not that she was eager to see him. Nah.

"I think they have CJ and Isabel," Henri said. "Garrett and Anna offered to pick up Sky, if I remember right. The carpooling plans got a little crazy at the end of the birthday party." She gave a happy sigh. "To think a year ago we were all at the hospital."

"Not yet, though," Ben said. "We were still at the Moose. Isabel's water didn't break until later."

"You guys weren't at Ed's?"

"We weren't." Henri looked at Ben. "Do you remember why?"

"I think she had some renovations that didn't get finished in time."

"Yeah, that was it." Henri gestured toward the massive house ahead of them. "And here we are."

"Wow." Penny stared at the lavish decorations as Ben drove past the gleaming stone steps and parked in a paved area to the right of the house. She quickly unbuckled and climbed out of the truck, eager to see the wonders that waited inside.

As she walked with Ben and Henri to the front porch, the scent of fresh pine wafted toward her. "Are those evergreen garlands wrapped around the pillars real?"

"Yes, ma'am." Ben gave the pillars an admiring glance. "Teague does a great job with that project. Usually we get a chance to compliment him on it."

"It'll be weird not having him here." Henri started up the steps. "But Teague's mom has already promised that she'll spend Christmas in Apple Grove next year."

Penny kept pace with her and Ben followed close behind. Where would she be next Christmas? Given a choice, not in L.A. The Buckskin was way more fun than—

"Hey, sis."

She turned and looked over Ben's shoulder. Leo and Fiona stood at the base of the steps. "Hi, guys! Isn't this fabulous?"

Leo smiled. "Ed spoils us. Listen, could I talk to you privately for a minute?"

What a confusing request. "Sure, but—"

"I thought we could sit in my truck."

Ben and Leo exchanged a glance. Then Ben descended the steps and offered his hand to Fiona. "Come on in with us, Fi."

"Love to." She gave Penny's arm a squeeze as she passed by.

Penny met her brother at the bottom of the steps. "I can't imagine why you—"

"I'd rather keep it to ourselves." He put an arm around her shoulders and hustled her back to the parking lot. Handing her into the truck, he jogged around to the driver's side, hopped in and closed the door. "It's about Sky."

She gasped. "Is he okay?"

"My God. Fi's right. You're in love with him."

"*Leo!* Has something happened? Is Sky—"

"I'm sure he's fine. On his way here with Garrett and Anna as far as I know. Fi told me you'd fallen hard, but I didn't believe her. Not in such a short time."

Thankfully, the dome light switched off. If he wanted to discuss her love life, she preferred the semi-darkness. "You scared me to death the way you said *it's about Sky.*"

"I wanted to get right to the point."

"That's how people talk when someone's had an accident."

"Sorry. I really didn't think you were in love with him, so I—"

"Stop saying that. I'm not in love with him."

"The hell you're not. You should have seen your face when you thought something bad had happened. You went white. Your eyes dilated. You could barely breathe. I'm sorry I scared you, but at least I know what I'm dealing with. This discussion just became more important."

"Discussion about *what*? You—"

"It's about Sky. He's terrific. Not only in a general sense, but terrific for you. If you're already in love with him, so much the better. Fi's sure he's in love with you, too. While everybody else was watching Cleo Marie, we were watching you and Sky. After the party we were discussing—"

"Stop." She pressed her fingers to her temples where a headache was building. "I don't know for sure where you're going with this, but I have an inkling. Sure, Sky and I like each other, but he's leaving on the twenty-ninth. I'm going back to L.A. on the thirtieth. End of story."

"Why?"

"*Why*? How can you even ask me that? He's not leaving his ranch and I'm not leaving UCLA."

"He definitely shouldn't leave his ranch. He's clearly very happy there. But you—"

"I'm very happy at UCLA!"

"Are you?"

"*Yes.*"

"As happy as you've been since Sky arrived at the Buckskin?"

"That's different. I'm on vacation for the first time in years. He's good company. I love being here for Christmas. Or I did, until you started in on this subject."

"Penny, I've never seen you so happy. You're glowing."

"I don't get you. First you lecture me about the dangers of a relationship with Sky and now you're all for it?"

"I'd forgotten about the horse thing. You always wanted one. I always loved the idea of being a cowboy and living on a ranch, but now I remember you wanted to be a cowgirl."

"Until I read *Lord of the Rings.* Then I wanted to be a hobbit and live in the shire."

"And have a pony like Handsome Sam? You freaked out watching Cleo and that Shetland. That's when it all came back to me — the bike you pretended was a horse, you begging the folks to add some Western riding lessons to the dressage thing, the horse movies you loved, the—"

"I was just a kid. I grew up. I wanted a challenging career that suited my talents and I found one. Now that I have my doctorate, I can—"

"Your accomplishments are incredible, Pen. I've been your cheerleader the whole time. But I just wonder—"

"Teaching English at UCLA is my calling."

"Is it your passion?"

She massaged her temples. "Absolutely. I worked hard to get where I am and I'm not giving it up to...." She ran out of words.

"Follow a childhood dream?"

"I told you." Her jaw tightened. "Those dreams don't fit me anymore."

"What if they could?"

"I don't see how. Last time I checked, they didn't allow horses on the UCLA campus."

"Ever hear of the University of Montana?"

She blinked. Then she sucked in a breath. "Are you serious?"

"It has a good reputation."

"You're suggesting I should leave UCLA, which is twentieth in the nation last time I checked, and get a job in Montana?"

He regarded her silently. "That's scary."

"What?"

"You sounded like Mom and Dad just then."

"No, I didn't."

"Sorry, sis. That's exactly how they would look at this. Prestige is everything to them."

"Well, that's not why I'm there, okay?" Icepicks jabbed her temples.

"Then how come you recently checked UCLA's ranking?"

She swallowed. "I didn't. Dad brought it up at their big Thanksgiving bash."

"I rest my case."

Great, now her stomach was churning, too. She reached for the door handle. "Congratulations, Leo. You've ruined my Christmas Eve." She scrambled out, slammed the door and headed for the house.

A truck drove by. Might even be Garrett's. She picked up her speed. She needed time to get her act together before seeing Sky.

Her brother caught up with her. "Pen, I apologize. You know me. I'm a bull in a china shop. I didn't mean to ruin your Christmas Eve. I just wanted to—"

"I'm not like Mom and Dad." She walked faster.

"No, you're not. And that's why I—"

"Drop it, Leo."

He heaved a sigh. "Yeah, okay. Sorry, sis."

31

Getting Georgie settled delayed Garrett and Anna, but that was okay. Sky made good use of the extra time. Now he and Penny wouldn't have to mess with creating their bed after they got home.

Home. It had always meant the big ranch house where he'd grown up. He had his own place, now, but it wasn't home. This bunkhouse, though, specifically when Penny was here.... Yeah, well, he might not want to continue down that rabbit hole.

Because he'd blocked the front door, he had to leave from the back and wait in front for Garrett and Anna. He paced a bit to keep his hands and feet warm. No problem. The prospect of seeing Penny generated plenty of internal heat.

Garrett and Anna arrived in high spirits. Although they'd attended several gatherings at Ed's, this was their first Christmas Eve party. The three of them spent the drive speculating what special treats and decorations they'd find at Ed's.

Since he wasn't driving, Sky took a video of the drive in and sent it to his mom, along with a suggestion that they might be able to do something similar with a light display. She was always on the lookout for new holiday ideas.

She texted back her thanks for the idea and a hug emoji. Yeah, he missed her. Missed being at the house with his family for Christmas Eve. But he wouldn't trade this time with Penny for anything.

As Garrett cruised past the line of parked vehicles, a woman who looked like Penny exited the passenger side of a truck, slammed the door and took off at a fast walk.

"That's weird," Garrett said. "Fiona stomping off as if she's upset."

"How do you know that's Fiona?"

"Has to be. The woman's blonde and that's Leo's truck." He glanced in the side-view mirror. "And there he goes, trying to catch her. Must be trouble in paradise."

By the time Garrett parked and they were headed to the front steps, Leo and Fiona were on the porch.

"Guess they worked it out, whatever it was," Garrett said.

Sky nodded. "Guess so." Except that wasn't Fiona with Leo. He'd glimpsed her profile. Penny had been in the truck having a private conversation with her brother, one that had ended in a fight.

Sky's jaw firmed. Leo had upset her. On Christmas Eve, no less. Not cool. He lengthened his stride, but Leo and Penny were already in the house by the time he reached the steps.

"Oh, my, the wreath on the door is as big as the ones at the entrance." Anna paused. "I need a picture of that."

Sky backed away so he'd be out of the shot. Fidgeting a little, he waited while Anna took several shots of the wreath and the decorated pillars.

Garrett leaned closer to Sky. "That was Penny, not Fiona," he murmured.

"Saw that."

"She didn't look happy."

"No, she didn't." And he'd find out why. Leo had seemed fine today. He'd even taken a video of the piggyback ride. Didn't make sense that he suddenly had a burr under his saddle.

"That's enough." Anna tucked her phone in her coat pocket. "I'm ready to taste all the fabulous food I'm sure Ed's laid out for us."

"Me, too." Garrett took her hand as the three of them started up the steps. "Wonder if she'll have the chocolate fountain going."

"Chocolate fountain?" The lights and decorations should have clued him in, but a chocolate fountain?

Anna glanced over her shoulder. "You'll think you walked into a resort. She sets up stations like they do at fancy buffets — salads at one table, bread and rolls at another, meat at the next one, and a dessert table that gives you a sugar high just looking at it."

"Can't wait." Except he'd lost his appetite. His first order of business was Penny. He unbuttoned his jacket as he climbed the steps. Didn't want to waste time on nonessentials once he made it through that gigantic carved wooden door.

Garrett held it for him. "You look like a man on a mission."

"Yes, sir."

"Good luck."

"Thanks." He stepped into a room filled with music, chatter and heady fragrances from the huge Christmas tree in one corner and the aroma of food laid out in the center of the room. He ignored it all as he stripped off his jacket and left it along with his hat on the nearest coat tree.

Scanning the room, he spotted Penny holding a glass of champagne and talking with Matt, Lucy, Jake and Millie. She laughed at something that was said. Putting on a brave face?

Then she glanced toward the door as if she might have been watching for him. Her smile bloomed. Whatever the deal was with that discussion, it hadn't succeeded in dampening her pleasure at seeing him.

He'd fight dragons for that lady. He'd rather not have to fight her brother, but if Leo was harassing her, he was asking for trouble. Sky held her gaze as he crossed the room.

"Finally!" Jake called out. "The prodigal son arrives at the feast. FYI, Charley was never late to a party."

"That's the truth," Matt said. "Charley always arrived early and stayed late."

"Good to know." Sky slipped an arm around Penny's waist. "Any other Charley behavior I should keep in mind?"

"I know one," Millie said. "Charley did himself proud at the Christmas buffet every year. The only person who could out-eat him was Nick, our other bottomless pit. Now he's unchallenged. I'm thinking Charley's son should be able to unseat him."

"Wish I'd had that info this afternoon. I wouldn't have had two pieces of Cleo's birthday cake."

Jake laughed. "I saw that. Which is what tells me you could be a contender. You and Nick were the only ones who went back for seconds."

"It was good cake." He'd keep up the banter until he could gracefully extract Penny and take her to a secluded corner where they could talk.

"Sky needed extra fuel." Penny gave him a nudge. "Piggyback rides take a lot of energy."

"Yes, ma'am. Gotta keep up my strength." If she was down in the dumps, she was very good at hiding it. "When am I supposed to start this eating marathon?"

"Any time," Jake said. "You guys were the tail end. We were forced to stand around drinking Ed's champagne while we waited for the guest of honor."

"Who's that?"

"You, hotshot."

"What?"

"It's a spur of the minute idea." Matt flashed him a grin. "So don't get too puffed up about it."

"I'd advise against any puffery," Jake said. "When we asked Penny to rate you as a roommate, she said you were *okay*." He made air quotes.

"Only *okay*?" He clutched his chest and gave her a stricken look. "You cut me to the quick, sweet lady."

Her gray eyes sparkled. "Didn't want you to get a swelled head."

"Hm." That just begged for a suggestive comeback. If they'd been alone, he would have run with it. He held her gaze until her cheeks turned pink.

"Okay, you two. Dial it back." Jake sent them a warning glance. "You can discuss that rating later tonight."

"But given Penny's lukewarm rating," Matt said, "we had to look for other attributes to justify your guest of honor status."

"We only found one." Jake gave him a once-over. "You look a hell of a lot like Charley."

"Not that he can claim credit for that," Matt said.

"No, but he hasn't disgraced the brand... at least not yet."

"And on that flimsy pretense—" Matt raised his glass in Sky's direction. "We decided to make you the guest of honor because Charley would have gotten a kick out of us doing that. Luce, got the medal of honor?"

"I do." She came forward with a flat tree ornament, a silver angel, dangling from a loop of red ribbon. "Lean down so I can put this on you."

Good grief. He ducked his head.

She put it around his neck and adjusted the angel so it rested near his breastbone. "I hereby pronounce you the honored guest of the Buckskin gang. Don't mess up."

"I'll do my best. Where'd this ornament come from?"

"Ed's tree. She wants you to keep it."

"Um, okay." The ornament was heavy, probably sterling silver. He glanced at Matt. "Did everybody agree to this?"

"They did. We polled the entire Buckskin gang. Garrett and Anna texted me their votes while you were taking off your jacket."

"And Leo?"

"Leo's text said, and I quote, *hell, yeah.*"

He glanced at Penny. Her smile was as bright as ever, but the slight tension around her eyes told him something was going on with her, emotions she didn't want to share with the group. They *really* needed to talk.

But it wasn't to be, at least not in the immediate future. He was instructed to lead off the buffet line ASAP, even ahead of Penny. That went against the grain, but she shooed him up there, so he grabbed a plate and filled it amid much teasing and heckling about his puny servings.

Cozy groups of chairs and side tables dotted the room. Since he had his pick of spots, he led Penny to one in a far corner. Henri and Ben joined them, along with Ed and Josette.

The minute Ed arrived, he thanked her for the ornament.

"You're so welcome. I figure a person can always use another angel."

"Yes, ma'am."

Henri beamed at him. "I love that the Brotherhood came up with this on the fly. They're right. Charley would have been tickled pink that they made you the guest of honor."

"I appreciate it. I also feel intimidated. I have a lot to live up to."

Her expression softened. "No, you don't, son. Just because you look like him, don't think you're required to be the reincarnation of Charley Fox. Just be yourself."

"So I don't have to out-eat Nick tonight?"

Her eyes widened. "Is that what they told you?"

"Well, it was suggested I—"

"Forget that nonsense. I suppose they also said that he was famous for being the last one to leave the party."

"That, too."

Ed chuckled. "And he was, bless his heart. Meanwhile, poor Henri would be dead on her feet, dying to go home."

"Fortunately I don't have that issue with Ben." Henri sent him a fond glance before turning back to Sky. "We'll be leaving at a reasonable hour. You're welcome to catch a ride with us."

That sounded like heaven, but he needed a signal from Penny before accepting the offer.

She gave him a subtle nod. "Going home at a reasonable hour would be lovely. It's been a busy day."

This time he had no trouble reading her. She was clearly relieved that he didn't want to be the life of the party.

"We'll stay for a few dances," Henri said. "Then we can shove off."

"Dancing?" Sky surveyed the lavish buffet that took up the entire middle of the room. "Where?"

Ed waved a hand. "We move all that. Most of it goes back to the kitchen. The desserts, the chocolate fountain and the champagne stay, but they're tucked out of the way on that far wall. Dancing is a tradition with this crowd."

"And a good one," Henri said. "Charley just took it to extremes." She grinned. "You look discombobulated, Sky."

"It's the first time I've heard anyone say that Charley...."

"Had faults? He was a good man, at times a great man, but he wasn't perfect. The Brotherhood has put him on a pedestal, and I understand why. Just don't believe everything they tell you."

"Thank you, ma'am. That helps." Sort of. Funny thing about finding out his dad had been a flawed human being. That made him more real, more approachable. Regret burned in his chest.

Conversation over dinner flowed easily thanks to the long-standing friendship shared by Henri, Ed, Josette and Ben. Sky relaxed enough to eat his meal and Penny ate hers, too. A good sign.

He glanced at all the empty plates and stood. "I'll take these to—"

"Back away from the plates, sir." Jake's arrival was so timely he had to be employing spies. "Our guest of honor will not be the busboy. I'll take those. The Brotherhood is clearing the dance floor. Sky, as our guest of honor you'll lead off the dancing. You get to start with Penny, but then each of the Babes will get a dance."

Henri stood. "Jake, that's excessive."

"But Charley used to—"

"Sky isn't Charley. Dancing with each of the Babes was only the beginning of his evening. Sky and Penny will be going home with us in about an hour. Plan accordingly."

"Yes, ma'am." He left with the plates.

Ed got to her feet and walked over to Sky. "You'll be coming back in a couple of months, I suppose."

"I'd like that."

"I'll claim my dance when you come for your next visit. Skip over me."

"I'll do the same," Henri said.

"*Moi, aussi.*" Josette patted him on the shoulder. "I can wait."

"Pam and Penny can, too," Henri said. "Anyway, their husbands are here. It's not like they don't have dance partners."

"That leaves Red." Josette glanced around the room. "There she is. I'll tell her to stand down. Then you can just dance with Penny tonight and save the Babes for another time."

Jake returned. "Lucy said she'd bow out of the Babes lineup for dancing with Sky, so that leaves—"

"Nobody," Henri said. "We've handled it."

"Alrighty, then. Matt's cueing up the music, so we're all set."

The Keeper of the Stars poured from Ed's top-notch speakers and Penny looked at Sky. "Did you—"

"Not me."

"I requested it." Henri held his gaze. "Charley adored that song."

_32_

Penny and Sky took the floor first, but thankfully others joined them soon after. Dancing in a virtual spotlight to a song about lovers brought together by fate would not be her choice.

The irony of it all. She'd fought for the right to enjoy a romantic fling with this gorgeous, generous cowboy. Thanks to Fiona and the ladies of the Buckskin gang, she'd won that battle. And lost the war. Now her brother, and likely many others, were pulling for a commitment she wasn't prepared to make.

Leo's accusation of snobbery stung. She wasn't that person. Her parents might brag about her accomplishments, but she never did. Unlike some of her colleagues, she didn't insist on her students using her title. In social settings, she never—

"I can hear you thinking," Sky murmured in her ear. "It's really loud."

She glanced up at him. "Sorry. I have a lot on my mind."

"And this song doesn't help."

"No, it doesn't." She sighed. "I still believe you and I were destined to meet, but these lyrics imply—"

"I know." He held her loosely, his touch firm enough to communicate his moves and pick up on hers, but he wasn't trying to snuggle.

"I usually pay close attention to lyrics, but with these, I like the song so much I've ignored the underlying message. Tonight it's hitting me in the face."

"Sounds painful."

"Sky, has it occurred to you that I could teach English at the University of Montana?"

His silence said it all.

"But you haven't brought it up. Were you ever going to?"

"No, ma'am."

Guilt punched her in the gut. She'd laid down the rules and he'd agreed to follow them. He would stick to his promise no matter what it cost him. How much was that, exactly?

He spun her in a slow twirl. "Did you have a fight with your brother?"

"I guess you could say that."

When he brought her back in, he tucked her in closer than before. "About me?"

"Not really. He thinks you're great. I'm the one he's unhappy with." And it hurt like the devil.

He tightened his hold, enough that the silver angel was caught between their bodies. "That doesn't sound right. He thinks the world of you."

"Yeah, well." Her defenses began to crumble. She'd walked into the party vowing she'd put Leo's comments aside and have a good time with these wonderful folks. He couldn't ruin her evening unless she allowed it.

She'd kept herself in party mode until now. But the warmth of Sky's arms created a safe haven for letting down her guard. One comment from him had released the anxiety she'd been holding back.

They were still in a public place, though. She didn't want to lose it here, and if she told him anything more about Leo's accusations, she might.

She cleared her throat. "I'll tell you all about my conversation with him, but not now, okay?"

"Okay. But if he's harassed you because of something to do with me, I need to have a talk with him before we leave."

The protective tone of that statement warmed her all over. But she couldn't have him confronting Leo, especially when he didn't have all the facts. "What he said wasn't harassment. He only wants the best for me. He and I happen to disagree about what that is."

"But it's your life. Yours is the only vote that counts."

"Thank you."

"Full disclosure, I feel like a hypocrite saying that. God knows I've been guilty of thinking I know what's best for Angelique."

"That's better than not caring what happens to her. You're coming from a place of love. And so is Leo. Please don't talk to him about this tonight."

"All right, I won't." Leaning down, he lowered his voice to a sexy murmur. "Can't wait to get home."

"Me, either." Her body stirred. In less than two hours, she'd be making love to this wonderful man. Okay, so he'd used the word *home*. She'd accidentally done the same thing this morning. In one sense, the bunkhouse was their home. For now.

* * *

Ben pulled his big red truck to a stop in front of the bunkhouse and Henri turned toward the backseat. "I just looked at tomorrow's weather. It could snow in the morning."

"I hope it does." Penny unfastened her seat belt. "I'm looking forward to riding King to your house in the snow. What time does everyone gather?"

"Whenever they want. Ben and I will make a couple of big egg casseroles and I have plenty of pastries. We stay loose. If it's snowing too hard, someone will come over and get you."

"Since I've never ridden in snow, it would be an adventure for me. If we get cold and wet, we'll just warm up by the fire. Unless Sky—"

"I don't mind snowy weather if Penny doesn't. But what about King? Would you rather we didn't take him out? I didn't ask if you had a good place to put him while we're there."

"We do, as it happens. Charley and I built a nice little two-stall shed a short walk from the house. That's where we're keeping Handsome Sam for the time being."

Penny looked over at Sky. "Then if you're game..."

"Sure am. Let's plan on it."

"But you'll call if it's nastier than you expect."

"We will." Sky reached for the door handle. "Thanks for bringing us back."

"You're welcome. Have a nice night."

Penny scooted over. "I'll just get out your side." She paused at the door. "Thanks for taking me to Ed's, too. What a fabulous party."

"You'll have to come to Montana next Christmas," Ben said. "So we can do it all again."

"Sounds great." She put her hand in Sky's and hopped down. "See you tomorrow." She shut the door and started toward the front of the bunkhouse.

"Hang on." He pulled her back. "Turn around and wave."

"Why?"

"Because we're going in the back door, not the front."

"I see." She laughed and waved goodbye to Ben and Henri. Ben turned the truck around, tooted the horn and drove away.

"Now we can go."

"Let's run."

"Works for me."

She arrived at the back steps breathless and laughing. "No fancy carrying maneuvers this time."

"Nope. Just go on in. It's unlocked."

She hurried up the steps and opened the kitchen door. "I love that you can do that, here."

"You can at Rowdy Ranch, too."

"Nice." Had he said that on purpose? *Stop second-guessing him. Enjoy the moment.* "It's dark in here." She shed her coat on her way past the dining table.

"Want me to turn on a light? There's another switch right—"

"No. That overhead is a mood killer. Just so you know, I'm taking my boots off so I won't walk across our bed with them on."

"Why just your boots?"

"Good point. Everything's coming off."

"Now I want the light on."

"Tell you what, once I'm undressed I'll walk carefully across the bed and turn on the Christmas tree."

"Good idea. Didn't dare leave those lights on."

"God, no. Glad you didn't." She stripped off her underwear and tossed it on the table.

"Turned up the thermostat, though. Figured we didn't want to take time to build a fire."

"Good call. See you in there."

"Yes, you will."

The gruff sound of arousal in his voice sent heat to her core. She hurried through the kitchen. Guided by the faint glow of the porch light shining through the front window, she crossed the spongy mattress, the army blanket scratchy under her bare feet.

She located the cord at the base of the tree and shoved the plug into the outlet mounted above the bedframe. Then she turned, and her breath hitched.

Sky stood framed in the kitchen doorway, a portrait of muscular, virile manhood bathed in Christmas lights. She swallowed. "You're beautiful."

"Funny. I was thinking the same thing about you."

She walked toward the bed, stepped on something brittle and yelped. Hopping away, she checked the floor for critters. Nope. Condom packet. "I believe this is yours." Scooping it up, she tossed it at him.

"Thanks." He caught it and tucked it behind his ear. When she started laughing, he shrugged. "No pockets."

"For future reference, that's not a sexy look."

"But inventive. And handy." Crouching down he flipped back the covers. "Looks like we're switching sides tonight."

"Not necessarily. I like the—" She spotted the gift-wrapped package on the pillow nearest the kitchen. It had been lost in the shadows until she focused on that part of the bed. "You did get me something."

"A little something."

"Looks like it might be a book." She dropped to her knees, reached over and picked it up. Too light for a book.

"Don't open it yet."

"Why not?" She shook it to see if it rattled.

"Just don't. Please." He crawled across the mattress. Still had the condom behind his ear. "Let me make love to you, first."

That condom made her giggle. "But you left it on my pillow like you wanted me to have it before we—"

"Couldn't exactly put it under the tree. You'd never see it lying inside the bedframe." He gently pried the package from her grip. "Later, okay?" Sitting back on his heels, he laid it in the kitchen doorway.

She smiled. "Are you trying to build the suspense?"

"Yeah, that's it." He stretched out on his side and wrapped an arm around her waist. "Come lie with me, pretty lady."

"Might as well, since I don't get to open my present."

"The thing is, I desperately need to kiss you." Rolling her to her back, he moved over her. "It's impossible to kiss a woman who's opening a package."

"Speaking of packages." Reaching down, she wrapped her fingers around his cock, just to tease him a little. The joke was on her. Desire slammed into her, making her gasp.

Leaning down, he feathered a kiss over her lips. "Trying to tell me something?"

All she could manage was a groan.

"Message received." Sitting back, he plucked the condom package from behind his ear. "See? Handy." His hot gaze touched on her lips, her breasts, her quivering stomach.

"Mm." Tension mounted in her core creating an ache that bordered on pain.

"Too bad it's not sexy." He ripped the package open.

She gulped. "I lied."

"I know." Tossing the package away, he glanced down. "You'll have to let go."

"Oh." She unclenched her fingers. Didn't want to.

After rolling on the condom, he moved between her thighs and hovered over her braced on his forearms. His chest hair brushed lightly against her sensitized nipples as he lowered his mouth to within a fraction of an inch from hers. "I like your hands on me," he murmured. "I want you to guide me in."

His soft words almost made her come. Grasping the base of his cock, she lifted her hips and urged him closer until he was... ah, right there.

"Thank you." He plunged deep.

And touched off an orgasm that spun her in a multicolored whirlpool of pleasure, sweet as a cotton candy machine and wild as a carnival ride. She held on, her hands clutching the bunched muscles of his back as he pumped faster, piling another climax on top of the first.

At last he claimed one of his own, her name on his lips as he surged into her and stayed, locked tight as his release blended with hers.

Her heartbeat had almost returned to normal when he lifted his head and gazed down at her. Leaning down, he kissed her, a long, deep and unhurried kiss. He ended it slowly, raised his head again and smiled.

"That was nice."

"The kiss or the—"

"The kiss. The climax, or rather climaxes, were more on the naughty side of things."

"Good." He took a deep breath. "I keep thinking we'll slow down, taper off."

"Not yet."

"Obviously. You turn me inside out, Penelope Marston."

"Backatcha, Skyler McLintock."

"I kinda like the long version of your name."

"Here's a secret. So do I."

"Then why not go by it?"

"Might be too pretentious."

"Not to me. What if I start calling you that in private?"

"That would be okay."

"Then I will. I need to make a trip to the bathroom, and then—"

"I can open my present?"

"Yes." He eased away from her. "In fact, you can open it while I'm gone."

"That's no fun."

"Seriously, do that. Then if you don't like it, you'll have time to recover from *oh, my God, I can't believe he thought I'd like this.*"

She laughed. "If you insist."

"See you soon."

As he walked away, she reached for the gift, untied the ribbon and pried open the taped ends. When it came to opening presents, she was the opposite of Cleo Marie.

After sliding a finger under the last piece of tape, she pulled the wrapping away from what was inside. And froze.

33

Sky finished washing up while trying to gauge what was going on in the next room. This morning he'd decided to get Penny a sexy nightgown, even though he wasn't wild about that idea. It would be more of a gift for him than her, and after they parted ways, she'd probably ditch it.

Then he'd seen this while he was in the collectible shop helping Rafe pick out the teacup cupboard for Kate. He'd spent way too much time debating whether to get it.

Taking a deep breath, he left the bathroom. She hated it. No other way to interpret her body language. She sat hunched over staring at what she was holding in her hand.

"Penny, I'm sorry. I shouldn't have given you something lame like that, but Angelique still adores her—"

She looked up. The tree lights reflected off her damp cheeks.

Damn, this must be the worst gift ever if he'd made her cry. "I'm so sorry. We'll have some time after Christmas. We'll borrow a vehicle and drive into town so you can pick out—"

"I love it."

"You *love* it? You sure as hell don't look like you love it."

She sniffed. "I do, though. Do you have some tissues around here?"

"I have a bandana." He crouched next to his bunk, yanked open the drawer where he'd stashed his stuff and pulled out a red one. "It's even seasonal."

"So it is." Her laughter was slightly choked and she cleared her throat. "I'm going to blow my nose on it, so then it'll have seasonal snot. I hope that's okay."

"I'll treasure your snot."

She cracked up for real. "Be quiet. A person can't laugh and blow her nose at the same time." She held the bandana to her face and blew hard. Then she folded it and wiped her eyes. "I'm keeping this in case I get teary again."

"Keep it forever if you want." *Keep me forever.*

"I thought you were going to treasure my snot."

"Depending on whether I get that back." *Please let me treasure you.*

"You'll get it back." She laid it beside her, retrieved her gift from the blanket and held it up. "This is awesome. I used to have a Breyer Shetland, but it wasn't a dapple grey. I can't believe you found this."

"It was in the collectibles shop."

"Huh. I haven't been in there." She ran her finger over the figurine. "Angelique collects Breyer?"

"She used to. She got so many that she decided to quit before her collection became unwieldy. But she still loves them." He sat next to her on the mattress. "I take it you have some?"

"Used to. When I moved to an apartment my sophomore year, I... gave them away."

"All of them?"

She nodded. "That part of my life was over. Gave away all my dressage stuff, too. Saddle, clothes, everything. I didn't have time for riding and I couldn't see myself ever having a horse. I needed my bookshelf space for books, not horse statues."

"I'm confused. If that's the situation, this little pony has no place in your—"

"I miss those little horses." She glanced up at him, her gaze filled with sadness. "Every time I think of them, especially my favorite ones, I wish I had them back."

"Then why not go online and hunt down a few?"

"Because it's ridiculous."

"Is it?" Her forlorn expression tore him up. She was making herself miserable. "Sounds to me like—"

"I still have a space issue." She turned the figurine around, examining it from all angles. "But I love this little guy so much. Maybe I will look for a couple more. My absolute favorites." She lifted her head and smiled. "This is a wonderful gift. Thank you." Laying it on the blanket, she leaned over and gave him a gentle kiss.

"You're welcome." Emotion crowded his chest. Could she see how her choices were leaching joy from her life? Did she secretly want him to throw her a rope? Is that why she'd brought up the University of Montana when they were dancing?

"Why are you looking at me like that?"

He took a deep breath. If not now, when? "Penny, I love you."

"Oh, Sky—"

"Marry me and come live at Rowdy Ranch."

"What?"

He had trouble breathing but he barreled on. "My house is loaded with extra—"

"Sky—"

"Your books, your research materials, your Breyer horses, it will all fit. You can have your own horse. You can ride whenever you want." Heart racing, he grasped her hands in his. "UM is less than fifty miles away. I know it's not UCLA, but I'll bet the students there would be even more excited about studying Western literature, and you—"

"Stop." She freed her hands and scooted back. "What are you doing?"

"I know it's crazy." His heart thumped so hard his chest hurt. "*I'm* crazy... about you. You could have it all. *We* could have it all."

The regret shimmering in her eyes gave him the answer before she said the words. "I can't marry you."

"Yes, you can." *Breathe.* "You think you can't, but—"

"It's only been a month and a half since I broke my engagement to Barry. I can't just turn around and—"

"You said you didn't really love him."

"I figured that out after the fact."

"Did you think what you had with him was *amazing*?"

"No." She met his gaze. "I'm dazzled by you. You're a fantasy come true. But letting myself get swept away, tossing aside everything I've worked so hard for—"

"That's not how I see it."

"I know." Her expression softened. "But it's how I see it."

He swallowed. She hadn't secretly wanted him to throw her a rope. She was satisfied with living her fantasy for a few days. After she left, she might even miss him... for a while.

He dragged in a breath. "Well, at least we got that sorted out."

"But it wasn't the response you were looking for."

"I miscalculated, that's all. You seemed to be yearning for the Buckskin way of life, which is a lot like mine. And since we get along so well, and I know you like me a little bit, I—"

"I like you more than a little bit."

"That's nice to hear."

"I've never had a fling with anyone before. I'll never do it again."

"Why not?"

"It's too easy to fall in love."

He glanced away. "I didn't mean to."

"Neither did I."

His breath caught. Slowly turned his head. "You—"

"I'm not going to say it. That will only make this worse." She sighed. "I should probably move back to Henri's until you leave. I can't do it now, obviously, but in the morning we can haul my stuff up there. It won't add that much weight to King."

"Is that what you want?"

"If it would be easier on you, yes, I do."

"It wouldn't. Please stay."

Her gaze was steady. "All right." She held out her arms.

"Are we going to have makeup sex, now?" Her smile was his reward for that remark. He'd dredged it up to lighten the mood. Seemed to work.

"You can't have makeup sex if you don't fight."

"You were ready to leave. I think that counts."

"But I didn't."

"Nope." Not yet. "So we'll celebrate by having makeup sex." He gathered her close and breathed in the sweet scent of her skin. From this moment until the one when they said goodbye, he'd make every second count.

34

Sky hadn't chosen separation and for that Penny was grateful. He'd laid himself bare and offered his heart. Rejection caused some men to retreat and nurse their wounded ego. Clearly Sky was made of stronger stuff.

Makeup sex was followed by toasting each other with warm cider. After midnight, they had Merry Christmas sex. On the surface, the playfulness was the same. Except it wasn't.

He didn't ask her about the heated discussion with Leo. Just as well. Loaded subject. Sated and drowsy, she fell asleep in his arms.

She woke up to the gentle glow of the Christmas tree lights and soft kisses on her cheeks and hair.

"Merry Christmas," he murmured. "It's snowing."

"It is?" She scrambled up. "Brrr."

"Here." He pulled the army blanket free and wrapped it around her. "Henri texted a minute ago. She thinks we should either get going or have them pick us up."

"What time is it?" Swaddled in the blanket, she shuffled over to the window.

"Past eight."

"Seems earlier." She used a corner of the blanket to wipe the condensation from the window. "Oh! It's beautiful! Big fat flakes. We're definitely riding to Henri's."

"Then I'll take a quick shower so I can go get King."

"Baloney. We're walking over to the barn together, buster."

"Then you go take a quick shower while I text Henri our approximate ETA and make hot chocolate."

"Do we have time to drink it?"

"We'll take it on our ride. I found a thermos in the cupboard yesterday."

"Perfect." She glanced at the mattresses on the floor. "Should we—"

"I checked with Matt during the party last night. He said nobody would be coming to the bunkhouse today, so we can leave it."

"Excellent." She hurried through her shower and dressing routine, straightened up their makeshift bed and placed her Shetland figurine on the small table next to the wood stove.

Sky was even faster than she was. Showered, shaved and dressed in record time, he unplugging the Christmas tree, picked up the thermos from the kitchen counter and ushered her through the back door.

She looked out on a world transformed, as if a giant hand had layered whipped cream over the ground, the evergreens, the woodpile behind the bunkhouse. Yet the lazy flakes drifting down seemed incapable of creating such a scene.

"How could these—" She gestured toward the feather-light snow. "Create this?" She swept an arm to encompass the landscape.

"It could have if the snow started right after we went in and kept up all night." He joined her at the bottom of the steps. "More likely it snowed harder early this morning and it's let up for now. That's why we need to make tracks. Literally." Taking her gloved hand, he started around the side of the bunkhouse and headed toward an opening in the trees.

"I almost hate walking on it. Like I'm ruining a fresh coat of paint." She stepped gingerly, snow crunching under her boots.

"If you don't, others will."

"I thought nobody was coming to the bunkhouse."

"No two-legged critters." He pointed to a trail of small divots in the snow. "Snowshoe hare."

"Oh, my goodness. That's cool."

He continued toward the trees. "To your right, those prints are likely white-tailed deer."

"What do they eat when it snows?"

"Pine needles, bark. They manage to find stuff. Sometimes we'll put a bale of hay out for 'em."

"That's thoughtful."

"We're all in it together when winter comes."

"Nice." She lifted her face to the snow as they moved along the path cut between the stand of pines. Then she stuck out her tongue and let the snowflakes land on it.

"Lucky snowflakes."

She glanced over. He was watching her, a gleam in his blue eyes. "Lucky me. This is beautiful."

"You've really never seen snow?"

"Only on TV or in the movies. I think that's one reason Leo chose to be a cowboy in Montana instead of Texas. He knew my folks wouldn't follow him here."

"I can't imagine living anywhere else."

"It suits you. When your mom describes the character of men who love the challenge of this country, she's clearly talking about you."

"And my brothers."

"And Charley?"

He hesitated. "Probably."

"Ben told me she would have married him in a heartbeat."

He gazed at her. "But it wasn't to be."

"No." She looked away and they walked in silence the rest of the way to the barn.

The clearing in front of it had been thoroughly trammeled by tire tracks and hooves. Horses frolicked in the snowy pasture, chasing each other and sending up white spray as they wheeled and dashed off in a new direction.

"They look so happy!"

"New snow is fun for them, too."

"Is King out there?"

"Garrett said he'd leave him in his stall for us."

"I didn't even think about barn duty. You didn't have it this morning?"

"Tomorrow morning." He let go of her hand and pushed aside the bar holding the double doors closed.

"Wait. I want a picture of the wreaths on the barn doors." She pulled out her phone and Sky stepped aside. She'd wanted him in the shot, but asking him to pose would be... awkward. Like she wanted something to remember him by.

She held the thermos while he brought King out of the barn and closed the double doors.

Holding the buckskin's reins, he glanced at her. "Front or back?"

"I like the front, if that's okay with you."

"Absolutely." He took the thermos, set it down, and helped her on.

She held it while he swung up behind her.

Then he asked for it back. "I'll be your barista."

"Aren't you supposed to keep me from falling off?"

"I can do both. I used to take Angelique into town in the winter and we'd bring hot chocolate along. Just requires cooperation. Off we go."

He had the routine down. She clasped the reins in one hand and the stainless cup in the other. He kept one arm firmly around her waist and used his free hand to pour hot chocolate into the cup. Without spilling a drop.

"I'm impressed."

"You get first sip."

She took a small mouthful to test the temperature. Ah, just right. The creamy sweetness bathed her tongue and slid down her throat, warming her all the way to her tummy.

Moist snowflakes kissed her cheeks and settled on King's black mane. She rocked in tune with the gentle motion of the gelding's stride as his hooves chopped a path through virgin snow. Wedged between Sky's muscular thighs, his strong arm holding her steady, she slipped into a state of bliss.

"You gonna drink that?"

She snapped out of her daze. "Yes, yes I am. I was just…"

"Yeah." His grip tightened a fraction. "This is good."

A chink opened in the wall of her resolve. She could give up incredible orgasms. She could give up his playful banter, his beautiful smile, the light in his eyes, his generous spirit.

But this… when he made all the pieces fall into place, when he created a moment so rich with joy that it radiated from her center outward to every atom in her body… could she give up riding bareback in the snow?

* * *

Ben's red truck was the only one in the parking area when Penny pulled King to a halt at the base of Henri's front porch steps. "Guess we're the first ones here."

"Looks like it." Sky swung down and helped her dismount.

"Merry Christmas!" Ben came out on the porch buttoning his coat. "Was watching for you. How was the ride over?"

"Terrific." Penny held up the thermos. "Sky made us hot chocolate to drink along the way."

Ben gave an approving nod. "Good man."

"Yes, he is." A wonderful man. The best.

"Why don't you head on inside?" Ben made his way down the steps. "I'll show Sky the way to the little barn."

"Uh, sure. Okay." She'd planned to go along and get another peek at Handsome Sam, but this worked, too. Henri could probably use some help with breakfast prep.

She walked in and was greeted by the smells and sounds of Christmas — pine, woodsmoke from logs crackling in the fireplace, delicious aromas coming from the kitchen and Henri humming along to Nat King Cole's *The Christmas Song*.

Nudging off her boots, she left her jacket, scarf and hat on the coat tree. "I'm here!" she called as she picked up the thermos and walked in her sock feet toward the kitchen.

"Are you an icicle?" Henri slid a casserole dish into the oven and straightened as Penny came through the kitchen doorway.

"I'm actually quite toasty. Sky made us hot chocolate."

"What a thoughtful thing to do."

"He proposed last night." Penny sucked in a breath. What was wrong with her?

Henri's eyes widened.

"Sorry. I have no idea why I just told you that."

"Because you didn't accept his proposal and now you're conflicted."

"How do you know?"

"Oh, sweetheart, I've been there. I said no to Charley when he asked me."

"You did? I thought you guys got engaged that week."

"Only after I asked him to marry me. Nobody knows that, Penny, not even Ben, so I'd appreciate it if you'd—"

"I won't, but why is it a secret?"

"That's my fault. Charley was such a charmer that everyone assumed he'd asked and I'd immediately said yes. That became the narrative. At one point Charley said we should tell everybody the truth, but I couldn't see the point so we never did."

"Obviously he accepted."

"He did. I wasn't sure he would after the way I'd reacted to his proposal."

Penny's stomach churned. "How did you... would you mind telling me—"

"I told him I couldn't imagine uprooting myself from an established job and a place where I had family and friends to marry a man I'd only known a few days." She gazed at Penny. "Sound familiar?"

"Yes, ma'am." She took a shaky breath. "What changed your mind?"

"For one thing, I was madly in love with him. That's not supposed to happen so quickly, but Charley... he was amazing. Everything I'd ever wanted in a man."

"That sounds familiar, too. But still..."

"Who throws away everything to run off with a man she's just met? Flighty women. Unstable women. I wasn't that woman. Such wild behavior would shock everyone I knew. And I was right about that."

"Why did you do it, then?"

"I figured out, luckily before I lost Charley forever, that all the voices in my head telling me not to marry him... not a single one was mine. They belonged to my family and friends."

"You mean like your parents?"

"Yes, and they were the hardest to ignore. They'd raised me, helped educate me, taught me to use my head and make sensible choices. Marrying Charley was based on gut instinct alone. And it was the best decision of my life."

The front door opened. "Gramma Henri!" Claire's voice was filled with excitement. "Can we build snow people in your backyard? Can we?"

"You bet we can! Let me get my coat and boots on." She gave Penny a hug. "So that's my story. I hope it helps."

"Thank you." She swallowed. "It helps a lot."

35

"The Brotherhood thought the video of Charley would be good for you to see." Ben closed the doors to the small barn. "But I told them I'd check with you and make sure you're okay with watching it."

"I'd like to." Sky fell into step beside him as they started down the path to the house. "It's one thing to look at photo albums, but I'm sure I'll get a better idea of what he was like from a video."

"Fair warning, you might get emotional. I always do, and I've seen it several times. You might not be as invested, though, since you've never met him."

"I feel like I have. Almost. I'm sorry I didn't."

Ben sighed. "Your mother's sorry about that, too. But what's done is done."

"Do you think my mom and Henri could ever be friends?"

"Hard to say. Henri's beginning to understand that Charley was the love of your mother's life, too. I won't say she's forgiven your mom for keeping you a secret, but... she's feeling more charitable than she was that first night."

"I didn't know how much Mom cared about him until this visit. She'd never let on. Seems like all these years she's been looking for another Charley."

"She won't find him. He was one of a kind."

"Evidently. And clearly I didn't inherit his charisma."

"What makes you say that?"

"I proposed to Penny last night. Charley was able to convince Henri after a few days, but I went down in flames."

"I'm sorry to hear that."

"So am I, but she has good reasons for saying no."

"And good ones for saying yes, if you ask me."

"Thanks, Ben. But to be fair, we haven't known each other long. Maybe, if we had more time...."

"Too bad you live so far apart."

"I knew it was a long shot. But I missed out on Charley because I wasn't proactive. I wasn't going to let that happen with Penny. At least I tried."

Ben squeezed his shoulder. "That's all we can do, son."

* * *

The day was packed, and Sky didn't have any time alone with Penny. Then again, he didn't make a big effort in that direction. His mom had instilled a belief that Christmas was about family, and Henri upheld the same tradition. Eating, playing in the snow and opening gifts kept everyone involved.

Sky managed to squeeze in a call to his family by going upstairs to one of the guest rooms. He must have picked the one Penny had used because her cinnamon-bun scent teased him the entire length of the phone call. He didn't talk long, but long enough to find out Jessica had broken up with Beau. That had to hurt.

When Sky came back downstairs, the gang was arranging seating in front of the TV.

Claire came over and took him by the hand. "Uncle Sky, you're in front with the new people. That's me, my dad, my momma Nell and Aunt Penny, plus Aunt Anna and Georgie. Uncle Garrett's not new, but of course he has to sit with Aunt Anna and Georgie."

"Of course."

"We all have to be on the floor so people can see over us. Can you sit cross-legged?"

"I'll do my best."

"I saved you a spot between my dad and Aunt Penny."

"Thanks." He lowered himself to the smooth wood floor and brushed Penny's knee in the process. "Pardon me, ma'am."

She flashed him a smile. "Pardon accepted, cowboy."

Claire crouched in front of them. "I'm gonna go sit with my dad and my momma Nell. Do you guys need anything before I go, like a drink or popcorn?"

"No, thank you." He glanced at Penny. "How about you?"

"I'm good, thanks."

"Just tell me if you need anything. It's easier for me to move around in this crowd because I'm small and limber." She hopped up and took her seat between Zeke and Nell.

Sky lowered his voice as he leaned toward Zeke. "That's quite a kid you have there."

He chuckled. "I'm aware."

"Have you seen this video?"

"I've seen the Charley one, but we're starting with Operation Santa."

"Oh, right. I heard about that. It's Ben's deal. Did he take videos while he delivered the toys?"

"No, these are the pictures the parents sent him this morning of the kids opening their presents. He hasn't been around much today because he's been putting them together. It's more like a slide show."

"Should be fun." If he hadn't said yes to Ben this morning, that would be the only thing shown. Now that the moment had arrived, he almost wished he'd nixed the idea. "So you've seen Charley's video?"

Zeke nodded. "Last month when I was initiated into the Brotherhood."

"They have a ceremony?"

"Yep. They take it seriously. So do I. The Brotherhood has been—"

"Okay, folks!" Ben walked in. "Prepare yourself for an explosion of cute." He clicked the remote and walked to the back of the room.

Sky looked over at Penny and held out his hand. She threaded her fingers through his and squeezed. The images on the screen were adorable, but as they flashed by, he spent most of the time looking at Penny.

Did she want kids? Her obvious enjoyment of the slide show indicated she might, but he'd never asked her the question. Would have been premature. Now it was a moot point, for him, at least.

The show wasn't long. Everyone applauded and congratulated Ben at the end. Feel-good stuff. Then Matt took over to cue up Charley's video and Sky's gut tightened.

Zeke leaned in his direction. "I heard you two are riding King back to the barn."

"That's the plan."

"I don't know if you've been watching the time, but you should get started after this if you want to make it back before dark."

"I do."

"We could give you a ride if you want to leave King here overnight. We'll be going home after this video."

"Thanks, but Penny and I are looking forward to the ride."

Zeke smiled. "Okay. It's romantic, that's for sure."

"That it is."

"If I can have your attention, please." Matt stood by the TV. "This isn't a normal part of our Christmas celebration, but since we have Sky here, it seems appropriate. Claire, Nell and Anna have wanted to see it, too."

"And Georgie," Claire piped up. "He wants to see it."

Matt nodded. "And Georgie. For the rest of us, it's a good time to pause, remember and be grateful we had Charley in our lives." He started the video.

And Sky saw himself, only twenty-some years older, facing the camera against a backdrop of blue sky and pine trees. The video was taken in Henri's backyard in the summer, since Charley wasn't wearing a coat.

Hey, there! Don't see the point in doing this, but Henri seems to think I'm mortal like everybody else.

Charley's warm, gruff voice startled him. Some throat-clearing told him Ben wasn't the only one who still got emotional watching this. Not exactly an upper on Christmas. But they were doing it for him and he was grateful.

Making a video about my philosophy sounds presumptuous to me, but that woman's persistent as hell. I love that about her.

A humble guy. That would have appealed to his mom. It appealed to him, too. His throat tightened. What if this man had married his mom? He would have had a dad instead of a vague image in his imagination. He would have lived on this ranch....

And he'd just missed part of what Charley was saying....

Be kind. Be fair. Keep your word. Basic stuff. I didn't invent any of it.

If Charley had married his mom, they would have had more kids, but nine more? Would Angelique exist? And damn, he'd missed another chunk of the video.

...reasons to laugh, especially at yourself, and you'll find a million of 'em. Don't get so busy that you forget to look at the mountains or the sunrise. Life is beautiful. People are beautiful. Count your blessings and love one another.

He glanced off camera. *Henri? Is that enough?*

Henri's words were too faint to understand but clearly she'd reminded him of something.

Oh, yeah. Have a hell of a good time! Every damn day! I sure do!

The video ended.

"Wow," Claire said. "What a great guy."

Sky swallowed. He'd missed a lot of the video. Next visit he'd ask to see it again. If they'd let him have a copy, he'd watch it over and over. He ached for what he'd missed, what he might have had if he'd come to the Buckskin years ago, if Charley Fox had been a part of his life.

But he wasn't sorry that things had turned out the way they had. He loved his brothers and his sister. Couldn't imagine life without them. Life had happened the way it was supposed to.

Penny cradled his hand in both of hers. "You okay?"

He met her gaze and took a deep breath. "Yes, ma'am." He gave her hand a squeeze. "I want to talk to some people, but after that—"

"We'll go. I heard you and Zeke discussing the ride back. Go see your peeps. I'll get our coats."

"Thanks." He helped her up. "See you in a few minutes." The Brotherhood had gathered off to the side of the room. He made his way over there.

"Thank you. That was…" He searched for the right words.

Matt put a hand on his shoulder. "You're welcome."

"I missed some of it. I was too busy thinking about what would have happened if things had turned out differently."

"We've talked about that," Jake said. "Until you showed up, we thought we knew Charley's story. But if he hadn't gone to that conference in Texas, if he hadn't met Henri…."

"None of us would be here," Rafe said.

CJ nodded. "I wouldn't have met Izzy." He swallowed. "There would be no… hell, I can't even say it. I can't picture it. Don't want to."

Sky took a deep breath. "It all worked out. I have my family and now—"

"Now you have us." Rafe smiled. "Whether you want us or not."

"Of course he wants us," Jake said. "Who wouldn't? I'd suggest a group hug, but seeing as how we don't do group hugs, Sky needs to get his ass out of here before things get sloppy."

He laughed. "Well said. See you guys tomorrow."

"Go see Henri before you leave, though," Matt said. "She has a little something for you."

"Will do." He turned and found her talking with Ben over by the tree. He crossed the room. "Henri, Penny and I are taking off, and I—"

"She told me. Good idea."

"I tried to talk her into letting me drive you guys back so you could stay longer," Ben said, "but she told me the ride was important."

Important? Interesting word choice. "Yes, sir. It's fun."

Henri reached in her pocket and pulled out a small package about the size of a tube of lipstick. "Merry Christmas."

But she wouldn't be getting him makeup. His heart rate picked up. "Is this—"

"Yes. Ben made you a copy."

He sucked in air. "Thank you." He glanced at Ben before turning to Henri. "Best. Present. Ever."

"Figured you'd want to watch it again." She hesitated. "Maybe even share it. Although...."

"I'll let her know I have it. I can't predict whether she'll want to see it. Probably."

"I know. It's complicated." She sighed. "And you need to get on the road." She gave him a hug. "See you tomorrow."

"Merry Christmas." He hugged her back, shook hands with Ben and headed for the door, calling out his goodbyes as he passed through the room.

Penny stood waiting, her gray eyes luminous, a smile on her sweet lips. "Let's go home, cowboy."

The best part of Christmas Day was ahead of him.

<u>36</u>

A few flakes of snow drifted down as Penny clucked her tongue and King started down Henri's driveway. Ben had scattered crushed rock so horses and vehicles could get better traction. King took his time.

She'd chosen the front seat again, but she barely had to neck rein the big buckskin. He knew exactly where he was headed and made the turn onto the road leading home without any signal from her. "He wants his dinner."

Sky chuckled. "Good guess. I think he was hoping we'd come out to the little barn to feed him, but instead we're making him work for his supper."

"Are you hungry?"

"Not really. Seems like all we did today was eat."

"That's for sure. I like popcorn, but I couldn't get excited about Claire's offer to bring us some. Which was a shame because she was so cute about it. *I'm small and limber.* What a hoot she is."

"And kind. She's so good with Georgie, making sure he's included."

"It was a good day. A good Christmas." She nestled against him, anticipation fizzing in her veins.

"And it's not over yet." He pulled her in a little closer. "Remember when you said how nice it would be to ride home bareback and then make love?"

"I do. And you promised to make it happen."

"I believe in keeping my word."

Just like his dad. "Looking forward to it." Desiree had kept Sky a secret from Charley, but she'd raised him with Charley's principles.

King's steady hoof-beats and easy stride never varied. She'd counted on the seasoned horse to switch into automatic pilot and move steadily toward the warm barn where he'd get a net full of hay for his efforts.

Time to put her plan into action. "I've been thinking about how you carried me into the bunkhouse that first morning."

"Got a hankering to have me do that again?"

"Wouldn't be the same. Sweeping me off Prince and carrying me into the bunkhouse was gallant. Picking me up after we've trekked the path from the barn lacks dramatic punch."

"Guess I'll have to throw you over my shoulder, then."

"Sounds interesting. Caveman-ish." And hot. "But I have a more immediate use for your impressive upper body strength. I'd like you to keep me from falling while I turn around to face you."

He laughed. "I see the advantages, but are you sure you want to ride down the road backwards?"

"Yes."

"FYI, I'm in for some kisses, but I'm not wild about having sex on a horse, especially in the winter."

"I don't want to have sex with you on this horse."

"Kissing, then?"

"And talking. It's more fun if I can see you."

"Okay, I'm game. Let me have the reins."

"How can you hold onto them and me at the same time?"

"I'll put them between my teeth."

"Like Rooster Cogburn in *True Grit*?"

"But without the gunfire."

"Then here you go, Rooster." She handed him the reins. "First I'll swing my right leg over his neck so I'm sideways."

"Go for it."

The maneuver was awkward but she made it. "I'll bet Claire could do this without breaking a sweat."

"And throw in a cartwheel."

She glanced at him. "You sound funny with reins in your teeth."

"Do I look like John Wayne?"

"No. You need the eye patch." She gripped his shoulder and hoisted her knee onto King's back.

He watched her progress. "Careful of the privates."

"I'll be careful. I have plans for those privates."

"But not while we're on the horse, right?"

"Relax, cowboy. That's not my goal. It's too cold. You'd have shrinkage."

"Thanks for bringing that up."

"That's the problem." She carefully worked her boot past the danger zone. "You wouldn't be able to get it—"

"Never mind."

"Okay, you can let go. I'll hold onto you, instead." She gripped him around the waist. "You'll have to handle the reins, though, since I can't see where we're going."

He transferred them to one gloved hand and smiled. "Think I'm up to the job?"

"I hope so." She gazed into his blue eyes and her heart stuttered. "I have something to ask you."

"Whatever it is, the answer is yes."

"You'd better wait to hear what it is. I could be asking you to go skinny dipping in Crooked Creek."

"I don't know where Crooked Creek is, but if you're in, I'm in."

"Crooked Creek runs through Buckskin land and I'm sure it's frozen over, so you're safe. What if I asked you to climb a twenty-foot tree and bring me some mistletoe?"

"Great idea. I'd do it."

"Share a peanut butter and anchovy sandwich?"

He winced. "Um, sure."

"Marry me?"

He couldn't have looked more shocked if she'd pulled a gun on him. The seconds dragged as he stared at her as if she'd grown an extra head. "Is this… a joke?" His face was pale and his voice sounded as if someone had both hands around his neck.

"No joke." Her heart drummed hard in her chest and she had trouble breathing. "I love you. I love you so much that it scares me. But what scares me more is that… you've changed your mind. That you don't want—"

"You're serious."

"Yes, sir."

His hands trembled as he knotted the reins and dropped them in his lap. Then he cupped her shoulders in his gloved hands and gazed into her eyes. "I'm very confused." His voice was stronger, but full of doubt.

"That's my fault. I confused the issue." She swallowed. "But I've got it straight, now." She cleared her throat and took a breath. "I want to live with you at Rowdy Ranch, if you'll have me. I want to get a teaching job at the University of Montana, if they'll have me."

"Why?"

"Because *The Keeper of the Stars* lyrics have it right. Destiny is a BFD. You don't want to mess with it." She dragged in another breath. "And because I love you. So much."

"You loved me last night, but it didn't matter. You still turned me down. Why does it matter now?"

"Because when I told you no, I was speaking for… other people."

"I don't follow."

"My parents won't approve. The head of my department won't approve. Some of my friends won't approve. All those voices were yammering at me. And like an idiot, I was listening to them."

"What if they have a point?"

"I'm sure they do. They're allowed to have their opinion and I'm allowed to have mine. And guess which one counts the most?"

"Yours?"

"Right! This is *my* life, *my* decision and I know, I *know* it's right for me."

Slowly a gleam of anticipation replaced the disbelief in his eyes. Color returned to his cheeks. "It absolutely is."

"See? You knew it, but I refused to let myself see it because I gave everyone else power. I've taken it back."

He sucked in a breath and slowly let it out. "About time."

"Just in time. I could've lost you. But speaking of that, you haven't exactly said yes."

The light in his eyes gradually turned into an intense glow. "Sure I did."

"When?"

"You said you had a question." His voice deepened. "I told you whatever it is, the answer is… yes."

Joy swelled in her heart. "You did say that. Now you're stuck with me."

"Completely. For the rest of my life. Yes, Penelope Marston, yes, a thousand times yes." Nudging back his hat, he gathered her close, so very close, and kissed her with a thoroughness that erased any lingering doubt.

She kissed him back, winding her arms around his neck as the swaying rhythm of the horse and the snowflakes on her cheeks filled her with more happiness than one person could hold. But that was okay. From now on she'd have Sky to help her hang onto the good stuff. And there would be tons of it.

* * * * *

Saddle up for an all new series of fun-loving
Western romances with the McLintock family
of Rowdy Ranch.

Beau McLintock gets the surprise of his life
from the woman who broke his heart at
Christmas in HAVING THE COWBOY'S BABY.

* * * * *

New York Times bestselling author Vicki Lewis Thompson's love affair with cowboys started with the Lone Ranger, continued through Maverick, and took a turn south of the border with Zorro. She views cowboys as the Western version of knights in shining armor, rugged men who value honor, honesty and hard work. Fortunately for her, she lives in the Arizona desert, where broad-shouldered, lean-hipped cowboys abound. Blessed with such an abundance of inspiration, she only hopes that she can do them justice.

For more information about this prolific author, visit her website and sign up for her newsletter. She loves connecting with readers.

VickiLewisThompson.com

CPSIA information can be obtained
at www.ICGtesting.com
Printed in the USA
BVHW070931291021
620251BV00005B/120